Maxim Jakubowski

is a former publisher and ow
Murder One bookshop in]
Road. As well as being a writer and cult
cult publishing imprints, he is acknowledged as a dis-
turbing and controversial voice in contemporary fiction.
His collections have sold massively, he is a regular on TV
and radio where he is an expert on crime, erotica and
film, a *Guardian* columnist and he writes on the arts for
The Times. He is literary director of the prestigious
Crime Scene festival held at London's National Film
Theatre.

First Published in Great Britain in 2004 by
The Do-Not Press Limited
16 The Woodlands
London SE13 6TY
www.thedonotpress.com
email: crp@thedonotpress.com

C-format paperback original
ISBN 1-904316-27-1

British Library Cataloguing in Publication Data. A catalogue record
for this book is available from the British Library.

1   3   5   7   9   10   8   6   4   2

Confessions of a Romantic Pornographer

MAXIM JAKUBOWSKI

To Natasha and Adam
from the tomb of the unknown father.

'I believe nothing of any beauty or truth comes of pieces of writing without the author's thinking he has sinned against something – propriety, custom, faith, privacy, tradition, political orthodoxy, historical fact, literary convention, or indeed all the prevailing community standards together. And that the work will not be realised without the liberation that comes to the writer from his feeling of having transgressed, broken the rules, played a forbidden game without his understanding or even fearing his work as a possibly unforgivable transgression.'

EL Doctorow
REPORTING THE UNIVERSE

CLIPPING THE WINGS OF YOUR MORNING FLIGHT

The day Cornelia turned thirty, she attended a funeral.

It was a day with no particular features, a sky with scattered anonymous clouds and a wishy-washy colour that veered like a seesaw between barely there pale blue and a dull shade of grey. A day that somehow belonged to no precise season. Waiting outside the crematorium building surrounded by a mournful crowd of utter strangers, Cornelia wore black.

She was not a friend of the family and had never known the deceased, the dead man, although she recalled after being given this particular assignment, that she had once read one of his books. She had found it decent enough for a lonely night in a hotel room out on a job, but it hadn't engaged any of her gut feelings, the way she sometimes reacted to stories that communicated basic emotions well beyond their plot. Neither had the writer been particularly collectable, so his novels fell outside of her parameters. Maybe now that he was dead this situation would change. If often did. She reminded herself to acquire some of his earlier titles while they were still cheap. Just in case. Once a book collector, always a book collector, although these days she bought less and less, having finally completed her runs of her favourite authors.

She wasn't wearing black because of the funeral, even though the colour was appropriate for the circumstances. It was just that she felt at ease in her Armani little black dress. It fitted her well, perfectly highlighting her long nylon-sheathed legs, moulding its strong but light material around her rump. She had never been much of a clothes horse or a designer label addict, but she had fallen in love with the dress from the moment she had spotted it on an end of line hanger at the Printemps in Paris a year or so earlier when she had been taken to the city by a now long forgotten lover. He had offered to pay for the dress, but Cornelia had insisted on using her own credit card. Presents from men always had some sexual taint about them and the little black dress, she knew from her first touch of its hem, was going to be with her much longer than him and could not be contaminated.

She looked up to the sky and followed the evanescent trail of a faraway jet.

Not all the other guests actually wore black, but neither was the crowd a feast of colour. Cornelia realised this was the first funeral she had attended since her own father's, and that went back to her now distant teenage years. She recalled how she had spent most of it holding back her tears, for fear of being thought childish, soppy. Only to burst like a dam with sorrowful grief when she had got back to the car after shaking the hands of every relative and stranger come to pay homage to her father. She had heard friends remark that she had appeared cold and indifferent throughout, which just showed how little the bastards knew. But then, how could strangers guess at one's inner life, its turmoil, its hurt, the hollowness inside?

It had been her first genuine encounter with the prosaic reality of death. All these years later, her familiarity with death was far more developed and it had become a strange, skewed relationship that she still found it hard to fully understand. Particularly the unmathematical equation that balanced sex and death on a similar level of visceral thrill. But over the past twelve months, Cornelia had grown tired of her relationship with death and had taken a secret vow to renounce killing for good as her thirtieth birthday approached. She reckoned that such a momentous road sign in one's life should be the occasion of mighty resolutions and change.

And, ironically, she now found herself on the very day that she had seen as a turning point, at a funeral. Or was that how they still called a crematorium ceremony. An incineration maybe?

Cornelia smiled.

Her absent gaze fell upon the eyes of an older man who stood opposite her, wearing a charcoal grey three-piece suit and sharply polished shoes.

'Miss…?'

She looked back at him with studied indifference.

'Smith. Miss Smith. Miss Miranda Smith.'

She'd pulled the name out of nowhere. Could have been Jones, she reckoned, less commonplace than Smith. But Miranda had somehow been conjured up by instinct. She'd never been a Miranda before.

'John Kerith,' he answered.

'Hello.'

'I don't think we have met before,' he said. 'Family? Acquaintance?'

'Neither,' Cornelia kept it vague. 'You?'

'I was his literary agent. A terrible loss.'

'Yes,' she nodded sympathetically.

'So, just one of his readers?' he suggested.

Cornelia demurely lowered her eyes.

'I understand,' Kerith said. 'There are a fair few people present here today who only knew him from his writing,' he added. 'Actually, I find that quite touching.'

'Really?' Cornelia queried.

'Indeed,' he replied. 'You just never know how someone's books will affect different people, do you? His stories were so, how can I put it, particular, that I was never quite sure who his public really was. His editors would always tell me that he was much read by women, which I find hard to understand. After all, his material was often somewhat explicit, as you well know.'

Cornelia silently pretended to acquiesce.

Kerith looked around at the small crowd milling around in groups of four or five and continued.

'I do believe it now, though,' he said. 'There are a lot of women here. So surprising.'

He sighed, as if mentally wondering how many women would one day turn out for his own funeral. His eyes faded briefly and he then switched on again and asked Cornelia:

'Satisfy my curiosity – did you have a favourite book among his?'

Cornelia frowned.

'That would be telling, wouldn't it? You are what you eat, what you read. And that makes your question rather personal, Mr Kerith.'

The man blushed.

'I'm sorry, Miss Miranda. You're right. Please accept my apologies.'

He stood there for an instant, awkwardly facing Cornelia, as if debating whether to run away or attempt to continue the conversation.

His face regained its composure and he finally said, 'Trust a female Conrad reader to be both beautiful and mysterious. I think he would have liked that. Liked it very much.'

'I'm not sure the timing for genteel compliments is quite right, Mr Kerith,' Cornelia pointed out.

'There never is a wrong time,' he answered, looking her up and down. She steadily withstood his gaze.

There was a swirling movement in the surrounding crowd of mourners and guests and small groups slowly began to make their way across the arched entrance to the crematorium's chapel. Cornelia hadn't heard any bell or a specific call to the assembled people waiting. It was all done so discreetly, she noted. So English. In the States there would have been some burly employee shouting out the name of the deceased (and no doubt mauling its pronunciation in the process) to corral them all inside. Here, a nod or a furtive gesture seemed to be enough to catch people's attention.

Kerith excused himself and moved along.

Cornelia realised there was one question she had wanted to put to him. It could wait until after the ceremony, she reckoned.

Earlier, Cornelia had overheard some of the guests complaining there would be no service, just a series of speeches about the dead writer by people who had known him well. Someone had complained that, at least, a humanist ceremony would have been a just closure to Conrad's life and accomplishments, but his family had felt strongly that he would have disapproved of this. Cornelia reminded herself to specify in her non-existent will that whenever she died, no priest or lay pastor should be allowed within a mile or so of her funeral under dire threat of damnation or whatever would scare her likely if unwilling appointed executors most. She was an orphan and didn't trust a mere lawyer or bank manager or whoever the authorities appointed in these cases in the slightest. She knew she was bound to go to hell in fifth gear if not overdrive anyhow, and in a perverse sort of way, she welcomed the idea; at least the hereafter could hardly prove boring, and the spilling of wrong words or any fulsome degree of piety at her own passing would invariably spoil the occasion, she concluded.

Soon, the forecourt had emptied and only Cornelia remained, except for a short, dark-haired young woman casually looking over the flower arrangements scattered across the concrete and thin grass. Occasionally, the woman knelt, peering down to read the messages that accompanied the wreath and bouquets. As silence settled on the small oval that served as a stepping-stone to the church-like redbrick crematorium main building, the dark-haired woman looked up and noticed Cornelia observing her from afar.

She nodded in acknowledgement.

There was the muffled sound of a burst tire on the main road half a mile away beyond the lush green expanse of the crematorium's grounds.

A moment's hesitation occurred as both women stood still, each reluctant to be the first to make a move towards the other. Cornelia finally took the initiative.

As she approached the dark-haired woman, Cornelia realised she was not quite as young as she had initially assumed – she was probably also about 30. Like her. Something about the thin lines on either side of her mouth, the shadow beneath her eyes, the way she wore her clothes. As befitted the occasion, the other young woman was also dressed in black, but her two piece ensemble had a business-like feel to it. The hem of the carefully tailored skirt fell well below her knees. She had thin ankles.

'Hello…'

'Hi.'

'Couldn't face going inside and listening to the speeches?' Cornelia suggested.

'Yes,' the other woman answered. 'But it doesn't mean I'm being disrespectful.'

'I know. These sort of occasions are always rather false, I think. Lend themselves to a surfeit of hypocrisy,' Cornelia remarked.

'I quite agree,' the black suited woman agreed. 'I assume you're not family, then?' she asked.

'No, just a friend,' Cornelia improvised.

'Me too.'

A cloud streaked across the sun and the area was bathed in momentary shadow.

'I'm Samantha... I prefer to be called Sam. Sam Hearn,' she extended her hand.

'Miranda,' Cornelia volunteered.

'It's a pretty name.'

'Oh, just a name,' she shrugged.

'Did you know him well?' Sam asked.

'Not really,' she reluctantly admitted, not wishing to be quizzed too extensively and found out.

'Oh,' Sam remarked and she briefly looked away, as if embarrassed.

'Why?' Cornelia queried, noting Sam's apparent discomfort.

'Me neither, to be honest,' Sam answered.

The dark-haired young woman brushed a stray hair from her forehead, breathed deeply and allowed herself, albeit reluctantly, to open up.

'He had me too,' she whispered.

'I see,' Cornelia acknowledged impassively, hoping the other would say more. She did.

'He never did pretend that I wasn't one of many. At least he was honest about it.'

Cornelia went along with Sam. 'He was,' she confirmed.

'And he was tender, which is not always the case. But it was soon obvious I wasn't the one he really sought, you know. When I heard he'd died, I long hesitated as to whether I should come but, you see, I was sort of curious. Wanted to see the others. You probably noticed how the women here outnumber the men. I wonder if his wife knew. Oh, I suppose she did. How couldn't she? I was looking around earlier trying to recognise which were the ones he'd fucked and those who were genuine acquaintances, not tarred by sex. But there's no way of finding out, is there? We all look so different. I suppose he didn't have a specific type. Just bedded us when the opportunity arose.'

She looked Cornelia in the eyes. Hers were nutmeg brown.

'But I was never angry with him,' Sam continued, as if this long, breathless speech had been bottling up inside her ever since her affair with Conrad. 'You just couldn't. He kept in touch, you know. A word here, a phone call there, as if he didn't really want to lose contact. Sometimes, I thought he saw me as a fallback fuck, should all else, all others fail him, but I don't think I'm being fair to him now. He did care, you see.' She slowed down. 'You?' she asked Cornelia.

'Just the once,' Cornelia played along. 'Some time ago.'

'But you came today, nonetheless?'

'Yes.'

'That's the sort of man he was,' Sam remarked. 'I reckon there are at least a dozen of us here, all with that one thing in common.'

'Maybe.'

'I'm still not certain why I came. Even now,' Sam said. 'Nothing is going to change. There are no faces to put on names,

names to put on faces. I'll… we'll never know what we really all meant to him.'

'A good fuck?' Cornelia suggested.

'No,' Sam reacted quickly. 'We were more, I thought I was more to him. You just know things like that. There were feelings, not just convenient sex…'

'But why so many of us then?' Cornelia continued.

Muted echoes of a melody escaped from the building, carried by the slight breeze of the early summer day.

'In a way,' Sam said, 'he was on some sort of quest, don't you think?'

'Could be,' Cornelia opined.

'Did you meet Conrad in America?' Sam asked, finally acknowledging Cornelia's accent.

'Yes,' Cornelia confirmed, building her tissue of necessary lies one step at a time.

'How?'

'It was at a reading at some small event in New York City,' she offered.

'Let me guess: even now, you're not quite sure which of you made the first step?'

Cornelia feigned a gentle smile. 'Yes, exactly.'

'Sounds familiar,' Sam sighed. 'Strange to realise we have so much in common, isn't it?'

'Yes,' Cornelia continued. 'And so do many of the others inside listening to hollow words of praise.'

Sam Hearn's eyes clouded, as if she were trying to hold her tears back. Her lips tightened as she attempted to retain control of her confused emotions. The hard, business side of her character took over and she succeeded.

'Well,' she said, 'I think I'll be on my way. I think I've seen enough. Staying here any longer is not going to make things better. Maybe I shouldn't have come…'

She gripped her handbag and once again brushed her hair back from her face.

'Do you know where they are all going after the ceremony?' Cornelia ventured. 'To his house?'

She had been hoping there would be some sort of reception at the dead writer's house. A chance to snoop around, ask more questions.

'No,' Sam answered. 'I was told his publishers have hired a reception room on the upper floor of a Soho pub.'

'But he didn't even drink,' Cornelia mentioned. She recalled reading that in one of the interviews with Conrad she had found online.

'Yes, that's true,' Sam remembered, her memory no doubt recalling a past time when she and Conrad had sat down some-where to drink.

She grinned.

'What did he usually have when you were with him?' Cornelia asked, out of idle curiosity, still beginning to assemble all the random parts of the jigsaw.

'Pepsi Cola – he said it tasted sweeter than Coke – with no ice, or tomato juice, mostly,' Sam answered.

Silence returned.

Sam stood there, not quite sure whether she should leave now. Cornelia realised the other woman still sought some form of closure from her brief affair with Conrad. Which she wasn't going to find here, if ever.

'Maybe, one day,' Cornelia suggested, 'when it's easier to think about him and the past, we could meet up, chat, no?'

'I don't know,' Sam said, and her features hardened.

Cornelia realised it had been a bad suggestion, as if she were offering the other woman the far-from-golden opportunity to start up a forlorn club of Conrad's old fucks. Not a good idea at all.

She would have to adopt some brighter methods to elicit the information she had been sent here to dig up.

Cornelia had accepted the case just four days ago back home in Manhattan. Her last job, a couple of months previously, had been emotionally messy and almost straight out of a book, ironically enough. Her target had somehow guessed who she was and why she had been sent to kill him and had offered no resistance or protest. As if he had welcomed death.

This had never happened to her before.

Had the guy read Hemingway's story 'The Killers'?

And it had made Cornelia think again about her job. Not a good thing.

So she had decided to take a sabbatical of sorts. She had enough cash in the bank to last a year or so if she kept a lid on her extracurricular expenses and, any way, there were no more books she actively sought for her collection. If an item of minor interest or of associational value came along, she would of course not ignore it, but neither would these titles strain her budget.

In truth, Cornelia was tired.

Of her jobs. The dancing. The killing.

The thrills were no longer there.

There must be more to life, but she had absolutely no clue as to where to find it, caught as she was in a familiar web of habits and the expectations of others. It wasn't meant to be that way, surely?

On one hand, she knew she was not the type of woman who would ever be fully satisfied with the humdrum routine of a 9 to 5 occupation, academia or domesticity. On the other, Cornelia was painfully aware that this secret life of minor evil she had somehow drifted into wasn't the answer either. The satisfactions, the inner thrill, the rush of adrenaline, the fear were all too fleeting and always made her come back for more, and she was much too bright, overeducated some of her few friends had said, not to realise that one day she would take that one step or risk too far and slip up to find her whole edifice of cards come tumbling down with a ferocious vengeance. She also knew she would die of both boredom and frustration in a prison cell, regardless of the other risks there, and that she was too much of a mental coward to even envisage suicide if she were cornered and bereft of alternate solutions. Between the metaphorical devil and the deep blue sea, indeed.

The man had slumped to the ground in a silent and empty street near Alphabet City with an enigmatic smile illuminating his resigned features and that expression still haunted her, damn it! Usually, the gift of death initiated some complex chemical process that raised her sexual senses to a wonderful state of arousal within, better than any illicit drug, and was how Cornelia often justified her murderous actions. But, on this occasion, there had not even been a flutter of excitement. Either he had somehow cheated her or she was losing her libido.

Not that she even remembered his name a few days later, it was the nature of the job, but she couldn't erase his face from her daydreams.

She had been involved in messy deaths, with blood spreading out of control, seeping, dripping, regurgitating; there had been dirty deaths with desperate pleas, vomit, bladders and entrails out of liquid and odorous control; her pulse had frantically raced at heart attack speed in chases, clumsy fights, struggles and she could live with all those side aspects of the assignment, but the sad death of her last prey had badly affected Cornelia, she realised.

She took a break.

As it was, the management at the club where she'd been doing a gig had received complaints about her new tattoo anyway. Somehow punters found it distasteful, not quite sexy. Philistines.

So, she had handed in her notice to the club and called Ivan, her contact, advising him she was going on vacation for a few months and wouldn't be available for assignment. She informed him that she would make contact again on her return. She was in fact unsure whether she would ever do so again. Maybe this was the right time and way to leave the killing business behind her. She'd looked at her well stocked bookshelves with pride. Her John Irving, Woolrich, James M Cain, F Scott Fitzgerald first editions and many others, each earned by the death of a man or a woman. She didn't even wish to think of the value of her collection. She just liked books.

And why not take a holiday?

In the sun?

Cornelia arranged for an expensive security system to be installed in her apartment, even though she knew that any break-ins in her absence were more likely to be of the opportunistic kind and that her hi-fi and TV would be in much worse peril than her book collection. Then she planned her stolen time in the sun. Yes, it had to be in the sun. Although her pale complexion would have to enjoy the protection of much cream.

She had never been to the Caribbean and, after much hesitation, chose the Playa Dorada area in the Dominican Republic. She landed at Puerto Plata airport with a single small suitcase full of T-shirts and an assortment of bathing costumes she'd swooped on at Century 21 and Daffy's. Her bulging tote bag was full of paperback editions of books she already owned in first printings but had never found the time to read until now. Whilst in transit at Miami International, she picked up a few more books in one of the airport's shops. One of them happened to be a collection of erotic love stories by Conrad Korzeniowski; an interesting name she'd recently come across in a review in the Village Voice book pages. This was Cornelia's idea of travelling light.

Non-essential items she could find locally, she knew. Toiletries, make-up, condoms, a hat or baseball cap to protect her vulnerable skin. She also deliberately left her laptop back home in her East Village apartment. She intended to distance herself from the world and go back in time by some strange quirk of thought. To the days before she had unwittingly taken up her killing trade, to the days when she still unknowingly swam in a sea of innocence, if such halcyon days had ever existed.

The hotel dining room overlooked a bay where Cornelia enjoyed watching the sun set first across the mountain to the east and then across the varying shades of blue of the warm sea. Daytime, she lay on one of the beaches, listening to the wavelets lapping the beach or crashing gently against the breakers of the stone jetty, reading lazily or sipping cold drinks from the nearby 24 hour bar that serviced the beach. It was slightly out of season, so the resort wasn't crowded. She relaxed by going to bed most evenings at ten or even earlier, deliberately ignoring the conducted festivities organised daily around the large swimming pool, blissfully falling asleep with her book still open in her hands, her long, lanky nude body stretched out beneath the thin white sheet while the air-conditioning buzzed away with metronomic regularity. She would awaken early in the morning and take long, solitary walks across the deserted beaches miles beyond the resorts, refreshing her body as the sun began to emerge over the distant line of the horizon by shedding her shorts and T-shirt and dipping naked into the still warm ocean. It was a sensation like no other. Playa Dorada was perfect, but it would have been even better if she had been able to sunbathe nude all day. Nudity gave her a wonderful sense of freedom, as well as exacerbating her dormant sexual senses. After a week of routine relaxation, Cornelia began feeling the need for some stimulation and allowed herself to choose amongst the occasional men who would nod in her direction during meals or even accost her at the bar. Truly, whatever they said was of no interest whatsoever to her and the words and needless sentences went straight in one ear and out through the other, while she checked up on them, their looks, their size. She bedded a few, never the same again twice, much to their dismay, treating each new lover as if he was merely there to scratch her lackadaisical urges. Some happened to be good lovers, filled her well, even made her come, while others proved mediocre, hasty or unfulfilling, but it made no difference to her. One day later, she could no longer even remember their faces, let alone the girth or hue of their cock, or the position they took her in. It was just selfish holiday sex, as far as she was concerned.

Soon, the sand and sea and meaningless embraces began to take their toll, and boredom set in. She'd changed hotels twice along the length of the resort, seeking new culinary experiences and bed partners as well as avoiding previous ones who couldn't take no for an answer, and the fun of being in the Caribbean was beginning to fade by the hour. After all, she was a city gal through and through, and she preferred her solitude at the heart of bustling crowds. She settled her bill and flew home a day later.

Even after several weeks away, there were barely a handful of messages on her answer phone, although her computer mail box was full to the brim, mostly with commercial spam. No she didn't require unlimited supplies of cheap Viagara or weight loss programs that came with ironclad guarantees.

Only one person had attempted to contact her both over the phone and by email. Ivan.

He'd been her contact for over a year now. Usually just a voice over the phone. Lingering traces of a Russian accent, or, at any rate, an Eastern European one. Once, out of curiosity, shortly after he'd appeared on the scene, replacing the Puerto Rican guy who had introduced her to the organisation, Cornelia had arrived much too early at a pick up point and observed him as he left her envelope. He was middle-aged, grey-haired and totally unremarkable. The sort of man who melts into a crowd. But she liked his voice, the silence between the words, the things unsaid. She didn't call him back, all too well aware he would know exactly when she had returned to New York.

He rang the next day.

'Ivan,' he said, not that he had to reveal his identity.

'Hi.'

'Good vacation?'

'Yes, I feel quite relaxed now,' Cornelia said.

'Good. The Caribbean is a good destination this time of year.'

'I never told you I was going there, did I?' Cornelia chuckled.

'No, you didn't,' he replied.

'So...'

'So...'

'Well, Ivan,' Cornelia said. 'I'm not quite sure I'm ready for an assignment quite yet.'

'What? No new book for Cornelia's wonderful collection?'

'Actually, there isn't right now. But that's not the reason...' She allowed herself a moment of silence.

'Tell me,' Ivan continued.

'I've been thinking about retiring, Ivan.'

'Really?'

'Yes. Losing my bloodlust, feeling tired, call it what you will.'

'Not your time of month, my dear?'

'Nor my time of year, Ivan,' Cornelia replied. 'It's just that I'm no longer certain that I want to carry on doing these hits you give me. Nothing personal.'

'I see,' Ivan remarked, his voice betraying no emotions.

'Is now the time you tell me that I'm not allowed to quit, that I'd miss the excitement?' Cornelia queried, with a mocking tone of voice. 'Once in, never out?'

'No. Not at all,' he said. 'It would just be sad. You're one of the best.'

'Thanks for the compliment. Maybe it so happens that I no longer wish to be one of the best.'

Ivan paused.

'Let's meet,' he suggested. 'Talk.'

In itself, this was highly unusual.

Cornelia couldn't help but be intrigued by the situation. How would he attempt to get her to change her decision? Would he cajole, threaten, plead?

She agreed. It was decided that the meeting should take place on Sunday evening in the foyer of the Angelika, the art cinema on Houston. It was always crowded, as people invariably queued for one of the half dozen auditoriums, while others sat at tables sipping coffee or juice.

At close range Ivan appeared older than she remembered, and his voice didn't have the seductive intonations she enjoyed over the phone line. He wore a heavy looking brown leather coat and a Vivienne Westwood black woollen scarf draped student like around his neck. He brought the drinks over to the table where Cornelia had settled, a lemonade Snapple for her and a dark coffee for himself.

His eyes twinkled.

'You're still somewhat young to be thinking of retirement, Cornelia?' he queried, a thin smile shaping his lips.

'Well, you know, it was never meant to be a permanent job,' she respectfully pointed out.

'I realise that, but I can't believe your dancing allows you to buy many luxuries, does it?'

She realised this man had in all likelihood watched her strip on stage, and knew every intimate hook and cranny of her body. He must have checked her out at least once. Made sense.

'It's not a question of money,' she answered. 'I'm a frugal sort of person…' she hesitated, 'apart from…'

'Apart from your beloved books,' he completed the sentence for her, and looked her in the eyes.

'You've done your homework.'

'Naturally,' he stirred some sugar into his coffee. Gazed at the tall young woman facing him across the small table, thin, pale, almost arrogant in her posture. 'You are really quite something, Cornelia. A fascinating beauty and most assuredly one of my favourite operatives.'

'You flatter me,' she replied.

'It happens to all of us, you know, this feeling of lassitude, an insidious tiredness in the bones and the mind that you interpret as a wish to change your mode of life. I've been there. I've done the same things you have, Cornelia. But I tell you, it passes, moods swing both ways.'

'Maybe,' she ventured.

'Let me make you a proposal,' Ivan said.

'Tell me,'

'Another job. But different end result.'

'Explain yourself.'

'No termination, just an investigation. You'd be assigned to find out information. Nothing more.'

Cornelia reflected.

'I'm no private detective.'

'I know that.'

'Can't you find someone with training, qualifications in that area?' she asked.

'We could, but on one hand, I should like to keep you onboard, not see you burn your bridges with our organisation, and on the other your love of books makes you an idea choice for this assignment.'

'I'm intrigued.'

Ivan told her.

Cornelia accepted the new assignment.

Sly old fox, she reckoned later, he had known all along that she would take on the job, almost as if had it been made to measure for her. She smiled. At the very least, she'd screwed a business class upgrade and some additional expenses out of him for the journey to London.

Chapter 17

I met Sam in Liège, at a conference on Georges Simenon. It was on the occasion of the centenary of the birth of Maigret's creator, and the whole Belgian city was celebrating the important cultural event with no holds barred. I'd written a few articles on his books for British magazines and had somehow hassled a freebie invitation for the occasion from the Belgian Ministry of Culture. There were endless speeches by local notables and politicians, the inauguration of a museum, countless panels of pontificating talking heads at the university, the unveiling of a statue in a big plaza by the train station and, on the second evening, the world première of a new opera about the affair Simenon had had whilst in his twenties with the famous music hall star and nude dancer Josephine Baker. All of Liège was Simenon-mad and remembering its prodigal literary son. I felt like mischievously reminding many present that I had read somewhere that Simenon had left his native city at eighteen or thereabouts and never returned.

If there is anything worse than a lengthy speech by a French politician it's one by a Belgian one. I'd craftily moved towards the back of the crowd of guests and hangers-on, and by the end of the second speech was ready to make a beeline to the door that led to the large salon where we would later be served the buffet. According to the programme notes I'd been given, there were at least four more speeches to come, as local politicians made way for national ones, and then actual regional prefects and ministers. Too many words altogether.

As I moved backwards I bumped into Samantha Hearn. It seems

we shared the same idea of escape.

We'd been briefly introduced the evening before as we were both part of the same British contingent of guests. She was associated with a literary agency specialising in estates and intellectual property. She had been instrumental in securing my invitation to the festivities and I'd always been intrigued by the sound of her voice on the telephone. There was a nicely ironic tone to it, as if she was always on the verge of laughing with you at something you might have said but never quite did, sharing a private joke with you even as the conversation carried no hint of irony or humour. On initially meeting her in the flesh though, I'd been slightly disappointed. Sam had dark brown hair which fell to just about her shoulders, a shy and insecure gaze and was dressed in an anonymous two piece business suit which concealed her shape. We hadn't had a chance to really talk, because of the throng surrounding us.

'Escaping, Conrad?'

''Fraid so. This is just all too boring, I fear.'

'Don't blame you, actually.'

I came up with a suggestion.

'According to this,' I pointed to the large format invitation I was holding in my hand, which listed the order of speeches and the timetable for the rest of that afternoon's proceedings, 'we have over an hour until they serve the canapés.'

'That's a lot of time.'

'We can have a coffee, or whatever suits your fancy. The railway station brasserie is just a block away, I noticed. Shall we?'

'Oh, why not? My job description certainly doesn't indicate I have to listen to speeches in French.'

'In Belgian, actually,' I pointed out. 'You should hear the accent!'

Samantha Hearn smiled.

'You know the language well enough to recognise the accent?'

'Yes,' I replied. 'Come on, I'll tell you all about it.'

She led the way and my eyes alighted automatically on her arse, slim but well rounded under the thin, grey material, her movements stretching the skirt as if it were a second flesh.

My mind quickly went into overdrive, my terrible imagination already constructing many scenarios. I just couldn't avoid this when meeting interesting women. Potential women. Awful, really. Not just a storyteller by trade but also a hopeless fantasist. But I could no more fight the galloping flights of my wishful thinking than I could resist the raging song of my loins.

The thought occurred to me that I hadn't even noted the colour of her eyes. Pale brown, I discovered later.

We sipped our drinks quietly. On the pavement outside, an old van was parked, adorned all over with peace slogans and hippie-like symbols, protesting for world peace, crude cartoons of current and past world leaders scattered across the rusting bodywork.

'You married?'

'No, but I live with someone.'

'I'm married,' I pointed out to her. Always better to be honest right from the outset.

'I know,' Sam answered.

'Checking up on me?'

She blushed ever so beautifully, a soft scarlet shade spreading across her cheeks.

'Maybe. It's common knowledge.'

'This guy you live with, do you have many plans? Happiness ever after, a gaggle of kids?'

She lowered her eyes as she replied.

'I don't think so. No, I really don't. It's been two years already and I think I made a mistake. We made a mistake maybe.'

'OK.'

Her skirt had rolled up to mid thigh as she sat on the uncomfortable leather banquette of the bustling brasserie. She was wearing black tights, or I would have seen the top of her stockings by now.

'So tell me,' she jump-started the conversation again as I'd allowed an uncomfortable break to settle as we both pondered about each other's marital or live-in situations,' where did you learn to speak French so well? I studied it at university but it's nowhere near as good as yours. You make me feel like a total novice.'

'Which university?'

' Brighton. Sussex.'

I explained, but I already knew our minds were on other things altogether.

The moment my tongue made just a first fleeting contact with her cunt, she reacted as if she'd literally been electrocuted, her whole body seizing up in spasm and her lungs emptied with one massive sigh.

'Are you OK?'

'Yes,' she whispered breathlessly. Hesitated, then revealed 'it's been ages since a man did that to me.'

'I haven't done anything yet,' I chuckled. And headed back down towards her intimacy.

As we'd left the brasserie to rejoin the group of Simenon guests in the town hall, her fingers had accidentally brushed against mine as we crossed the Grand Place. We both knew right then that we would end up sleeping together that day. We had to endure the final speech and a ponderous, never-ending banquet overflowing with fine brandy where we stole too many glances at each other across separate tables as we had been unable to engineer a change in the seating plan. By dessert, I wanted Sam badly.

We'd first kissed in the back of the taxi driving us back to our hotel. She had put her hand under my arm, the moment we had crossed the threshold of the wood panelled smoking lounge, to which most of the guests had retired for conversation and digestion following the extravagant, drawn-out meal. As we hailed a cab, her hand had settled inside mine.

Her breath tasted sweet, with an underlying hint of Grand Marnier and coffee. The darting movements of her tongue inside my mouth betrayed her hunger. As we kissed silently, my hands steadily moved across her clothed body. Sam felt ever so soft.

Inside my hotel room, I'd asked her if she wanted the bedside lights left on or off. You never know with some women the first time how brazen or shy they will become in private. She left the decision to me. I preferred to keep them on. I wanted to see every inch of her flesh as I undressed her and every cloud that moved imperceptibly across the horizon of her eyes as we fucked.

She was thin, pale but exquisitely built. The way she dressed, brand manager extraordinaire, did her no justice. Her dark nipples like a welcoming oasis in the desert of her white skin. One touch of my fingers, then my lips and they hardened instantly. She obviously hadn't envisaged a sexual encounter on the occasion of this trip and her jet black curling cunt hair was untrimmed and luxuriant. As I pulled her sensible Marks and Spencer panties down, she was looking down straight into my eyes to see my possible reaction to the generous spread of her bush.

I like all cunts. Made no difference to me. A veritable slave of lust. A fool for lust, you'd even say, and you'd be right.

I firmly pushed her back onto the bed, rose from my knees where I had initiated the tentative taste of her cunt and spread her legs wide. My breath hovered just an inch or so from her opening and a quick tremor again raced across her skin. My fingers parted her slowly; she was already quite wet and her lips sticky. I inhaled her exhilarating musky fragrance and lowered my lips towards the warmth that rippled out from her opening. Anticipating my forward motion she shifted her rump across the bed cover and instinctively raised herself slightly towards me. My tongue buried itself into her folds, as my left hand took advantage of her movement and slid under her arse, a finger seeking the tightness of her anus, positioning itself at her puckered entrance.

Sam moaned in response.

My mouth now engulfed her cunt, methodically licking it along the ridges of her engorged lips and making deliberately slow but systematic progress towards the elevated nub of her clit, which already peered at me, pink and shiny and minuscule, from under its fleshy hood.

I paused for a brief moment to catch my breath and her drowsy eyes showed signs of panic, as if fearful that I was about to tease her and do no more down there.

'You OK?' I whispered reassuringly.

'Oh, yes,' her face was flushed with sexual greed and neediness.

I looked down again into the parted leaves of her cunt, my tongue finally reaching the tremulous and visibly swollen peak of her clit.

Sam let out a guttural sound from deep inside her throat, both of relief and pleasure and I nudged my well lubricated finger deep into her arsehole at the same moment. Her hand gripped the bedcover on both sides. I took the small fleshy excrescence between my teeth and chewed gently on it as her pale body stretched out before me began to writhe and wriggle in response. With my free hand, I took hold of hers and steadied her while I worked on her with both my mouth and my gyrating finger inside her anus.

I was still mostly dressed myself, and could feel my cock straining hard against my boxers.

A quick pretend bite of her clit and Sam came for the first time, a loud sigh rushing out of her lungs as her whole body shook and initially dislodged my mouth from her nether parts. As her trembling slowly began to subside I returned to her cunt, just licking the periphery of her opening now, allowing her to settle down.

'That was nice,' she said, her muscles relaxing, the first step in our dance of lust now taken, her mind and body now ready for more excess.

I swiftly rose from between her legs and pulled my shirt off and unbuckled my belt.

As I slipped off my underwear, I could see her spying my cock as it emerged and unfurled promptly from the tight cotton boxer shorts. She straightened herself, moved across the bed, positioned herself on the edge facing me.

'Let me…' she asked.

Right now, she looked just like a little girl, her delicate features coloured almost scarlet by the waves of desire she had willingly succumbed to, her small, hard breasts jutting out in parental defiance, her cunt flowing with inner juices, her body vibrating in unison with all the sexual fantasies she might ever have imagined. The inner Samantha had been released. Right now, I knew, she would do absolutely anything. Not that I had any particular deviant ambitions for her. As much as she touched something inside me, I already knew this was just sex, a divertissement. My senses responded to her, to the way she moved, smelled, reacted, would fuck, but my heart was on a separate wavelength and that was something one always knew from the outset. At any rate, I was hungry for the experience and determined to enjoy the moment.

She took my cock into her mouth.

It felt like home.

*

The affair with Sam continued back in London and lasted just over four months. We never actually found much to talk about, and restricted ourselves to recreational sex in hotel rooms rented for the afternoon, or in some cases just the morning, or even on a couple of occasions, the plush sofa in her office after hours, both anxious about the possibility of the cleaners bursting in on us because of an unpredictable change in their schedule. Halfway through the liaison, her live-in boyfriend moved out of the small flat they shared in Temple Fortune. She only informed me of this after the fact and didn't gloss over it or explain whether the decision had been his or hers, or even been influenced by our regular meetings. She made it very clear to me this would have no bearing on our meetings and that she had no further ambition to see our relationship develop into any other dimension than that of sheer lust. She knew we were not intended to be happy ever after in the conventional sense. In the final month that we saw each other, conversation between us began to flow better, our sex took a more experimental, extreme road, and she even confessed that when I was not available she would pick up other men in bars and fuck them, as if she had become addicted to casual, no-strings-attached sex. The thought did not make me jealous; in fact, I found it rather exciting and mentally pictured her slight, if flexible, pale body being ravaged by other cocks of all shapes and sizes and Sam, humiliatingly, begging for more, a slave to this craving I had inadvertently introduced her to. Not to be outdone, although it occurred naturally rather than being the result of a conscious decision, I was already seeing Victoria at the time, and uncomfortably juggling two extramarital affairs. How did I find the energy? – this was the period when I also was writing the Seattle novel – but then I was younger, and full of stamina and foolishness.

But we had just become two separate emptinesses desperately attempting to create a whole and both Sam and me silently acknowledged we were travelling on a road to nowhere, albeit a highway with sometimes alluring pit stops.

The break came as no surprise. She was attending a marketing conference in Paris and I had joined her there for the weekend. She had been booked into a room in a small hotel particulier just off Notre-Dame and through the window we had an interrupted view of the gargoyles guarding the outline of the old cathedral. It was summer and sultry and we kept the window open, allowing the stone monsters to watch us fuck with abandon. I was taking her doggie style and vigorously smacking her rear as I ploughed in and out of her, watching with relish the wonderful spectacle of my wet, juice coated penis moving in and out of her stretched red meat-like cunt, and the darkening scarlet imprints of my hand criss-crossing the taut surface of Sam's white arse. I'd discovered some months earlier that she enjoyed being spanked. A minor perversion I had never been into before, but which had its charms I found, if allied with extra sexual activities. Like Kay, there was something inherently submissive about Sam I perceived, although it just didn't touch me in the same way. With K it was a total abandon of the self, evidence of the fact she gave herself so fully and came to belong to me totally, whereas with Sam it was merely an adjunct to feelings of sexual satisfaction, probably more in her imagination where her sexuality was whipped into a gentle frenzy by thoughts of slavery and being treated rough by me, or more likely some pirate or slave master in antique times. Sam's was a safe form of submission. She would never have had the guts or the will-power to explore it fully.

I was about to come but wanted to hold back a bit longer, enjoying not just the wave of pleasure racing through my loins but also the beautiful vulgarity of Sam's moans of pleasure, and slowed the movement of my cock inside her, my eyes alighting on the pulsating, browner ring of her anus (which she had never suggested I breach, although I suspected she'd be incredibly tight there) and, just like that, my mind wandered off on a tangent and I looked up and spied one of the distant stone gargoyles at at quarter to eleven.

'What is it?' Sam asked, sensing my sudden absence.

'Nothing,' I replied.

'Are you OK?' she continued.

'Yes,' I said, but already my bulk inside her was shrivelling and the moment was gone.

I withdrew from her, turned her round and proceeded to bring her off orally. As I did so, I realised her inner taste was no longer so welcoming, had changed somehow.

Afterwards, Sam sucked me off after I'd slipped into the bathroom to wash my penis; she wasn't keen on a cock still coated with her own secretions. By now, my balls were full and she found it easy to bring me to a conclusion. Returning from the wash basin where she had spat out my seed, she remarked:

'You taste different.'

'But you don't swallow?'

'I can still taste your flavour over my tongue.'

We'd eaten oysters at a restaurant in the Rue Buci that evening. I joked that this had affected the savoury manifestation of my come. I'd read about that somewhere. At least I hadn't had asparagus…

But as we dressed separately the next morning, ready to take a taxi to the Gare du Nord where we were booked on the Eurostar train back to London, I reflected that the changing flavour of our genitals was betraying the dead-end nature of our affair. I didn't quite decide there and then that this was the last time with Sam, but the decision was on my mind. And the same probably applied to her. We parted with a kiss at Waterloo and went our own way, with traditional promises of a phone call soon.

I never called her again. And neither did she call me. Not with a further tryst in mind, at least.

Sam had left Cornelia her business card and the two women agreed to keep in touch and maybe talk again. 'When the wound wasn't quite so fresh', as Sam had put it, still assuming in the absence of denial that Cornelia was another of Conrad's past conquests.

Another plane continuing its descent towards the Heathrow runways passed overhead. Cornelia shifted her bodyweight onto her left foot as she stood in the crematorium forecourt wondering why in hell she had accepted this particular assignment. She was no detective. Just a part-time hit woman with deceptive airs which made the job easier. What next? she wondered as the distant plane sunk over the flat horizon and silence returned.

She watched Sam's silhouette move steadily towards the crematorium car park and finally overheard the muted sounds and whispers of the mourners beginning to file out of the chapel in small groups. A middle-aged blonde woman, flanked on one side by her now grown-up children, a young man and a young girl, quietly nodded as others trooped towards her to shake her hands or embrace her. The widow. The children.

From her vantage point. Cornelia noted that many of the single women were moving away, deliberately missing the line of condolences that led towards Conrad Korzeniowski's family. As Samantha Hearn had assumed, other past fucks come here to utter a final good-bye, and with no wish to confront the dead author's wife. Cornelia studied them, their faces, some in tears, others impassive, their varying ages and style of clothing, their bodies. If this had been a proper funeral they would have been queuing to throw their handfuls of dirt onto the sunken coffin of this man who, seemingly, loved women too much. But as his dead body burned to ashes no doubt right now on the industrial side of the peaceful chapel, the women were left without a proper ritual to express their sorrow, expunge their memories of an erstwhile lover. Surely his wife must have known he was playing the field?

Some of the women, at a loss, just stood there, as if caught at night in lights on a dark road, while others milled around, perusing the garlands arranged around the chapel's front. Some eyed each other suspiciously, others averted their gaze in a bad imitation of discretion.

The mourners finally began to break up, making their way towards their cars or walking in the direction of the grounds' gated entrance.

Cornelia was in two minds over whether to approach the widow, when a foreign hand quietly tapped her right shoulder.

She turned round. It was John Kerith, Conrad's literary agent.

'Still here?' he inquired.

'As you see,' Cornelia answered, deciding there and then he was as good a lead as any other considering the circumstances. He would surely know about the book if it existed.

'Do you live over here or did you cross the pond especially for the occasion?' he asked.

'I was visiting anyway,' Cornelia said. 'I just happened to hear about his death.' She remembered the Guardian obituary she had read on the plane over. 'The newspaper I saw didn't say how it happened.'

Kerith covered his mouth and coughed.

'I'm not quite sure,' he said. 'I think the family don't want any rumours to spread unnecessarily.'

Could it have been suicide? Cornelia was aware that it was a subject that often appeared in Korzeniowski's books and stories. But surely the obituary would have highlighted this, particularly when an author was concerned?

'I see,' Cornelia nodded.

'I was told it was a stroke,' Kerith continued. 'It surprised me, I must say. He was in good health. One of that rare species of writer who never drank or smoked. Wasn't into drugs either. Actually once wrote a rather funny piece for a magazine about the fact he'd tried some soft drugs when he was still young and they just did nothing for him.'

Most of the mourners had by now dissipated and they were part of the final stragglers. Cornelia caught a glimpse of Korzeniowski's wife and offspring moving away.

Kerith allowed himself a short, almost embarrassed smile. 'Maybe it was sex,' he ventured. 'An appropriate way to go for Conrad, I'd hazard.'

'Sex, no drugs and no rock 'n' roll' she added.

'Oh no, not at all,' Kerith interjected, 'he loved rock music.'

'That's true,' Cornelia said, remembering the books of his she'd actually read.

'Do you require a lift back into town, maybe?' Kerith asked.

'To the wake?' she responded.

'No wake. Not the sort of thing he would have approved of. Not his style at all, Miss Miranda. We've hired a function room at the Groucho for a small get together to honour his memory; bookish friends, people he knew.'

Cornelia was disappointed. She had hoped they would all congregate at Conrad's house after the funeral, and that she could smuggle herself in. A chance to snoop around a bit.

'Would you mind if I hitched a lift, then?' she asked Kerith.

'Not at all,' he replied, a broad smile lighting up his florid features. 'It would be a pleasure.'

'Thanks.'

'We can talk more as we drive along.'

'Exactly.'

Cornelia recognised Kerith's type all too well. She also knew she could deal with him. Whatever information he could provide, she would obtain sooner or later. So she didn't protest on the couple of occasions during the slow drive into the centre of town when the literary agent's fingers grazed her knee as he changed gears. It would only serve to encourage him.

Didn't he realise how much better Cornelia played this game than most?

As the metal grey BMW methodically zigzagged its way into the congestion zone, Cornelia's mind wandered off. Away from the topic of the day, her assignment.

She had seldom given the process of ageing much thought before. Even as a child and, later, a teenager, she had lived for the day and not worried too much about the future. And now, all of a sudden she was thirty and spending her birthday in London. Wondering where all the days had gone, the years. As if they weighed nothing. She had her memories of course, her apartment, her cherished book collection. But that was all. She sighed, and Kerith looked round at her.

'OK?'

'Yes,' Cornelia replied. 'Just thinking…'

'Conrad?'

'Yes,' she lied.

'I understand,' he said, and his hand alighted once again on her right knee as he manoeuvred around a sharp corner, controlling the steering wheel with his other hand.

Oily bastard, she thought. But ignored him and delved again into her own thoughts. Realising at the same time how unusual this was for her. She just wasn't the analytical type, she knew. She was a woman who responded to music, to rhythm, to the expression of emotion, even if most would have described her as having a cold heart, not realising that was just a construction she had built up to cushion herself against the realities of her recent past: the jobs, the deaths, the indifference of silence.

Damn it, she thought, teach me a lesson to attend a funeral on my bloody birthday. And quickly dismissed the feeling. This was not the occasion to feel sorry for herself. Cornelia snapped out of it.

'Nearly there?' she asked Kerith.

'Almost,' he said. 'I'll park the car in the Chinatown NCP and it's a short walk from there.'

'Good,' Cornelia said.

The game was on again.

MANHATTAN LOVE SONG

No one at the farewell party appeared to know much about an as yet unpublished book by Conrad Korzeniowski.

Cornelia had managed to speak briefly with his publisher and another guy who also worked at the same house and both stated categorically that Conrad was not working on anything at the time of his death. His last novel had appeared some two years previously, and he had since seemingly restricted himself to newspaper and magazine pieces. There had been rumours of a future science fiction book, marking a return to one of his first literary loves, but nothing had materialised.

'Whenever he started on a new project, he would always let me know so I could initiate a contract, and more specifically a delivery deadline,' James Green had informed her. 'It was the only way he could work. It helped Conrad's commitment and discipline to have a deadline looming. And he never failed us. Never was early delivering, but neither was he late. Some authors tick that way.'

John Kerith had also denied the existence of a new novel.

'When he'd wrestled long enough with the idea, only then did he actually begin to write a book,' he'd informed Cornelia. 'He'd phone Jim and me, and we'd negotiate the contract. Just gave us a title, that was enough. We both trusted him implicitly. Sometimes just a hint of a story or theme, but then as you well know he always had the same obsessions and subject matter. Although, every single time, it would turn out to be a brilliant new variation. I can't pretend that dear Conrad was one for striking originality, but there was no one better than him at providing new angles on the man meets woman, man fucks woman with a plethora of four letter words and then things go wrong story.'

Seeing the surprised expression on Cornelia's face as the two of them stood in a corner of the Groucho first floor function room lost to the subtle hum of the other guests, Kerith quickly added:

'Don't get me wrong, Miranda. That's how Conrad himself once described his books to me. I wasn't being dismissive. Far from it. Rather a witty way of putting it, don't you think?'

'I've not read them all,' she replied. 'But it fits the formula, I suppose. Although a touch simplistic.'

'Of course, he was always very self deprecating was Conrad.'

Cornelia altered her angle of attack.

'How well did you know him?'

A faint smile crossed Kerith's lips.

'I didn't, in all fairness,' he replied. ' It was just a business relationship. His books did OK, sometimes better in foreign markets, France, Japan, Italy than they did here or in the USA, but he was never a major earner for our agency, so our contacts were limited.'

'I see.'

'He was an essentially private person. Kept himself to himself.'

Cornelia nodded in acknowledgement.

'Back at the crematorium, I saw you talking to that other woman, another of his readers?' Kerith inquired.

'Yes, I think so,' Cornelia said.

John Kerith grinned. 'A man with a lot of readers.'

'Indeed.'

44

'And mostly women.'

'If you say so.'

'Well, it's obvious he loved women. It's all over his pages.'

'Yes.'

'You know, Miranda…'

'What?'

'It makes me wonder which one you might be?'

'Really?'

'No harm in it. Nothing to be ashamed of. So many of his stories were set in America. There must have been some American women. Maybe you?' he asked her.

'Just a reader, Mr Kerith,' Cornelia answered. 'Not a lover. Although I'm flattered that you might think I was one of Conrad's conquests. It must really be something, to know you've been immortalised in prose. But I haven't, you see. I'd know…'

He blinked once, dismissing the fantasy.

'Subject closed then, Miranda. Will you accept my sincere apologies?'

'There was nothing to apologise about.'

'How long are you in London?' he asked.

'It's open-ended,' she replied.

'Might I convince you to join me for a meal, maybe?'

'Perhaps,' Cornelia said. The literary agent could still prove useful, she knew. It was too early to dismiss him out of hand. 'Let's talk again before this is over.'

'Certainly.'

She moved towards the cash bar to get herself another vodka and cranberry juice and began to work the room.

Cornelia swam from group to group like a svelte dancer on a random mission. Here and there she would catch snippets of conversation, but no one appeared to be discussing the dead author. She was aware that most of the men here quietly noted her passage and no doubt speculated as to her identity. Or did all of them mistakenly assume she was yet another woman from Conrad's past, and just cast envious eyes on her body?

She realised by now she would have to embark on a lengthy session reading Korzeniowski's books and stories. If clues were to be found, it would be within their pages.

And she would have to speak to Sam Hearn again.

The only specific information she had was on a print-out from a web magazine interview, which Ivan had passed over to her at their Angelika Film Centre meeting. It was dated six months ago. In answer to the traditional question about what he was working on right then, Conrad Korzeniowski had confided to his questioner that he was vacillating between two very different book ideas. One was the science fiction time travel tale she had been told of earlier that day, and the other was a memoir, to be titled *Confessions of a Romantic Pornographer*, which he revealed would shed much light on the elements of fiction and reality in his previous books. That was all the information she had.

And Ivan's client was paying hard cash for her to discover whether the latter book had in fact been written and, if so, to obtain its manuscript and prevent it from being published.

From her brief conversations with Sam Hearn, John Kerith and Conrad's erstwhile publisher, and her cursory knowledge of his books, Cornelia now assumed the client must be a woman, who could not bear being named in the hypothetical memoir. Reputation? Wealthy husband? Privacy?

Her initial assumption was that the client must be American, but she knew of past jobs she'd worked on with a European connection, and the fact that Ivan was based in Manhattan meant nothing more than coincidence.

Cherchez la femme? Could the best way of uncovering the whereabouts of the hypothetical book lie in discovering who the client was?

Moving between less than animated groups.

'Hello.'

A short guy with a moustache and a bald patch Cornelia could look down on.

'Hi.'

'And you are?'

'Miranda. Miranda… Jones,' Cornelia said, for one just instant uncertain whether she'd been Smith or Jones earlier today. Getting rusty, girl.

'Barrington Shaw. But don't call me Barry.'

'I won't.'

'Hello, Miranda, then. This is Eve,' pointing to a short Asian women standing next to him.

'I was just about to leave,' Eve said, setting her empty glass down on the window ledge.

'See you around.'

'Bye.'

'Have we met before?' Barrington asked.

'No. I'm from New York. Just visiting.'

'Haven't been there for ages. Fascinating place. So what brings you here?'

'A bit of a fan of Conrad's writing. I was thinking of writing something on him. I teach in a private college back home. Maybe a good subject for my Masters, I'm not sure. I have to tackle that soon,' she improvised.

'I edit a magazine called McGuffin. Maybe you should write

something for us. It would have to be a bit less academic. There's been very little written about his books actually. A fascinating man.'

'You knew him?'

'Not very well. Often saw him at launch parties, literary dinners and such, but can't say he ever opened up very much. Always pleasant and ready with a quip, but a somewhat private individual. I suppose he preferred his books to speak for him.'

'So I gather,' she confirmed.

'A loss to our small community, though,' Barrington concluded.

'Did you ever publish anything of his?' she asked.

'Yes, a few times. A short story once, before we changed the magazine's mix and stuck to non fiction. Also a couple of pieces each time on the occasion of a new novel. About how the books had come about. It's something we often do.'

'I'd love to read them. Particularly the short story. I've only ever read his novels.'

'In that case, you might well already have read it. Conrad had this infuriating habit of cannibalising his stuff over and over again, expanding short pieces and integrating them into the books. It was sometimes like a hall of mirrors. As if the story took on a second lease of life the next time around as it fitted into the novel like the additional piece of a jigsaw puzzle.'

'Fascinating.'

'He was a bit obsessive like that,' the magazine editor said.

'There's a rumour he was working on a new book,' Cornelia ventured.

'I've heard that too,' he said. 'Maybe he didn't finish it. Jim Green, his publisher, knows nothing about it. Also, in that article he gave us for 'Sadly', Conrad did indicate it was the end of a cycle and anything to come in the future would be radically different. Wrote that he had nothing left to say. Sounded rather final.'

'Do you know anybody who might know more about it, maybe?'

'Not sure,' he paused.

The party was winding down.

Cornelia felt a gentle tap on her shoulder. Kerith had joined them. The two men knew each other.

The conversation veered off her chosen track as they began to exchange the latest London literary gossip, metaphorically burying Conrad Korzeniowski a second time at his own wake.

Small talk exhausted, Barrington Shaw made his excuses and left them. They were now amongst the final stragglers.

'Where are you staying, Miranda?' Kerith asked her.

'The Cumberland Hotel, by Marble Arch,' she answered.

'A bit of an impersonal place, no?' he said.

'It's functional. It was arranged at rather short notice, through a travel agent,' Cornelia said truthfully.

'You could have stayed here.'

'The Groucho?'

'Yes, they have rooms, you know. Not many people know that. Very convenient for the media crowd. Has character, although maybe not as much as Hazlitt's round the corner.'

'I'm not a member anyway,' Cornelia shrugged.

'You don't have to be,' Kerith said. 'Anyway, I am. Also a shareholder. Good little investment. Want me to check if there's anything available?'

Cornelia agreed. It would be a more central base of operations. And she wanted to keep on the literary agent's good side. There must be more information in him somewhere about

Conrad Korzeniowski. In the files at his office, with his staff maybe. She realised she might have to fuck him to get that one step nearer to her goal. Just a minor infelicity. She looked over at him, as he strolled away to ascertain the availability of rooms at the club. At least he appeared fit for his age. She ordered a final drink; a soda water to clear her mind.

Chapter 9

It was a bad time in my life.

It was like a cycle I couldn't escape from: weeks up and days down, a pattern to which I was condemned by forces seemingly outside of my control.

I was feeling decidedly mortal. People I had known, friends, acquaintances, were dropping dead almost like flies all around me or else being rushed to hospitals in a frantic rush for desperate life-saving emergency operations. My back hurt every single morning when I woke up and I couldn't function properly until I had a couple of Ibuprofen's down my throat. My writing was still sinking down in fifth gear toward an abyss of despond, and every single time I read back something of mine, I was appalled by the sheer hollowness and lack of consequence of my own meagre talent.

I couldn't get K out of my mind.

And God, did I try.

I didn't like myself in the slightest.

It was early spring and the occasion of my regular New York trip to do the rounds of American publishers and book clubs. I had no wish to go. The trip wasn't that necessary that year; I had my contracts and enough commissions and the rest could easily have been done by phone or email.

But then I thought I would just be miserable staying at home in London, confronting my inadequacies and my family. Surely a change of air would do me good. I'd always loved New York rhythms and opportunities. It revived me, gave me a new sense of purpose. So I flew out on the wings of optimism.

I was wrong.

My bad vibes followed me there and after a couple of days cruising between editorial offices, exchanging meaningless small talk and pitching ideas I didn't even believe in myself I just ended up feeling so damn empty. Watching two movies in a row at the Union Square multiplex most evenings, following a sushi at Taste of Tokyo on 13th Street, became a predictable routine. After three days I'd run out of movies worth seeing and still not released in Britain. I wasn't one for theatre shows and plays and even less of a social drinker, so cruising the East Village bars was out.

I'd gulped down a hearty early evening meal of mushroom and barley soup and pierogi at Veselka, a Ukrainian restaurant on 2nd Avenue and had drifted back to my hotel off Washington Square, thinking of writing my daily allocation of 800 words of the novel then in progress on my laptop, and getting a day ahead of myself, or maybe catching CNN on the room's TV. But my mind was elsewhere. I'd always found the atmosphere of hotel rooms insidiously sexual and tonight was no exception. The air conditioning had been reset by the maid while I had been out, and within a half hour I could feel the sweat from my armpits seep through my T-shirt. I adjusted the settings, stripped and walked to the bathroom to take a shower.

I'd left the plastic shower curtains open and watched in the mirror as the soapy water pearled down my body and splashed about the bath tub. My cock was already partly hard. Jesus, did I need sex all of a sudden. Badly. Irrationally. A need that jerking off to a porn magazine couldn't satisfy by a lustful mile. It was only 8.30 in the evening. After drying myself, I impulsively decided to shave.

Naked on the edge of the bed, I sat with the gleaming Titanium Apple Power Book on my knees and logged on to the net. My first thought was a lazy one, to trawl a bi or gay site where the odds of finding sex within the hour were naturally better, but tonight I knew cock would not suffice to calm my longings. Anyway, I felt it was a phase I'd travelled through and seen the back of. Initially it had just been a curiosity, no more. I'd never been attracted to men. Just the idea of cocks. And the submissive concept of having one inside me. To know what it felt like. To be like a woman. To experience what she did, what she felt. But cocks always came attached to a body, a voice, and this just complicated the feelings involved. It had been months already. There was no point exploring that territory again now. Been there, done that.

I located an adult chat room I'd once played on a few years back in the immediate aftermath of the affair with K, when I had plunged headlong into an orgy of self-pity and meaningless debauchery as a sop for my despair. Curiously enough, that awful self-pity born of her rejection was often mistaken by some women for unalloyed romanticism and made my task easier. Conjured their instinct to nurture and console. Beggars need not be choosers and why should I have contradicted them if they chose the wrong reason to bed me? There is never a wrong reason.

I stroked myself gently as I thought of the right handle to use tonight.

'Melancholy'?

'Londonwriter'?

'Naked in NYC Hotel Room'?

'Romantic Pornographer'?

I settled on the first nickname, typed it in and prefaced it with 'Manhattan', then systematically scrolled several times up and down the list of current members of the adult forum in the room. There were a few with 'NYC' identifications as well as a handful of Long Island ones.

I buzzed a couple in Westchester and a self-proclaimed nympho sub from New Jersey. Neither answered.

It was then that Sarah Jane contacted me.

Advertising melancholia either attracted similarly lost souls or horny men who would invariably ask why I was sad, mistaking me for a woman.

It didn't take long to hold her full attention.

Within a half hour of continuous if halting dialogue she consented to call me. It was better to offer one's own number rather than request theirs. Made them feel safer from possible stalkers or freaks. They didn't always phone back. Sarah Jane did.

She sounded young. I sounded British. Which she found wonderfully exotic and reassuring.

She was shy and it took me ages to extricate direct answers out of her. I really hoped this would lead somewhere as I'd had to disconnect the laptop as the hotel room only had the single telephone line. She had recently completed a journalism course at Hunter College and was presently an intern at Time Out New York. She had been born in New Orleans and when I questioned her as to her reasons for frequenting this particular internet forum, she was honest enough to admit to her dark side, a manifest attraction to anonymous sex and dangerous encounters. A trait I recognised all too well. You know that the pleasures and joy are fleeting, and the degradation, guilt and mental anguish will tear you apart, but you can't stop yourself from going back to the well. Again and again. The sexual animal has no respect for sense or logic. I'd been there. I was still there, up to my ankles in it.

I suggested we meet.

'Tomorrow evening?'

'No, tonight,' I insisted. 'I'm only in New York for another two days.'

'Oh.'

'Before you start thinking about it too much and begin a hesitation waltz.'

'I understand.'

She lived in a sublet on the Upper East Side.

'Get a cab,' I said. 'I'll reimburse you if you wish.'

'Fine,' she decided. 'Where do we meet up? Is there a bar, a place that's convenient for you?'

'No bar. Come straight to my hotel.'

There was a brief pause on the other end of the phone line.

'You have to trust me,' I continued.

'I suppose so,' Sarah Jane answered.

'I'm not asking for your heart, just your body. As we discussed earlier: no strings, just an indulgence of the senses. You did say how tempted you were. Tomorrow I might have changed my mind.'

'Or found another gal?'

'Who knows, Sarah Jane?'

'It's crazy,' she replied.

'Totally,' I agreed.

'All I know is your voice.'

'Yes, you don't even know what I look like…'

She laughed softly.

'Actually,' she pointed out. 'I do. While we were chatting online earlier, I looked you up on Amazon.com, just to see if you were who you said you were. Checked on the titles you'd mentioned and then, through Google, looked up a photograph of you on your publisher's web site.'

'Ah, Watson, we'll make a proper detective out of you one day.'

I could almost hear her smile all those two or three miles up North from me.

'I'll come,' she finally said, full of resolve.

'Good.'

'How do you want me to dress?'

I then knew we understood each other and what she sought from the encounter.

'You know that already, Sarah Jane. With humility. To please me.'

'I understand.'

'Should I bring any… toys?' she inquired.

'Do you like toys?'

'Sometimes,' she answered.

'I'll leave that to your discretion then.'

'OK.'

It was nearing ten at night when we both hung up. I sat there for a few minutes, watching the emerald green screensaver flicker, then I switched the computer off. My cock was still semi-tumescent, expectant. She'd mentioned she had auburn hair and wasn't very tall. She was only twenty two. I estimated the chances of her actually coming here tonight were two to one. Reasonable odds.

I settled on the bed with two cushions against my back, and began reading a new crime novel I was scheduled to review, but gave up after a few pages without ever managing to concentrate on the text.

She arrived a half hour later and called my room from the lobby.

'It's Sarah Jane. I'm here.'

'Good. Take the elevator at the back of the lobby and come present yourself, Sarah Jane. The room is just down the corridor. The door will be open. Come in without knocking and kneel.'

'I will,' she acquiesced, her voice just a whisper.

I was still naked, but felt that would be too obvious, so I pulled the white cloth robe from the bathroom door and wrapped it around myself. I switched the room's main light off, only leaving the two small reading lights on each side of the bed on.

I sat on the edge of the king-size bed and awaited the young journalist's arrival with measured trepidation.

'Hello.'

She assumed her position, as I'd instructed. It was just a game. But we had to follow the conventions. Over the course of our online chat, she had revealed she had formally been with doms on a few occasions and had undergone some training. It wasn't just the sex that turned her on, it appeared, but the loss of control, sometimes the humiliation. Made sense. A genuine submissive thinks and reacts in ways that vanilla society can't understand.

I had never pretended to Sarah Jane that I was a genuine dom, let alone a Master, as some preferred to call themselves. I had explored my own submissiveness in a different context on occasion and was conscious that when not with women I had a strong streak of submission deeply ingrained in my soul. It confused me.

'So this what you look like.'

Her gaze stayed downwards, fixed on the hotel room's parquet flooring.

She was very appealing. Small and frail, with a face that reminded me of an even shyer version of the actress Renée Zellwegger. Her complexion was deadly pale under the light reddish hair and she had a few awkward pimples on her forehead and right cheek. She wore flat black slip on shoes and a flimsy floral dress that would have been better suited to the Tennessee backwoods than Manhattan. Her long hair was parted in the middle. I could smell her. Anaïs Anaïs I thought, or maybe it was a Givenchy fragrance whose name I couldn't recall. A perfect china doll; her pale brown eyes were narrow and gave her a whiff of the Orient too.

But her determination and strength broke through. There was a ferocious intelligence at work here behind the little girl facade.

My stomach tightened up. I had not expected this wonderful vulnerability. Just one look at this small woman kneeling at my feet and I was responding in ways I shouldn't.

I had to remember we had agreed this was only sex. Use. A commercial transaction in which money took no part, just the hard currency of lust. I must not get involved.

She misinterpreted my lengthy silence for possible disapproval and mistakenly assumed I was just sitting there waiting for her to make the initial move. She did.

She lowered her head to the floor and kissed my bare foot, as a sign of obedience, of total submission.

'No,' I whispered. Aware that under different circumstances, a social meet, a hello in a bar, on the next seat on a plane, I might bleed to love her.

This was no time for raised voices.

Again Sarah Jane got me wrong, straightened herself and her hands moved towards the belt of my robe and opened it.

Call me shy but it was all happening too fast. She took my cock in her warm hands and caressed it with silky tenderness and brought her face close to it. Her tongue extended and grazed my tip. I shuddered. I wanted to stop her but the beast inside me silenced both my heart and voice and allowed her to lick the tip of my cock with obvious expertise.

I extended my arm in her direction and combed my fingers through the fine curtain of her hair as she began to service me.

Her mouth was exquisite as she mapped every contour of my penis with slow deliberation, her small fingers clutching my stem and balls like a velvet glove. This was a young woman who had sucked cock before and visibly enjoyed it, never too fast or over eager to punctuate the rhythm and rise of the blood within and accelerate my automatic reactions to her ministrations.

I should have been enjoying this moment. Her mouth working away on me, her docile position below me, her utter submissions and desire to please me, but I was still half hard. Not that Sarah Jane said anything or remarked upon it.

The sight of her delicate face, the lost expression in those eyes was still having its effect one me. I was touched by her presence. Already

I knew that I somehow wanted more out of Sarah Jane than sexual congress, use, what have you. The fact that for one so young she appeared to have come to such an early understanding of her submissive nature and the likely history she must have behind her made me yearn to know all about her, even though I was sadly aware that many of the details would hurt me deeply and stay carved in my mind forever, marking me with their desolation. I remembered how K had once remarked that the problem with the two of us was that we just thought too much. Life would have been so much easier if we thought less, and just lived in all simplicity, savouring experiences, episodes. But we hadn't been built that way. Did it make us an exception?

Would we have been happier as drones, a mindless part of the crowd, fucking like rabbits, abandoning ourselves freely to the flow of animal lust?

Sarah Jane lowered a finger and stroked my perineum.

My pulse rose.

Hell, this girl had been trained by better dominants than me.

She was well on her way now to coaxing my whole bloodstream into my jutting cock.

'Stop,' I ordered her.

She obeyed instantly. With no hesitation, totally compliant to the whims of my pleasure rather than her own.

Where did she come from?

'Rise.'

She lifted herself off her knees and rose, stood upright facing me with eyes still lowered towards the hotel room's floor. She couldn't have been much taller than five feet. And thin as a rake. The sort of kid you felt you could snap in half with barely a strain. She had almost no breasts. The thin cotton fabric of her loose dress fell across her slight stature, the faded flowers of its pattern shapelessly framing her.

'Look at me,' I said.

Her distant eyes focused on me. Both expressive and sad. Knowing and resigned.

I closed the robe, concealing my cock again. I could still feel its clammy wetness, the lingering quicksilver liquid touch of Sarah Jane's tongue meandering across it.

In the room on the other side of the wall, someone had a radio or the TV on. I recognised David Bowie's 'Let's Dance'.

It was at times like this, with or without soundtrack, that you want the moment to last forever, for time to achieve an eternal sense of elasticity, expanding ever outwards. Never ending, its inevitable climax receding as fast as you moved forward.

I ached for her voice and words of explanation but knew that if I allowed her to speak it would break the spell, the tenuous relationship game we were playing. That I was playing badly.

'Raise your dress,' I asked her.

She bunched the material across her waist and pulled the dress up.

She wore no underwear.

Her cunt was smooth. Cleanly shaven.

A straight, barely reddish vertical scar across the alarming pallor of her stomach. Unlike other woman whose labia protrude erratically from their openings, Sarah Jane's cunt looked as if its lower lips had been cleanly excised by the sharpness of a razor blade, and her private portal was no more than a thin line in the landscape of her body.

There was also an irregular pattern of deep bruises moving from blue to yellow across her upper thighs and lower stomach.

I gulped.

She noticed my reaction.

'It's OK,' she said. 'They don't hurt. I don't mind them.'

'But…'

'Pain is OK,' Sarah Jane said. 'It keeps you alive.'

'Who?' I asked her.

'My boyfriend. He's also my Master.'

'You didn't mention him,' I remarked.

'His name is Daniel,' she answered. 'We don't live together. He's studying corporate law in Washington DC. He visited me the other weekend. It was just play, you know.'

'Very rough play,' I couldn't help remarking.

Sarah Jane ignored my negative reaction.

'Why did you agree to see me if you have someone like Daniel,' I asked her.

'I'm allowed to see others while we're apart,' Sarah Jane said.

'How liberal.'

'But I always tell him everything,' she added.

'I see.'

There was a moment of silence. In the neighbouring room, a different song was now playing, with a strong bass line, but I strained to recognise it.

'Take the dress off altogether.'

Her breasts were like small buds. Just one old fading bruise on the lower flank of her left one. A few freckles seeded her minimal cleavage.

Were it not for the pattern of marks dotted across her flesh, she would have looked completely like a child, with her hairless vagina and lack of hips. But her melancholy face had, despite her youth, seen things I couldn't imagine even in my most fantastic feats of sexual writing. The pools of her eyes, the angle of her mouth told me all this. Later, I would find out how true my guess had been.

'I'm anything but opulent,' she remarked.

'No matter,' I said.

61

'Do you still want me?' Sarah Jane asked.

'Yes… Most definitely.'

Right now, I was the one who wanted to kneel at her feet and explore her cunt with my lips and tongue, spread her open, absorb the colour of her insides, taste her and imbibe the memory of every single violation she had endured. Become her in order to know her fully, absolutely.

'Come here,' I beckoned her towards the bed.

She approached, stopped, 'Don't say words you might later regret, Conrad. This is just a fuck. I can't be anything more, you see. I have my life, whatever you may think of it and I have no wish to change it…'

'Sarah Jane, I…'

She stopped me.

'No more words.'

Her skin was cold as she came to me and allowed me to embrace her within the hesitant cradle of my arms. I'd left the air conditioning on and she'd been standing there naked for a while now. There was a switch by the bed that controlled the temperature and I flipped it off.

I kissed her forehead, reached for her lips, but she remained passive and didn't return my kiss.

She disengaged from our initial clinch and pulled on my bath robe's belt. I stepped out of the heavy white garment. We were now both nude. In my overweight condition, I must have towered like a clumsy giant next to her. Probably at least double her weight. She climbed on to the bed and renewed acquaintance with my cock, sucking on my balls and slipping a finger into my arse. Damn it, she wanted to be a whore while my senseless guilt dreamed of innocence. But her calculated move had the required effect and I pulled her down onto the bed cover and slipped a couple of sharp nailed fingers into her cunt. She didn't even flinch. She wasn't particularly wet.

We wrestled a lust dance for ages across the bed, tangling limbs, stretching extremities, teasing, fighting. All along, I could feel how Sarah Jane's whole being called for me to control her, rough her up, but I resisted. It was not an instinct that came naturally to me. Gentle, playful spanking, some element of restraint on occasion, maybe. But the way she reacted to my touch betrayed her longing for heavier use. I felt myself approaching that perilous slope all too easily.

We were in a sixty nine position, my cock lodged deep inside her throat, almost gagging her while my eyes feasted on her splayed open cunt and half of my fist engaged into her tight snatch, straining her sinews almost to bursting point. There was not a murmur of protest from her, even though I was sure I must be hurting her. Worse, she shifted her body and raised herself as if to force my hand further inside her, ready to take all my fist, encouraging me, my violence.

I retreated from the brink, withdrew from her, mouth and cunt.

Held my breath.

She slithered round me and positioned herself behind me. I was still on hands and knees, a posture both inelegant and indecent.

I felt her tongue lick the periphery of my arsehole, drawing unimaginable feelings from my soul and body. Methodically she circled my opening, untiring, voracious. Then her tongue darted inside my softened opening and she penetrated me by half an inch or so and ate me out. My throat was dry, my thoughts scattered to every remote corner of my soul.

I relished the wonderful obscenity of the moment.

An eternity passed. Finally, she tired. Her jaw must have been killing her.

'Fuck me now,' she said.

I moved around. Sarah Jane assumed the doggie position. I guided my wet cock towards the slim opening of her cunt and rubbed it a few times against her engorged edges.

'No,' she said. 'Not my pussy.'

I flinched. She was so small in build; my cock was rather thick. Could she take me there?

'Are you sure?'

'Yes, I want to feel thoroughly used.'

Earlier, online – or was it over the telephone? – we had mutually agreed we would not use condoms. We would fuck raw. A risk, I knew. But the thought of protection felt wrong in the circumstances. It was a question of trust. Instinct also.

I had some cream in my shaving kit. I fetched it.

She raised her rump, presenting her dark puckered entrance to my gaze in all its wonderful indecency. I thoroughly applied the Boots baby cream (I'd always found it to be the best cure for heat rashes or any kind of skin irritation) across her anus and pushed a second smear of cream inside with my finger. Her anal temperature was close to boiling. I lubricated the tip of my cock with saliva and positioned myself to breach her. It took a few back and forth movements but her fleshy ring opened easily for me and I was quickly half embedded inside her.

I could hear her breath slow and a flush appear across her shoulders and, no doubt, her front as I began ploughing her hot hole with added energy. Soon there was little resistance to my advance and her rear opening had all the pliancy of a cunt. The vision of my dark, fleshy cock plunging in and out of her gaping opening was exhilarating.

'Fuck me harder,' she rasped.

I accelerated my movements, my heavy balls slamming against the pale cheeks of her heaving arse with every forward surge.

'Yes, yes,' she encouraged me. The harder I dug deep into her with my member, the more frenzied and vocal her response became. As I sodomised Sarah Jane, my eyes moved manically between her engorged opening and the irregular patterns of bruises her previous lover had left across her rump and thighs.

I lovingly caressed the silken flesh of her arse as I still kept on fucking her, capturing the vibration of my lovemaking as it skirted over the surface of her skin.

Then I slapped her right arse cheek. Hard.

It just came naturally. Not something I'd even planned.

Sarah Jane's response was electric. Her whole body shook as if I'd applied leads to her.

I slapped her again. Harder.

I was half-heartedly hoping she might ask me to stop. But she didn't and I continued to mark her pale rump with the image of my hand as I defiled her anal opening with even stronger thrusts. Silently, she kept on encouraging me, her whole body responding whole-heartedly to my double pronged assault.

I had never hit a woman before. And I couldn't even justify my actions by pretexting any form of playfulness. I was now smacking Sarah Jane hard enough to know I was doing her harm and would leave marks. God, she made me do it. So, I realised, this was the way to really know her. I didn't, right then, know whether I should laugh, cry or just keep on fucking her like a crazed animal.

The dilemma quickly resolved itself as my lust, out of control, took the ascendant and with every movement inside her crashing against the soft barrier of her boiling innards brought my own release closer and closer, I soon could no longer hold on. No need to count sheep and delay the moment. A furious wave of both pleasure and anger rose from my loins and I literally exploded inside her arse, bathing her faecal corridors with all the pent-up juice of my sins. Then collapsed over her, flattening her slight body down onto the hotel room bed. I gasped for air as the tide of lust kept on ebbing and flowing inside and outside of me.

Neither of us said anything for several minutes.

Finally:

'You OK?'

'Hmmm…'

'Sure?'

'Yes.'

I could feel myself begin to shrink inside her rear cauldron, my still madly sensitive cock uncomfortably bathing in what was probably an unholy cocktail of come, shit and assorted secretions.

I prepared to withdraw from her.

'I'll go clean myself,' I said.

'Don't,' Sarah Jane remarked.

Rotating on the spot where she had been open to me on all fours, she turned to face me.

'I'll do it,' she said, her angelic face nearing my dangling, and humid penis.

'You don't have to,' I said to her, 'but I'm quite…'

She interrupted me.

'It's not a question of cleanliness,' she said. 'I want to.'

And, yet again, took the full length of my still dripping cock, so liberally coated in our respective emissions into her mouth and proceeded to lick me clean with appetite and application.

It was now past midnight and in Washington Square, outside the window, isolated groups of evening revellers walked by the giant arches, some furtive and others boisterous, at the end of another drinking day in the many bars of Greenwich Village. In the next room, they had switched the radio or TV off.

'Stay the night,' I asked Sarah Jane.

'Sure,' she replied.

I pulled the cover from the bed and slipped between the sheets. I indicated to her she should do the same and she pointed out that my come was still seeping out of her.

'The sheets,' she said.

'You said it, it's not a matter of cleanliness. It's a hotel room anyway, no need to bother. I'm sure they are quite used to stains, and worse.'

She joined me, cuddled up and set her head on my reclining chest.

At last a picture of normal intimacy.

The quiet after the war.

We spoke until halfway through the night.

Sarah Jane told me her stories. I provided an abbreviated version of mine.

The patterns were awfully similar.

Back in high school in New Orleans' Garden District, that disquieting feeling of not fitting in, the profound lack of understanding of how others could feel satisfied by their lot, by what the world landed on their doorstep. The frustration of normal relationships or, at any rate, their tentative building blocks.

One night, lingering too long in search of she knew not what in the French Quarter and killing time at the Café du Monde and striking up a conversation with another girl in goth make-up and colourful clothes. Agreeing to sleep at her nearby apartment off Burgundy and being coaxed into a threesome and mild bondage.

University in Texas, already aware of her submissive temperament and embarking on an ill-advised affair with a married professor who collared her and would offer her to friends in his bdsm circle.

All along the realisation that she didn't feel exploited or sexually used and that these depredations excited her more than anything and kept her spark alive amongst the boredom of her English Literature studies.

Indiscriminate and often rough sex with both men and women.

Being gang banged at a party with her own friends cheering along. Cigarette burns. Whips, tawses and paddles. Being filmed sucking a succession of strange cocks and being made to watch the ensuing video while being spit roast by two anonymous Hispanic guys recruited off the street by her dom. The Chinese (or was it Japanese?) symbol for 'slave' was tattooed in the fall of her back, which had fascinated me as I fucked her earlier. Oh, the stories. Of the time when she was peed on or made to defecate in public after being paraded nude, led by a leash attached to her dog collar. Like a race towards oblivion on a road full of sexual servitude or humiliation. Maybe at times it sounded like a scenario for a bad stroke book, an O-like calvary trail, a parody of real life, but I didn't question her appalling tale. I could see the truth in her eyes. This crazy yearning for the extreme things that made her life worth living.

In her final year, she had come across Daniel and moved in with him. She had met him at one of the rather particular parties she often had to attend and he was therefore aware of her past and sensibility. She knew he had other women and sometimes had even been asked to watch when he used them or even was ordered to find new meat for him. She wouldn't even always be allowed to participate. Now that they were in different cities, she had license to play elsewhere as he no doubt did, but she still found it difficult and only permitted herself one night stands. No, she didn't know what the future held. Following this final year of studies in Manhattan, she would try and get a job on a regional newspaper somewhere, to learn her craft. Maybe Daniel and she would live together again. Maybe they wouldn't. But she would remain at his beck and call. She had willingly submitted to him. This was her life.

It was obvious by her tone, however sad its accents, that she was not seeking a white knight to rush to her assistance, to set her on the path to normalcy.

I kept my mouth judiciously shut throughout her quiet monologue, stroking her hair, grazing her white skin with all the delicacy
my heart could summon, feeling the heat of her body against mine,
our combined warmth stored between these grey hotel room sheets,
savouring her bittersweet presence.

'I didn't bring any toys after all,' Sarah Jane said.

'It's not a problem,' I said.

'But there is something…' she added, and pushed the sheet away,
revealing her pale body in all its splendour, small dark scarlet
nipples, flat stomach (with bruises), smooth baby-like pudenda and
round arse. She stepped over to the door where she had, on arrival,
dropped a Barnes & Noble canvas tote bag.

She returned to the bed and handed me a large red candle and a
lighter she had taken from the bag. She handed them to me.

'Tie me down first,' she asked.

My silence betrayed my doubts.

'Please,' she insisted.

I had never played with hot wax before. With a woman. Or
myself. Frankly, the prospect scared me.

I had only known Sarah Jane just over six hours since our first
electronic hello.

As happened so often in my life, things were moving too fast and I
was no longer in control of the situation. But I had no choice, had I?

I now wondered about the provenance of those many marks on
her body. Obviously, they had not all been caused by hands alone. I
had naturally been involved with a handful of truly submissive
women before today, but never an authentic masochist.

The thought was dizzying.

I arranged Sarah Jane on the bed, spread-eagled and we managed
between us to find enough belts, neckties and scarves to immobilise
her four extremities in an obscene parody of nude crucifixion. I

looked back at my handiwork and, frankly, found her so beautiful it almost made me cry.

I held the candle above her taut stomach and lit it; very quickly the liquid wax accumulated in the small pool surrounding the wick and I slowly angled it downwards. The first drop fell onto her skin. She shivered. Then another. And another. With every drop falling onto her, her whole body convulsed quietly. I stopped. There were half a dozen so red stains dotted across her tummy, on either side of her navel. I could see the wax drying as I watched.

'My breasts,' she asked.

I moved upwards and proceeded.

Her reaction to the searing initial contact with the hot wax there was even stronger. Each drop extricated a deep sigh from the very depth of her lungs. The drops continued dive-bombing her almost non-existent breasts as I manoeuvred the candle in a circular motion around her nipples. Then, instinctively, I centred my aim and allowed an initial droplet to fall onto her right nipple. Sarah Jane shuddered and a deep moan escaped from her throat.

'Enough?'

'No. NO.'

The torture continued and I became more proficient. Learning to delay the moment just that one instant too long, to betray her expectancy of pain or accelerating the aerial bombardment so she had no respite between the savage injections of pain, no time to relax, eliminating the lows and concentrating on a continuous assault of highs. Soon there was no clear skin left on her upper body.

My mind was racing.

I set the candle aside, found a final scarf in Sarah Jane's tote bag and tied it around her head, covering her drowsy eyes, blinding her. The silence in the room was isolating us in a bubble of lust and unspoken violence. Both she and I knew what inevitably came next.

I lit the candle once more. Its muted fire was fierce and hypnotising and drew me like a magnet.

First I scraped most of the dry wax away from her breasts and stomach. I had left barely a mark, which surprised me. Just a few fading blotches here and there. Sarah Jane's aroused nipples were darker and harder than hell itself. Which only served to encourage my folly.

I delayed the moment as long as I could, precariously balancing the hot wax pool at an angle. Then the first boiling drop fell in slow motion towards her cunt and splashed down on her hairless mound. Sarah Jane hissed, an expression of both plain and pleasure. I was ashamed to say I was now enjoying this.

I had noticed during the course of the exercise that the sensation the wax caused in her was stronger if its descent was shorter, so I approached the burning candle nearer to her exposed cunt and soon smothered her whole pudenda. There was sweat on Sarah Jane's brow but never did she utter a word to halt me.

By now I had run out of skin to attack with the hot wax and after a few desultory flights over her open thighs, perversely extended my hand towards her caked cunt and splayed it open with my fingers.

And liberally sprayed her pink insides with the hot wax.

Sarah Jane almost screamed as the first droplet of incandescent wax hit the delicate inner wall of her cunt, but bit her tongue and convulsed with pleasure. The wave of inner ecstasy hit her in overdrive and she came like an earthquake, squirming on the spot in rhythmic thrusts and sideways movements, both embodying the sheer utter pleasure of the moment and instinctively trying to evade the further drops of wax coating her exposed walls and her roaring, uncovered clit.

I held my own breath, quickly extinguished the candle, threw it aside and swiftly dug my cock into her, past the waxy coating and deep inside her. This was my first time in her cunt. Also, in all likelihood the last. I fucked her with anger, every forward movement a rageful assault, an ersatz rape. I didn't last very long and my orgasm was one of the strongest I'd experienced in ages. It obliterated me, cleansed my mind, forgave all my sins.

After I'd untied her, we stayed together another hour or so, but didn't talk much. There was little left to say. She gathered her crumpled floral dress at around five in the morning and made her way back to the Upper East Side. I offered to come down to the lobby with her and help her get a cab, even pay for it, but she declined.

We parted with a chaste kiss.

I returned to London a couple of days later.

Sarah Jane and I kept in touch by email on and off for almost two years after that momentous meeting. She did move to Washington and worked as an intern on a local political magazine. Lived with the evil Daniel again. Then she was offered a job on a small local newspaper in Cedar Rapids. We drifted apart. I don't even remember whether it was her or me who failed to respond to a final email. I just hope she's alive and happy somewhere. Living in her private version of hell. Just like me.

It's easy: you just don't think about it too much.

Isn't the zombie life seductive?

'Y ou're in luck,' Kerith said, 'they have a few vacancies. You'll see, it's so conveniently situated. Soho never sleeps. The place to be.'

Cornelia thanked him and followed him to the club's reception where they made the necessary arrangements. She would move in the following day. She would book out of the Cumberland tomorrow and move her sparse luggage.

Kerith suggested they celebrate.

'It's a bit dead through there,' he said, pointing to the club's bar area, where the crowds were thinning.

'Anywhere in particular you'd like to go?' Cornelia enquired.

She could hazard a fair guess as to the eventual destination he had in mind. But she had to humour him. An idea suddenly snaked through her mind. Yes, that was it. She had to obtain access to his office. The literary agency must have bountiful files of correspondence with Conrad Korzeniowski stacked away somewhere. Maybe there would be a paperwork trail of sorts leading to this hypothetical book of his, this manuscript she was being paid to track down.

'Did you have something in mind?' she asked Kerith.

'Hmm...' he pondered loudly.

'Yes?' she insisted.

'We could go over the road to Soho House, might be more lively,' he suggested. 'Or then again, a change of scene. I know this small club just off Ladbroke Grove…'

Cornelia pouted. Maybe the little girl mode would excite him?

'I'd prefer somewhere a bit more… private, you know.'

'Definitely, definitely.' His eyes had lit up.

'Not a bar or club.'

The middle-aged literary agent frowned, visibly advertising his dilemma.

'It's already late in the day. Not that many places left open, you see.'

'Exactly,' Cornelia said. 'I was thinking we could go back to my hotel. I've a bottle of duty-free malt. It would be nice to talk in peace.'

'That would be nice,' Kerith confirmed. She already knew she would not have to ask him twice. She had no such bottle, JFK duty-free or not, in her room. But she did have the right pills for the occasion in her toiletry kit.

'Good,' she agreed with him.

'Perfect,' he added, beaming.

'I'll just freshen up before we go, shall I?' Cornelia suggested.

'Please do,' he said.

She slipped out of the function room and made her way to the powder room. She had noticed a public phone there earlier. She called the Cumberland and arranged a quick deal with the head porter, so that the mythical bottle of malt whisky would magically emigrate to her room.

The only decision that remained to be taken concerned Kerith and how far she would allow him to take things. It had been a few months since she'd had a decent fuck, and it felt almost like a matter of sexual hygiene to get laid sooner or later, but on the other hand there was also something oily about him that she disliked at some primeval level. Allowing him to mount her would only serve to boost his innate arrogance.

She'd play it by ear, she decided, and returned to fetch him.

'Wonderful,' he said as she walked up to him, as if the recently applied make-up suddenly enhanced her beauty in some obvious way. All she'd done was wash her hands clean! Hypocrite.

'I'll get us a cab,' he said, leading the way out of the club onto the bustle of Dean Street. Darkness had fallen and the evening light had the acrid urban fragrance of neon.

'A lady with a laptop!' Kerith exclaimed as she ushered him into her spartan room at the Cumberland. Their cab had snailed its way through the Oxford Street traffic, while his fingers repeatedly explored the uncovered territory of her left knee during the slow drive. His breath already reeked of stale alcohol.

Her Power Book lay closed on the bedcover. She still had to find a universal plug that would allow her to connect but had had to rush to the funeral straight after her morning arrival from the airport. The jet lag part of the trip hadn't yet kicked in.

'Could be worse,' Cornelia said, 'could be a lady with a gun…' The whisky bottle was on the small table by the window as she had instructed. With two clean glasses. She just hoped there was ice in the mini bar fridge. He was just the sort of man who'd insist on ice in his drink and, unlike American hostelries, London ones didn't automatically provide ice machines on every floor.

Kerith settled himself down in the room's lonely chair as Cornelia dropped her imitation Burberry handbag in one corner and excused herself, moving towards the bathroom.

'Help yourself,' she said, her back already turned on him.

'Excellent choice,' he said, grabbing the sacrificial bottle of malt.

She freshened her face under the cold water tap and explored her toiletry kit for the pills. The label on the small plastic container described them as a form of aspirin to be taken twice a day, under medical supervision. She'd printed the bogus label herself a few days prior to the trip. She was always finding new uses for the computer and its attendant technology.

Kerith was slowly sipping the malt in his glass with unctuous deliberation when Cornelia returned. There was no other chair in the exiguous hotel room and she sat on the side of the bed, carefully hitching her black dress up to mid thigh, no doubt allowing the older man a good view of her underwear.

'Would you pour?' she ordered him, presenting her glass.

'A pleasure,' Kerith said and served her a generous amount from the bottle.

'So…' Cornelia said, with an enigmatic smile.

'So,' the agent replied. 'Miranda?'

'Yes?' Cornelia said.

'Tell me; it's just the two of us here and I'm curious.'

'Tell you what?'

'Just a fan of his books? Or did you actually know Conrad?'

'You mean did I fuck him?'

He coughed and blushed, taken back by her directness.

'I suppose that's what I was trying to find out in my stumbling way, yes,' he finally admitted.

'Would it make a difference?' Cornelia asked.

'I suppose not,' he replied. 'It's just that… hmmmm…,' he hesitated. 'Hmmm… all these women he wrote about, one sort of assumes he knew them, that they do exist in real life.'

'So, in which book of Conrad's am I supposed to appear?' she questioned him.

'Not easy to say,' Kerith replied. 'I haven't read all his stuff.

One of the younger agents in the office dealt with him most of the time. But you seem a sort of amalgam of many women.'

'Really?'

Kerith took another slow sip of whisky.

Cornelia still hadn't sampled hers. She wasn't into booze.

She had to kill time harmlessly until she had the opportunity to do the deed.

'What do you do, back in America?' Kerith asked her.

Cornelia chuckled and, mischievously, decided to tell him the truth. Or at least part of it. She knew that would keep him hanging on.

'I'm a stripper,' she said.

'You're kidding me, Miranda?' he reacted.

'Not at all, although some of my colleagues sometimes prefer to be called exotic dancers. But the phraseology doesn't bother me.'

'I'm amazed,' he said. 'I never would have guessed. I would have known of you, of course, if you'd worked in the publishing world, surely, so I had you pegged as an academic. Amazing.'

'I did go to university,' Cornelia pointed out. 'So your intuition wasn't totally wrong,' she pointed out.

The literary agent hastily emptied his glass, still absorbing the impact of Cornelia's revelation. She promptly offered him a refill.

'You're incredible,' he remarked. And inevitably, 'Why do you do it?'

'Do what?'

'The stripping,' he confirmed.

Men invariably asked that. Even the bright ones.

'No complex motivations,' Cornelia pointed out. 'I enjoy it. It's sexy. it's fun. You might say it empowers me, if you have a liking for clichés.'

'So that's how you met Conrad?' he continued.

'Why won't you believe me, Mr Kerith? I never met Conrad. I'm just a fan, someone who would read his stories.'

'Call me John,' he insisted.

'OK, John.'

'Could actually make a great book, the journey from university to striptease,' he remarked, his professional nous returning. 'You sound like a girl who could even do her own writing...'

'Maybe,' Cornelia said. 'And I suppose I'd need a literary agent?'

Kerith roared with laughter. And half emptied his second glass. His features were reddening by the moment as the alcohol coursed through his body.

'Did you come to London to... work?' he asked her.

'No, it's just an open-ended holiday, a spur of the moment thing' she answered. 'But maybe, if I run out of cash, I might freelance a bit. I've been given some contacts in London should I feel the need.'

'I'm sure you have.'

'Yes.'

'I... I...' he stumbled over his words as he grew hotter under the collar. 'I hope I don't offend you by saying I'd be most interested in witnessing your... act, if that's what you call it, Miranda...'

'Not at all,' Cornelia replied. 'I'm not ashamed of what I do. Although,' she added, 'I wouldn't pretend it's art either.' She smiled.

Then decided that this ridiculous cat and mouse game had gone on too long and went on the offensive.

'As I'm still unsure whether I'll be doing any gigs in London, John, maybe you'd like a private performance? We call them lap dances back home, do you have those here?'

His eyes lit up.

'Don't you need music?' he queried.

'I'm sure I can find a suitable tune on the radio,' Cornelia said, pointing to the fact the television also had a choice of radio channels.

'I don't know what to say. It's a most... generous proposal...'

'Well,' she said. 'If I am to write a book about my idiosyncratic life story, surely my literary agent must have some evidence of my professional talents, shouldn't he?'

'Of course,' he agreed.

'It's a deal, then,' Cornelia concluded.

She moved to the television set, brushing her legs against Kerith's as she did so and squeezed past the chair he was sitting on. She hunted down a music station.

'Maybe someone will be playing Conrad's song?' she joked.

Kerith beamed at her, and downed the rest of his second glass of malt.

'Look,' Cornelia said. 'Maybe you should refresh yourself in the bathroom for a minute or so, while I try and adjust the lighting. You'll be more comfortable. And, ' she added, 'we don't want you to have to take a break midway through my little show, do we?'

'Quite,' Kerith agreed and hurried off.

'I'll pour you another glass,' she shouted out. 'It'll be ready for you when you get back. And so will I, of course.'

The two small white pills dissolved instantly. She knew their taste would be undetectable in the alcohol. A double dose like this would have floored an elephant. She just hoped he hadn't misinterpreted her too much and would emerge from the bathroom stark raving naked and with his cock at salute stations!

He had taken his jacket off, and visibly washed his florid face, but that was all. She ordered him back to the chair and dimmed the hotel room's lighting.

And danced with agonising slowness, her eyes fixed on him and observing his pleased reaction. Initially, it was some electronica tune, with synthesiser washes surrounding a faint melody; then it was a mid tempo Elvis Costello song with a tasty chorus she could hum along to as she moved in front of him, every movement dictated by the ebb and flow of the music from the tinny speaker.

By the time she had rid herself of the little black Armani dress and was down to her Myla underwear, Kerith had lapsed into unconsciousness. Even his initial, and noticeable erection had subsided behind the woollen material of his dark trousers. She gave him a sharp prod to check, but he was out for the count.

She had at least six hours.

And would no doubt think of some explanation for Kerith, when he woke up the next day with a raging headache and little detailed memory of the evening before.

Cornelia slipped on a pair of jeans and a promotional T-shirt advertising her Caribbean holiday resort, and pulled her black leather half-length coat from the wardrobe. She took a bunch of keys from the somnolent man's jacket pocket and made for the door and the London streets. It had been easy. She knew the address of the literary agency; it was on the business card he'd given her earlier.

SOME KIND OF HAPPINESS, SOME KIND OF LONELINESS

Cornelia had the rare luxury of several hours to search through the dark offices. She'd bought a small torch at a 24 hour convenience store just off Marble Arch before catching a cab here.

Had she known how many files, how much paperwork she would find scattered across desks and filing cabinets in the twin set of rooms, she would have had second thoughts about coming here. She quickly located the folders containing all the correspondence between Conrad Korzeniowski and his publishers, but they only appeared to go back two or three years. However, she guessed that the apocryphal book she had been dispatched to find must be recent and was unlikely to be mentioned in earlier correspondence anyway. Most of Conrad's communications over this period were in email format, but had scrupulously been printed out for the record.

The majority of it related to commercial transactions, offers from foreign publishers and negotiations about advances, book club deals and royalty rates, and there was little reference to any work in progress.

Damn.

Who said it was going to be easy, though?

It appeared to be a relatively small agency; there were only three computers.

Cornelia quickly located Kerith's desk, switched on his PC and ascertained through a cursory search that there were files on or about Conrad stored away in its labyrinthine memory. There was no time to read them now, let alone print them out or copy them. She didn't have the technology of 'Mission Impossible' at her disposal, she reflected. This was real life and things were just that touch clumsier and more realistic. She managed to open the computer and pull out the hard drive. She then remembered Kerith mentioning that a junior agent had sometimes dealt with Conrad's affairs. She checked out the other two computers in the suite of offices, quickly located the one that had further Korzeniowski related files, and duly appropriated its disk. The final computer belonged to the resident accountant and only displayed financial data and royalty calculations. To give credence to a possible burglary or vandalism scenario, she also broke it open and threw the vital component to the floor and systematically trampled it until she heard pieces break off.

She then proceeded to sweep phones, files, unsteady piles of manuscripts and books off each desk there, and also attacked some of the shelves, disgorging their contents over the ancient shag pile carpet.

It would just confuse the police and point to an opportunistic burglary. Which it was. On departure, she took care not to lock the door with the keys she had borrowed earlier.

She headed back into the night with adrenaline flowing freely through her veins. It had been a new, enjoyable experience. Always a first time for everything, she reckoned. Now she would have to find some helpful computer geek to enable her to retrieve the good stuff from the two computer hard drives she carried in the canvas tote bag she had brought along to the break-in in expectation.

The night porter at the Cumberland helped her place the bag in a night safe, no questions asked, and Cornelia returned to her room.

Her whole body still vibrated from the thrill of her clandestine endeavour, combined no doubt with a zest of jet lag from her flight to London barely 24 hours earlier. Cornelia ached for some relief. She'd shot a quick glance at the hotel bar on arriving, but it was almost empty. No available man. A fuck would have been good, she thought. And there was now no way she was going to get a rise out of Kerith upstairs. Not that he attracted her in the least.

He was still slumped back on the chair where he had gone under as she walked quietly into her bedroom, his third and final glass of malt whisky having slipped out of his right hand and fallen first on his thigh, and then the floor. She picked up the glass and took it to the bathroom sink where she thoroughly washed it. She dropped his bunch of keys back into the jacket draped over the back of the chair, collar now crumpled and splattered with dandruff.

He would still be out for several hours, she knew.

Ignoring Kerith, she freely undressed in front of him, this time even disposing of her underwear. Which of course failed to wake him.

She stretched her long limbs, a minimal form of pre-bed gymnastics. She looked down at the middle-aged man snoring peacefully in his corner. Damn, she felt horny right now. Always did after a job, whatever its nature. She trailed a finger across her gash. Yes, she was wet.

And slipped between the bed's covers, switched the light off and promptly fell asleep.

Kerith woke up mid-morning.

He looked around, saw Cornelia's long limbs lazily extended under the crumpled sheets, her bare shoulders emerging like a pool of light from the bed. He could smell alcohol on his breath and clothes. His throat was dry. Had they or hadn't they? He just couldn't remember for the sake of him, and as he attempted to dig further into his memory cells, he felt the hangover of all hangovers swirl across his brain and body. He rose slowly from the chair, unfolding his arms and legs with painful deliberation.

He was still fully dressed and couldn't help but notice the young woman's underwear scattered across his shoes where she had lazily dropped the flimsy, silk garments. Again, he vainly searched his memory but could only come up with a gaping blank. Miranda moved in her sleep and the cover slipped, revealing a tantalising expanse of pale flesh.

He stood up, straightened himself out and taking care not to disturb her, he made his way towards the hotel room door. Cornelia vaguely heard him move. Yes, please, she thought, don't say anything, just go. He opened the door and she closed her eyes again.

Cornelia slept.

In her dreams, she swam in a sea of books. Every cover displayed the face of a different woman. Like a parade of humanity. And on the elusive soundtrack, a man laughed. And sometimes cried. As Cornelia danced across the waves, shedding her clothes like an angel of abandon, light as a feather, she somehow became conscious of a sudden burst of heat taking birth in the pit of her stomach, as if her whole body had caught fire right there and then and the weird feeling was expanding through her in concentric ripples. And could no longer be stopped. The conscious part of her mind resisted the whirlpool of thoughts and images and feelings and helplessness, but all she could manage was to slow it down and make the experience even more agonising. If there was one thing Cornelia detested, it was not being in control. She forced herself to open her eyes. Timid shafts of light from Oxford Street were peering through the blinds of the bedroom. She was in bed, her forehead was glistening with sweat and the sheets at her feet were a tangle of material.

'I should have found a guy to fuck,' she quietly muttered to herself and then smiled, aware of how ridiculous she was. She peered over at her Tag Heuer watch on the nearby dressing table. It was nearly eleven in the morning. At least she had caught up with her sleep.

Time to change hotels, as arranged.

Later that day, showered and fed and back on track following her momentary mental lapse, Cornelie found herself an Internet café near the corner of the Euston Road and Warren Street Station at the end of a long and rambling, exploratory walk casing out the immediate surroundings and beyond of the Groucho Club where she was now installed. Past experience had taught her to familiarise herself with the territory where she had to work. As well as avoid to use her own computer for the majority of her research. Anonymity had its uses.

She paid for a couple of hours and treated herself to a cappuccino.

She quickly located a company in Wandsworth, south of the river, who claimed to be able to retrieve anything from a failing hard drive. Those she held were, she assumed, in perfect working order, which would possibly provoke some inconvenient questions. She called them up.

'It's just that the… material is somewhat confidential,' she explained to the guy with an Indian accent who took enquiries.

'No problem, Madam, for us it's all just data and we have no interest in the contents we retrieve.'

'I realise that,' Cornelia said, hesitantly pleading in a little girl manner. But, you know…'

By now, the technician probably assumed she was hoping to retrieve compromising material, maybe porno shots of herself and was ashamed to admit to it.

'I realise it's delicate, but what precisely can I do for you, Madam?' he inquired.

'I was thinking…'

'Yes?'

'A private transaction, maybe?'

'I'm not sure what you mean,' he answered.

'Well, I'd like to avoid having the material retrieved publicly, so to speak. I was sort of wondering if you knew anyone who could do it, for an increased fee of course, privately. Off the books. Surely, you know someone, a friend, a colleague, maybe you?' Cornelia suggested.

There was a half of minute of silence on the other end of the line. Cornelia fed some extra coins into the phone.

Finally, the man quoted a fee.

'But it would have to be at the weekend,' he said. 'Saturday. I'd borrow the necessary equipment, though. Remind me what type of computer the drives come from? Not an Apple, I hope, they're tougher to crack.'

'Just normal PCs,' Cornelia informed him.

'Good. What about Saturday?' he suggested.

They agreed on a time and place. She jotted down the details on a small notepad she always carried.

Cornelia returned to her computer station. She still had over an hour's worth of online time. Time to kill, time to use up, play maybe. She had picked up a couple of Conrad Korzeniowski's early novels from a second-hand bookshop on the Charing Cross Road, but was in no hurry to read them. Even back in college she had not been an assiduous researcher, relying all too often on her innate instincts, her natural unformed intelligence. Others might have called it laziness.

This was not her first time in London; she'd visited a few times before and still couldn't decide whether she liked the city or not. Or rather, she couldn't quite grasp the essence of the sprawling city, where every area had its own personality and architecture, and never gave up its true nature to the casual stranger. Cornelia lacked curiosity when it came to places, new and old, and couldn't see herself filling up dead time with tourism or therapeutic shopping.

She exited Google and gazed at the blue screen on the green, semi-transparent iMac. Then, on a sudden impulse, summoned up the web browser again and called up an alternative adult chat forum with which she was familiar. The familiar logo emerged, initially in bits and pieces, then metamorphosing into the image of a blonde woman, not unlike Nicole Kidman, in leather collar wielding a whip. Cornelia typed in her screen name 'DeathAngel' followed by her four-letter password and entered.

She looked at the time in the top right hand corner of the Imac's screen. She had just over an hour to make a connection.

Chapter 2

I was asking her, as you do, about other men.

I already knew about those who had come before she met her present husband. What am I saying? Her only husband. Three in all, a modest figure. I was number five. Or did husbands maybe count double?

But surely, I inquired, there had been temptations, infatuations, attractions, even if nothing sexual had actually occurred?

'Well,' she hesitated, lowering her eyes with false modesty, 'there was a man in Wales. He was a bit like you in looks. Dark haired, intense. I just saw him staring at me in a strange, insistent way from across the room at a reading I attended. It was last year. October. At a library event in Wales.'

'Really?'

'The way it goes. A look in someone's eye and you think, it could actually happen, there could be sparks. Sort of wondering what it would be like to fuck him, be fucked by him… But we never even spoke.'

'Oh…' Somehow I was both disappointed and reassured. 'Anyone else?'

'Well,' her eyes again avoided me.

'Come on,' I insisted.

'The bass player in Grant Lee Buffalo,' she spat out, her tone almost breathless. It was at their gig, just last week at the ICA. I was standing towards the front of the crowd and he was on stage. Our eyes met. Jesus, he could have had me right there. It was crazy. I felt like a slut. I think Christopher must have guessed, or something, because he wanted us to leave at the end of the set and wouldn't stay for the encores. He's never too keen to go to music gigs these days, thinks he's too grown-up for that sort of thing.'

I smiled. The next day I looked up the American musician's name (and physiognomy – rough trade with an intellectual bent) in the CD liner notes. But never remembered it later.

'Was it the music?'

'No, just him, up there, it was his eyes, they just cut through me, I swear. He was deathly thin, even gaunt, not even my type of man. But I knew, and I think that he also knew that something was in the air that night. I even guess my husband had some second sense of it, because he also behaved unusually at the end of the concert, annoyed, frightened maybe.'

Frankly I couldn't see what she saw in him. Too American, too rock n' roll. But there was an element of danger present. The lure of forbidden fruit? But then I was still amazed that she was even having an affair with me. How did I even compare to a rock musician with tight trousers and charisma to spare?

Would I ever understand women?

Even as I slept with them, gazed voyeuristically at their features in repose as they dreamed next to me in the illicit beds of the hotel rooms we mostly inhabited, I felt I could read in their soft breath the seeds of their future absence or betrayal.

This was the summer of Grant Lee Buffalo. After our break-up I discovered Counting Crows and ached with the knowledge I would never play their music to her or whisper into her ears the lyrics of a couple of songs on the CD which just broke me up inside. Much later, I'd come across Matthew Ryan. And others. Singers, groups, musicians. Funny the way rock music punctuated the major events in my life, the women who hitchhiked with seeming insouciance across the irregular landscape that was my life.

This was K, of the tousled hair, the porcelain skin, the repressed anger, for whom I would buy a Leonard Cohen CD and prepare an assortment of compilation tapes she would only be able to play on her Walkman on her way to work near Goodge Street.

'Was' being the operative word.

A summer that lasted into early winter as lust made place for love and then desperation, as embraces grew in intensity and the fucking took on an aura of violence as I realised my days with her were numbered. It was already there, in her voice, in her eyes, in the subtle twist of her lips as she shied away from passion, her cold cold heart turning away from more serious involvement than sweaty copulations on office floors or adulterous hotel rooms rented for the duration of the lunch break. Those things you can't help but feel inside, can you? So, you turn the screw on your anger; you tighten your hold on her wrists as you hold her down and thrust inside her and she feebly protests that you are hurting her. You thread out the belt from your black trousers and, one night, tie her hands and render her helpless. She does not protest. Allows you to do it. You raise the ante. Order her to close her eyes, and circle her fragile neck with the dark brown leather belt. Just like a slave collar. You position her on hands and knees and forcefully take her from behind, watching in fascination as your thick, dark member breaches her openings and makes its savage way through into her wet intimacy, all the while holding on to the belt and pulling firmly, keeping her head in a vertical posture. With every new fuck, you feel her migrating still mentally further away from you. But within her silence she still submits to those perverted whims of yours.

She comes, again and again, under your ministrations, with a soft moan, a deep sigh and, torturing yourself, you imagine her being taken in a similar sexual position by another man, maybe the bass player from Grant Lee Buffalo even. You have used a piece of black silk to cover her eyes and theatrically arranged her over the bed cover, spread open, obscenely gaping, then led him to the room and indicated to him she is fully his for the taking. You watch. Of course he is bigger, longer and thicker than you and as he makes his way past her lips, his cock brushes the folds of her labia away inwards, and every in and out movement that shakes her whole, white body as he pumps into her bruises her engorged skin, marking her for ever. And, God in heaven, does he stay hard so long and never tire! The sweat glistens on her back, her breasts swing gently under the impact of his attack, and the animal sounds that rise from deep inside her are unlike any I have ever heard come from her before. Or, at any rate, not with me.

Ah, isn't my imagination vile?

Or, had I actually shared her with another man in real life, whored her for the sake of my madness, would she not have returned to silent Christopher, her husband? Maybe it was something she actually craved?

Two years later, Grant Lee Buffalo, having failed to achieve greater commercial success, broke up and Grant Lee Phillips, the singer and songwriter in the group would launch a solo career. But his music on its own somehow never recaptured the intensity and gut wrenching impact of that initial year.

I never discovered where the bass player went or what he did. Another minor casualty of the rock and roll wars.

The French Lycée in London's South Kensington was the first school I attended where the sexes were not segregated and my initial few months attending classes there proved highly distracting. I soon lost my fascination for the Tour de France and continental bicycle riders and discovered that new race: girls. Somehow, before, they had never really meant much to me. They were just there, another gender, a mere curiosity.

To celebrate the end of the first term, the headmistress organised a small party, where all final year students, of which I was one, were invited to sip soft drinks, mingle socially and even dance, albeit under the watchful eye of the staff.

Thinking back on the occasion, I reckon it must have been shortly before the Christmas break, when many of the students from France and overseas would return home for a couple of weeks or so. I was awkward, had no social graces, moving from group to group of students and not-quite-friends, making small talk and stealing furtive glances at Catherine Guinard, Rhoona DeMole, Elizabeth Lavelle and the myriad girls who'd caught my attention during the course of the term. Some were from my class, some from other groups in the same year. They were all supremely exotic, unreal in a strange sort of way, emerging from the cocoon of childhood into womanhood, stirring new, unknown emotions inside me that I was irritated to find I couldn't fully control. Creatures I wished to befriend, but knew not how, or even what to do with following the first insignificant conversation.

The headmistress worked the room, dispensing biscuits and cakes, helping to thaw out our shyness. Sensing failure, she finally signalled it was time for music. This was the year of the twist. Chubby Checker reigned supreme.

I hadn't truly wanted to go to the school's party but my mother had convinced me a change of atmosphere would do me good. I had fervently argued I couldn't even dance, so she had given me a twist-made-easy lesson a week before and I had been practising my movements in the bathroom every day since, using a bath towel as the centre of gravity for my graceless movements.

Six months later, the cancer inside her got the better of my mother and she died.

But the Chubby Checker tune was the song I was prepared for that day and when the first strains of its melody sounded, I swiftly moved onto the dance floor and studiously began dancing.

And oh, how I danced, and Catherine Guinard even joined me, with a wry smile on her face which just melted me inside. We twisted again like we did that winter and it felt wonderful and at the old age of 16 I entered the world of women in earnest. Forever. Never to leave it again, for good, for bad, for joyful, for heartbreak.

Encouraged, I even invited Catherine out a few weeks later after classes resumed in the New Year. Small Catherine who looked like a bird and made my hear flutter. But that's another story altogether. A sad one of course, but then it wasn't Chubby Checker's fault so hey ho let's twist again in a circular motion and close your eyes and imagine you are drying yourself after a shower and your body gyrates against the soft contact of the bath towel against your skin. Oh yeah.

When I returned to Paris I finally drowned in the sea of sex.

It was a mixed soundtrack, blending the studious sounds of jazz my flatmate would play non-stop, making me feel so damn guilty I could find no pleasure, no celebration of the senses, in its arty tones, together with the latest hits I would import from back home, early Beatles songs, the Stones' 'It's All Over Now' which would start the adrenaline flowing inside me like few other rock tunes. A feeling I would soon grow accustomed to, opening myself to the sheer emotional power of music and being amazed by the fact some melodies could affect me inside so strongly and scar my soul forever.

It was a time of folly, of foolishness and shattered ideals.

Lois had blonde hair the colour of straw and looked, to my inexpert eyes, like a svelte and beautiful model. Her breasts were small but full and her skin the colour of porcelain, and I would feel like fainting every time I entered her, believing it was all a dream and this was too good to last. Of course it didn't, and she quickly tired of me.

When I remember her these days, it's to the sound of the Four Tops' 'Reach Out and I'll Be There', the Tamla Motown hymn that kept on being played at the party at which we met.

Nicole and I never even had sex. We spent hours naked together on my bed but never crossed that momentous Rubicon. Did we have a song, a group? I hate myself now for not remembering the soundtrack of our relationship. She had high cheekbones, short, thick, light brown hair and a compact body. Her nipples hardened under the mere breeze of my breath. She was the first woman ever to say 'I love you' to me.

And then there was the time I even went out with a singer on the folk circuit. When her career hit a roadblock in England, she decided to move to Nashville from where she would send me occasional demo tapes. She later married the much older owner of a Greenwich Village club and settled down to have kids before we lost touch. I still have her albums, gathering dust with the rest of my vinyl collection up in the attic.

With Melinda, we spent hours together listening to the fey but then rather exotic sounds of the Incredible String Band on my deficient hi-fi and slowly fell in love in a quiet, unassuming way, later setting the seal on our relationship with a bus ride to the Hackney ABC to watch Franco Zeffirelli's film *Romeo and Juliet*. Perfect romantic fodder for the now unlamented late 1960s.

Elaine was a classical buff, dressed most conservatively and sucked me off with zeal of a common whore.

Tabitha liked Duran Duran and most of the New Romantic bands and liked to have her hands bound when we fucked.

Leonard Cohen's melancholy tunes punctuated the long, on-of

affair with Mimi, although she was also partial to Metallica and isolated opera arias, a woman of diverse tastes and moods and sexual cravings.

There is something about Cohen's music, I suppose, that strikes a resonant chord inside my heart and my loins. I would often include his songs on the various compilation tapes I used to record for her-who-must-no-longer-be-named, alongside music by the Walkabouts, Counting Crowes, Springsteen, Peter Gabriel, Oh Susannah, the Handsome Family, Matthew Ryan and, again, Grant Lee Buffalo.

Music, sex and heartbreak or the Reader's Digest abridged (and expurgated) story of my life. The people at Sony, Virgin and other record companies must be laughing all the way to the bank at my excuses for keeping them in business.

But when I suddenly wake up at three in the morning in an alien hotel room in some American city or other and the world outside is cold and silent and the emptiness inside me is just too much to bear, random thoughts evoke faces, bodies and tunes from yesterday with uncanny poignance.

Mimi's so pale blue eyes.

A tune from 'Aida'.

K's cunt. Her gash like a blooming flower of blood.

'Truly, truly, truly.'

Nicole's uneven teeth. A smile designed to launch a thousand hips.

Gainsbourg's 'Melody Nelson'.

And on and on.

Maybe I'm just a sexual romantic who's seen too many movies and feels that every life, every relationship requires a soundtrack?

Or a disgusting, self-deluded pornographer, who believes that the shocking intimacy of every act of sexual excess can attain unknown heights of sheer beauty if provided with the right musical accompaniment?

I can live with both theories I suppose.

And already my shameless mind is busy speculating on what Claudia's soundtrack will be. Forget the hotel room, the railway station we meet at or the foreign city that will shelter our bodies, the colour of the wallpaper, whether she keeps her eyes open or not when we fuck, what I want to know already is how I will remember her when it is all over, as it inevitably will be one day.

I vainly try to guess what sort of song will go with those breathless phone tones of hers, that unsaid longing, that sadness that is already bringing us together despite all the obstacles.

A dance tune from Jamiroquai?

A melancholy dirge by Goldfrapp?

I do wonder if Claudia has ever listened to Grant Lee Buffalo in their glorious heyday, and whether she might fancy the bass player? Not that I have a threesome in mind, I assure you…

They had agreed: no names.

She would remain 'DeathAngel' and he was 'AngelTamer'. He had adopted that persona to page Cornelia online, and she hadn't had the opportunity to check what he had called himself earlier, before adopting that nickname in response to hers. It made his intentions clear from the outset. Which suited her fine. Those who made the initial approach were either plain stupid role players or else happened to be just right. This was as good a way of meeting as any. In real life, in a social environment, men tended to be reluctant to approach Cornelia. Maybe because of her looks, her icy coldness; it was a problem. In her mind's eye, she reckoned she looked quite normal and that nothing about the way she normally dressed or acted betrayed her second, or even her third life, if you considered the stripping work an arcane escape route from the reality of day-to-day living.

His forum profile had been left blank, so she had no choice but to accept whatever tenuous information he had provided in the course of their brief on-screen chat. So was hers. It was par for the course. Better the unknown than a pack of self-serving lies.

They had agreed to meet in Camden Town late that afternoon, opposite a furniture shop which specialised in heavy, rustic wooden furniture. It wasn't a weekend so Camden High Street wasn't its usual thoroughfare of teeming humanity populating all the colours of the rainbow. As Cornelia stood on the corner waiting for AngelTamer, she couldn't help but scan all the passers-by, hoping maybe to identify her 'date' before he could spot her. Which she knew was unlikely anyway. How could he miss a six-foot blonde with gorgon hair? She realised he had not even provided her with a description of himself.

Young women in tummy-baring T-shirts, many of them pushing baby buggies, swept by at regular intervals, punctuated by earnest couples hand in hand and the occasional more mature specimen. There was an older man, in his fifties perhaps, but age was something Cornelia found increasingly difficult to evaluate at a glance, as most people no longer dressed according to tradition.

He slowly came towards her but didn't even give her a glance, and passed on by. His hair was swept back in bouffant fashion, badly concealing a cavernous bald patch. Cornelia caught herself checking up on the back and top of the head of every man walking in her proximity, up and down the High Street. And was surprised that seven men in a row all sported bald patches. An anomaly or a sign of the times? All but two of them had made a concerted effort to disguise their evolving condition. Some of the styles were elaborate, others desperate, and a couple quite casual and outspoken in the way the remaining strands had been manipulated into place. Cornelia smiled. She just knew she'd never be able to get on with a man who was not only going bald, but also tried to conceal the fact. Call her intolerant. She hoped that the mysterious AngelTamer didn't fit into this dreaded category.

A woman brushed past Cornelia and made her way into the furniture shop. Cornelia's eyes followed her, scrutinising her back and, particularly, her shoes. Pale beige and pointy with thin straps lacing their way up the woman's thin legs. Interesting, but not quite enough to convince her to ask the stranger where she had bought them.

'Hello…'

A man's voice, smooth, a moderately deep baritone, confident, but with an unexpected American accent. Not quite New York, but neither Boston. Geographically halfway between the two cities.

Cornelia turned round.

'I'm AngelTamer',' he said. 'You must be DeathAngel'.'

He was in his early forties, hair greying but all there, with warm brown eyes and an enigmatic smile spread across a pair of thin lips.

'I am,' she replied.

'And quite an angel, too,' he remarked.

Cornelia snapped out of her earlier reverie.

'You're…'

'American,' he confirmed. 'Yes. Disappointed by the lack of Hugh Grant accent? I see you're from the States too…'

'Yes,' she said, still taking him in.

'Visiting or resident?' he asked.

'Just here for a few days.'

'And in search of some fun?' His smile was neither conceited or triumphant. Just the right degree of knowing mischief, she felt. Almost a smirk but not quite.

'As we discussed earlier,' she curtly confirmed. 'So what brings you to London?' she inquired.

'Research. A job,' he replied.

'OK.'

She found it deeply ironic that they should both have crossed the Atlantic to meet here, just for a scene.

Maybe those dark needs inside her would be better catered for in an alien environment?

Their first moment of silence came and went almost as quickly.

He wore a seemingly expensive black leather jacket and a dark grey Pierre Cardin shirt and slacks. His shoes were slightly scuffed. Visibly not the sort of man who worried too much about his appearance. His hair was parted on the side, but generally unkempt.

Yes, this could work, Cornelia estimated. Just the right distraction.

'No more questions?' she asked him.

'No,' he said. 'That's fine with me. It's what we agreed.'

'Yes,' Cornelia said.

'Shall we?' he proposed.

He was renting a small apartment half a mile up the road in a block near Belsize Park. Few words passed between them during the fifteen minute walk there. It was better that way. They were total strangers and it had to be kept thus. Cornelia was buzzing with muted fear and expectation. It had been a long time since she'd allowed something like this to happen to her so breezily; voluntarily relinquishing all control. Putting herself into the hands of a total stranger. But there was also something deeply exciting about this set of circumstances. And, as much as she reluctantly admitted it to herself, something she craved. Nor needed to reason why.

'Ready?'

'Ready.'

They both walked into the elevator.

'It's just two floors up,' he said.

They waited in silence.

'We could walk,' Cornelia said.

'So not even freaky elevator fantasies?' AngelTamer asked her, a fleeting trace of mischief in his voice.

'No, but give me time… Maybe I've been watching the wrong movies,' she suggested. The elevator smelled of disinfectant. Pine scented. Fear. It rose only two floors. They exited into the penumbra of a grey hallway with a parade of darker doors punctuating the straight walls. He indicated left.

'This way,' he said. Ordered.

Cornelia caught her breath as the man twisted the key into the lock. It was always like this, she knew. Would be wrong if she felt any other way: nervous, aroused, dead scared, totally exposed, but irremediably committed to what was about to happen. She knew the risks, but every time she played this dangerous game, she knew something inside her would always compel her to return to these troubled waters of her sexuality. Like an addiction that impaled her whole body. Much as she tried to reason matters, it was an integral part of her being, one she couldn't escape. And the worst part of all was the awareness of this deep and bruising failing.

AngelTamer pulled the door open.

'Come in.'

She took the necessary few steps forward into the apartment's entrance hall. White painted walls, a coat stand. She stopped. AngelTamer turned and looked to her.

'Take off your clothes.'

Without waiting for her to even acknowledge his order, he moved on to the nearest room on the right.

Cornelia bent over to take her shoes off. Then her stockings, slowly rolling the silken sheathes down her unending legs, enjoying the tactile sensation of the static electricity generated in the process.

The man returned. She couldn't quite see what he was holding in his hands. He looked down at her.

He raised his arm and, unfolding his anger, suddenly smacked her cheek. Hard.

'Too slow.'

'I'm sorry.'

'Shut the fuck up. I'm not here to listen to your sorry excuses.'

Cornelia lowered her eyes.

'Pull that up. Now.'

Cornelia exposed herself. As she had been ordered, she was not wearing any undergarments.

Her small breasts jutted outwards.

'Not quite a picture of opulence,' he commented. 'No mind. I like small tits.'

AngelTamer scornfully gazed at her cunt now revealed, offering no sign of either pleasure or disapproval. Looked to the floor where the black nylon lay in an anthill heap. He moved a step nearer to her. The contact of his hand against her already reddening cheek was sharp and stung.

'Bitch. Who said you could take those stockings off?'

This time, Cornelia knew not to offer an answer or an explanation. She had clearly already disobeyed his orders. Taking her clothes off clearly did not entail dispensing with her stockings. There was visibly a ritual involved and she had forgotten the unwritten rules. How should she slip the stockings on again, she wondered; must she keep her genitalia still exposed or allow the skirt to fall down again?

She somehow manoeuvred herself into an awkward position which allowed the man to still peer at her cunt while she rolled the nylon back up her white legs.

She guessed rightly that the outline of the man's hand on her sore cheek was the shape of a scarlet continent. She had no wish to see it expand an inch further across her face. She swiftly undid the buttons of her white blouse. Again she wore nothing underneath, but then she never did, even in normal circumstances.

Only in her stage act when it was just another garment to relinquish in the pursuit of titillation.

Now, she was quite naked, apart from the stockings. She had briefly pondered whether to put her flat shoes back on too, but intuited that the equation of flats and stockings did not have the sensual power of stockings and heels in the predictable eyes of men, let alone dominants.

She waited for what would occur next.

That's when AngelTamer hit her again, on the other cheek. For no reason or visible sign of disobedience or lack of satisfaction with her progress or anything she had failed to do or say. It was just to let her know he was now in charge and that she had agreed to submit to his will, whatever happened.

'Posture,' he barked.

Cornelia straightened her body, stretched every sinew in her elongated frame, but kept her eyes demurely lowered, avoiding his gaze as she stood before her new momentary master in all her pallor and nude glory.

She kept her eyes fixed on his shoes, brown moccasins held together by rough leather laces. She could feel the man examining every visible inch of her. Judging, evaluating, weighing every one of her flaws. He circled her. She remained glued to the spot. She could hear the shuffle of his feet on the shiny laminated floorboards of the apartment's entrance area, could feel the muted heat of his breath as he looked over her shoulders and, gently, pulled her hair up to uncover her thin neck.

' A fine specimen,' she heard him say. Grading her like an antique, or a slab of meat. It seemed that she was passing the inspection. She would do.

There was a lengthy silence while he continued his appraisal of her body; a police, or maybe it was an ambulance, siren raced by on the main road, ascending Haverstock Hill at accelerated speed.

'Come,' AngelTamer finally said, tapping on her shoulder for Cornelia to look up again, and indicated for her to follow him into the main room. She obeyed.

'There,' he ordered, pointing to the centre of the living room where he had shuffled away a low slung coffee table to make space for her. Discreetly, Cornelia took in her new surroundings, noting every irrelevant detail of furniture, fittings and minute cracks in walls and ceiling, as if this effort was about to delay the inevitable. The man threw his jacket down onto a leather sofa against the far wall.

He approached her.

'So, DeathAngel...' he whispered in her ear.

Cornelia knew better than to respond.

'You may answer,' he added.

'It's just an Internet name, a handle,' she said.

'No death wish, then, I hope?' he remarked.

'No.'

'Submissive women fascinate me. What they allow, get from it, ultimately seek. You see?'

Once again she refrained from comment.

'Oh, I could tell you stories...' he continued.

Somehow already Cornelia's mind had switched off and her body was in another dimension altogether, anticipating the man's whims and demands, however sadistic they might turn out to be, at one with the likely pain and pleasure he would choose to inflict. She tried to recall the first time she had recognised the roots of submission in herself, buried deeply into the most secret part of her soul. Early teenage years, she remembered, after reading 'The Story of O' and some Anne Rice books in quick succession and vicariously imagining herself in the clutches of Masters and torturers, being turned into a willing slave and fuck toy and more. The waves of pleasure so carefully hidden behind the curtains of propriety had been momentous, lasting, heart shattering and even though she never went back to the books, her own imagination had taken the relay and could now conjure up images, acts and situations which went so much further, she thought, than the s&m novels that had acted as an trigger for her feelings. She allowed a neighbouring schoolboy to fuck her at fifteen and, even though the act was arousing and satisfying to a degree, it would never equal the savage, necessary intensity of total submission. Only that brought her truly alive, she realised. She quickly understood, knew it was a part of her that must remain forever concealed, and took great pains never to allow both parts of her life to come together. Initially, she was the model student, the brilliant academic (in whom one canny lecturer recognised her true nature and elected to train her quite forcefully for a year or so, introducing her to the demiworld of dominance and submission, before passing her on to others with more experience and imagination), and later, the dilettante stripper, book collector and occasional hired assassin she had become. She had become a woman of two worlds. Which could never meet. The Internet and its murky hiding places and easy communication had proven a godsend. Part of her realised that the river she swam up was a dangerous one, but her soul also knew she could not live without the episodes of submission, pain and humiliation (although she was never a great one for pain, and fainted the first time a dom attached sharp, serrated nipple clamps to her delicate breasts). After all, she was now responsible for the death of 12 human beings in her new career, so what was there to be afraid of? Just herself.

His hand again made brutal contact with her cheek and roused her from her thoughts.

'Don't go all dreamy on me, bitch,' he said quietly, definite menace in his voice.

She returned to the present world. Her cheek stung badly.

'Spread,' he said.

Cornelia shifted her legs wide apart.

The man moved behind her, his hand roving rapidly over her bare flesh.

He withdrew for an instant and then, suddenly, Cornelia felt his hand move between her legs and cup her cunt. He slipped a finger across her lower lips.

'Decently wet, I see,' he commented.

The finger continued its exploration inwards and breached her. It felt cold, but only, she knew, because as the fever moved in overdrive through her body, she was reaching boiling-point inside.

She knew the symptoms all too well. Another finger joined it, then a third. He was now stretching her and she had to adjust her stance a touch to accommodate him. He finger fucked her quite steadily for a minute and, for a brief moment, she even thought he was going to fist her right there and then, but the thought seemingly had not occurred to him.

He pulled his fingers out of her vagina. She felt her cunt wide open and still gaping from his absence. Sighed.

'You want it that badly, do you?'

She refused to answer.

He raised his hand to her face and she readied herself for another blow but he shied from contact and merely advanced his fingers towards her lips.

'Open,' he summoned her.

Her mouth was dry and the lips stuck together briefly as she opened her mouth for him.

He forced all three of the fingers that had just now been rummaging inside her cunt past her teeth.

'Lick,' he said.

Her tongue recognised the familiar taste and heated fragrance of her own juices still coating the fingers. She methodically licked them clean as he expected.

'Good girl,' he said.

His hand returned to his side and he took a step or two back. Cornelia was still standing in the centre of the small room, her bust thrust ahead, her strong but shapely legs wide apart, the silk of her stockings taut across her flesh.

'Bend,' AngelTamer ordered.

Cornelia arranged all her weight on her awkwardly positioned feet and lowered the top half of her body forward, bending at the waist. Soon her rump was at a complete angle from the split tree trunk of her legs. Involuntarily, her legs moved slightly back together.

His hand brutally smacked her left buttock.

'Spread! I said spread, didn't I?'

The position was uncomfortable and her balance precarious. He kicked one of her ankles sideways, widening the angle between her outstretched legs. She almost fell over but quickly recovered her balance.

'That's better,' he said.

Unless she had been on her knees in a similar position, there was no more revealing stance, one in which she could have felt more exposed. The man knew that.

His hand gently caressed her arse, lingering insistently over the white skin, moving from globe to globe, assessing its smoothness, its softness.

Then his other free hand slipped into her arse crack and slid

107

down its valley to her anal opening. She knew the overall white-ness of her rump there made way to a subtle shade of pinkish brown, more suitable to a breast's aureola, where the skin of her backside began to pucker at the approaches of the small crater of her sphincter.

A finger delved over the rim of her back opening, testing her, it.

Cornelia shuddered. It was difficult to conceal the sheer sensi-tivity of that area of her body.

'Hmmm…' he said.

The finger suddenly dug into her and broke through into her arse and she felt its short invasion. He kept it there a minute or so, while the outer muscles of her sphincter began to relax and loosen after the initial, and natural, shock and resistance to the unnat-ural breach.

'Rather tight,' AngelTamer commented. 'I like that in a woman. I see you're no virgin, but you haven't been used there too much. Good.'

He moved his finger inside her in a slow, circular motion.

Then, as suddenly as he had entered her there, he pulled his finger out. The feeling was painful and for a moment, Cornelia again felt she was about to lose her precarious balance and tumble unceremoniously to the ground. Had she done so, she knew from the rules of the game that it would elicit some serious punishment. Somehow, she managed to stay in her undignified position.

There was a moment's grace as AngelTamer reflected no doubt on the next step of her ordeal. Cornelia could smell the pungent odour of bacon wafting through one of the apartment's windows, no doubt from a kitchen nearby. This mundane everyday fact and its incongruous juxtaposition with her situation made her smile.

She heard a gentle sliding sound behind her which she couldn't quite place, but soon recognised as the man's belt appeared in his hand. It was a thick black leather belt with a silver buckle. He had just taken it from his trousers.

'Shit,' she muttered under her breath. What had she done to deserve this? Had she not obeyed all his instructions so far. But there was no point protesting or claiming a lack of fairness. The dom positioned himself a foot or so behind her and she listened to the silent sound of the leather belt making its first ascent into the air.

The blow on her ass cheeks still caught her by surprise, sending a lava flow of excruciating pain through her whole body. Cornelia was unable to repress a deep moan.

Again, just a few inches above the first point of impact of the leather.

And again, this time below, almost at the point where her ass cheeks folded into her thighs. This hurt even more.

'Ohhh... she couldn't help crying out.

'What a lovely sound,' the man said and raised the belt again.

And made contact. This time she couldn't even guess where the blow landed. Her whole arse was on fire.

Jesus, she reflected, this is going to leave marks for days. The natural pallor of her skin meant she marked easily. Which excited men even more. They loved to witness the deep red welts they could inflict on her skin, their own special way of momentarily branding her. Making her uniquely theirs.

Cornelia, fighting the pain, grabbed a memory like a fishing line. The first time she had suffered severe corporal punishment. Her second year at University, when her then Master decided she was ready to be presented to his local circle of acquaintances. In the vestibule of the country mansion, just a few miles outside Boston, he had ordered her to strip and then led her into the large room where a a couple of dozen men and women were already congregating. They were all dressed in elegant finery while she was stark naked. She was paraded around the room like a prize filly, and then asked to perform. She had not understood what was requested of her. This was her first time in public as a submissive. Once the instruction was, she thought, explained to her, she reluctantly moved towards the man who had brought her here and, all too aware of the gaze of the whole audience upon her, began unbuttoning his trousers.

Angrily, her trainer had pushed her away and explained she must chose any man but him. Cornelia quickly acknowledged this cruel subtlety, but already the promise of later punishment was inevitable. She randomly chose another male member of the group, kneeled before him and quickly serviced him with her mouth while the audience watched. Then it became time for to pay for her mistake.

She was placed against the back of a tall, padded chair with her hands tied in front of her, as her posture was adjusted.

They flailed her with an assortment of implements : rope, leather straps, thin canes, tawses; it seemed to her that every participant had a weapon of choice. It seemed to go on forever. She moaned, cried, even screamed, but their ardour was unceasing and with every new attack on her back, buttocks and rear thighs it felt as if she was crossing through yet another of Dante's circles of hell, until she knew her fevered mind had conjured up even further circles than he had possibly envisaged. By the time they finished with her, she was a wreck. She had truly been broken and would have said or agreed anything, however foul or extreme it might have been. Which, fortunately, was not required. They weren't sadists. Just intent on training her.

The pain stayed with her for days and the memory of every

single minute of the episode was like a thorn in her battered flesh. She swore she would never be broken again that totally. And never would be. But soon she became aroused by the memories, and part of her sought for the inner pleasure the occasion had somehow provided her with again. Like a need, a drug, deep inside. A vice that defined her, her very nature. She was not nostalgic for the pain, but for the situation. The helplessness and total vulnerability that had defined her. She never sought out that dom again, though. There was too much independence and pride colouring her personality. She recognised the need for submission, abasement inside her but knew she could never agree to be the property of just one Master again. She wasn't 24/7 slave material. Part time slut would have to do. She would submit again, but on her own terms. A precarious balance which now guided her private life.

AngelTamer finally threw the belt aside and stopped.

Cornelia drew a deep breath, while the accumulated pain slowly spread from her marked buttocks to the rest of her body in concentric circles. She gritted her teeth against the ebb and flow of the pain on the exposed surface of skin. Her rear must look like a red and white crossword puzzle, she thought. But she also knew that the man had been artful, and she was not bleeding. The marks would go.

'So,' he said, 'that should soften you up, no?'

She refused to comment.

'You submit, DeathAngel, but somewhere inside that pretty head of yours, I sense there is something very rebellious. Oh no, there's nothing meek about you at all, young woman. Most interesting...' he added.

Cornelia stung abominably, as if a whole hornet's nest had been set loose on her arse cheeks and the raw top of her thighs.

He had spared her back and she was grateful for small mercies.

'Straighten up,' he ordered.

She picked herself up, overcoming the lassitude creeping through every sinew of her body as the warmth from the beating kept on invading her every nook and cranny.

His hand went to her cunt and sampled her increased wetness.

'Nice,' he said, mentally comparing this to his earlier examination. 'Almost ripe, wouldn't you say?'

Finally, she was standing tall again, although, from past experience with doms, she was careful to keep her legs wide apart and not decrease the angle that exposed her so much.

'So what shall I do with this whore now?' he wondered aloud. 'I don't think she deserves to be fucked quite yet.'

Cornelia swallowed. He had a good sense of her needs and seemed intent on foiling them, making the ordeal last longer.

'Maybe some toilet training?' he suggested. Then answered his own question. 'No, that would be a bit messy. It's a rented apartment, after all.'

The sting in her flesh was beginning to subside just a little. She'd be raw for a few days, she was aware, but the worst was over. There, at any rate.

'On your knees, slut,' he finally commanded.

Once she was in position, he approached her. Installed himself in front of her. The wooden laminate floor was both smooth and cold under her knees.

'Worship me,' he asked.

Cornelia moved her hands upwards and unbuttoned his trousers and then unzipped him. He was not wearing underwear. His cock was already partly erect. She helped the trousers down his legs and he stepped out of them. She pulled his thin black socks off and looked up again. His penis was darker than the rest of his body, not specially long but quite thick, uncut, ridged, veiny. Its mushroom head reared out of the wrinkled skin of his sheath and loomed purple and regal. His balls sack was shaven. She moved her face nearer. He smelled of soap. She was about to take his cock in one hand to facilitate its insertion into her expectant mouth, and wetted her lips in anticipation. But he suddenly drew back and slapped her cheekbone.

'No,' he said. 'You'd like that too much, I feel. Not quite yet.'

He pulled his shirt off and now stood there fully naked, towering over Cornelia's prostrate form. A moment he had purposely been delaying until now, enjoying the superiority his clothes automatically afforded him over her fragile pale nudity, the sheer vulnerability of her exposure.

The man who called himself AngelTamer turned round and presented his rear to her. She noted he was only moderately hairy. She'd seen more hirsute in her days.

'Now,' he shouted with a breath of authority.

Cornelia neared her mouth to his buttocks and parted his crack with both her hands with abominable gentleness, avoiding any movement that might anger him, surprise him. She unveiled the cratered depth of his rear hole, sheathed in a thin forest of humid, short hairs. She approached her tongue.

'There,' he continued.

The tip of her tongue made a dart's eye into his opening.

'Yes,' he moaned. 'Good girl.'

Once in position, she began licking outwards, rimming the slow gradient of darker flesh that ran down from his arse cheeks to his opening. She tasted nothing.

Through her lips, now attached to his anal perimeter, she could feel a noticeable tremor running through the man's body as she licked him, cleaned the flight path to his sphincter with deliberate, humid movements of her quickly tiring tongue.

The man shuddered.

'Inside,' he whispered.

Cornelia knew this was an order.

She moved her tongue away from the now wet perimeter she had prepared around his hole, and darted her tongue into the tight, closed opening. For a brief moment, her mind strayed, and she wondered what her own rear opening looked like to the men she had allowed to gaze into that most private place; those who had breached her, fucked her there with fingers, toys and cocks. At least, she knew she had no hair there.

Just above her buttocks, in the small of her back, a thin layer of delicate blonde fuzz, some men had told her. She had often been tempted to ask one man or another, at any rate those who she thought she could trust, to take a photograph of her anus, at rest or even play. A weird fascination, she knew. But the moment had never been right or, more often, they had been in too much of a hurry to use her there to make a pit stop for a potentially dangerous souvenir.

The extremity of her tongue now dug forward and her nose couldn't help but lodge itself in his crack. The customary smell of man, of shit, of lust; at times deeply revolting but also fascinating and spellbinding.

'Deeper, girl; deeper,' he said.

She pulled his arse cheeks even further apart to facilitate her progress within him. His rear muscles relaxed and offered less resistance to her pliant assault. AngelTamer moved downwards a further few inches, bending his knees, almost squatting to widen his availability to her. Cornelia had to move in unison with him and lower her head along with his splayed open body.

Her tongue was now well inside his hole. The texture of his inner walls was both rough and smooth with an unholy mixture of his secretions and her own, liberally-generated saliva. Amazingly hot as she drilled through him, every movement of her tongue occasioning another invisible tremor to course through his whole body. The taste grew stronger in her mouth, the smell more pungent, the pain in her neck more acute as she strained to bury her mouth, her face into his hard flesh.

Guessing he would now not object, Cornelia moved one hand away from his outstretched buttocks and advanced under his perineum and cupped his balls. They were full, almost vibrating. She could feel his cock was now fully erect, hard as steel, a lethal weapon soon to attack her, to waste her.

The movements of her tongue were by now relentless, on automatic pilot, inching somehow closer to the stench of his bowels, drilling towards his distant heart with an energy which was born of despair, her mission to please him and generate his orgasm now a condition of her own survival. Her mouth could no longer breathe, like a deep-sea diver she now had to remember to specifically use her nose to catch her breath every time she felt her lungs were about to burst. Her knees were killing her, scraping rhythmically against the laminate floorboards of the flat; the muscles in her crotch were screaming at her because of the discomfort of her kneeling position and her thighs kept desperately apart.

Soon, Cornelia felt she could continue no more and was about to slowly withdraw her tongue from his arsehole for at least a minute of relief, even if it meant unspeakable punishment later, when AngelTamer suddenly roared and she felt him come, heard him spurt well across the floor to collapse on his haunches, displacing her face and giving her time to breathe normally again.

Both man and woman sat still for a couple of minutes in deep silence, inches away from each other, sweat pearling down their exhausted bodies.

Finally, AngelTamer spoke 'That was nice, DeathAngel. Very nice. Very talented girl indeed. I just shudder to think how wonderful a cocksucker you must be... But we have all the time in the world, haven't we?'

They had.

Cornelia knew the ordeal could go on so much longer and that there were so many variations still to be spun.

'Stay there,' he told her. 'I must wash.'

He rose from his prone position, his cock still dripping, still semi erect, and made a beeline for the nearby bathroom.

Cornelia shivered. Outside the windows the sun had set and evening was approaching, another London night full of expectancy, desire and danger. She sighed.

She heard the water from the shower head splash about while this ferocious man she had met on the Internet washed the sweat and the come from his body. She sensed the water was scorching hot. Which only made her feel colder, but she was aware she must not dress, even partly; she must remain bare and fully available to him. For the next instalment of her calvary.

She thought back to her childhood.

The street in Philadelphia where she had grown up. The smell of apples in the fall, and the stagnant ponds in which she and other kids from the neighbourhood would timidly dip their toes when the summer heat was just too much. Cornelia thought back to the turning of the seasons and the voices from the past. To the events that had marked her, mostly minor, even insignificant but all still rich in her memory. She wanted to understand this illness she harboured within, these shameful needs, this race for a flawed nirvana in which she appeared to wish to immolate herself in a frenzy of defilement that was also a cry of joy because it meant she existed, she was alive.

And others were not.

The men and women she had executed back home. For money. For books. With her brain switched off from the realms of morality and decent society. She hadn't been born bad. But she had become an instrument of her own lust and terrible desires, so that others would suffer.

She seldom thought of her past victims. Didn't actually think she was capable of guilt.

She also remembered, shards of thoughts peeling across her eyelids, those she had wanted, even loved and how she had not been able to connect.

And instantly realised this was precisely what all Conrad Korzeniowski's books were about. How could she not have seen it before? She could so easily have been one of his characters, she recognised, one of the beautiful and the damned.

'A lovely sight, indeed,' AngelTamer said, looking down on her. He had returned from his ablutions. He was wearing trousers now, a tight fitting pair of jeans with washed out paler areas around the knees. Shirtless.

Sometimes, silences last forever; full of things unsaid, undercurrents of fear, expectation and puzzlement undulating agonisingly slow to the surface of reality.

The Belsize Park room was pregnant with untold possibilities as AngelTamer and Cornelia observed each other in the fading light of the day. Both pensive, but also attentive, like insects on an autopsy slab, watching the arc of the threatening scalpel in slow motion.

Something inside her brain, no doubt under direct orders from her cunt, ached to scream out. Wanting to say aloud, shriek, explode, 'Take me, use me, now! Tear me apart, crucify me with that cock of yours and turn me into the worthless slut I am...' But Cornelia controlled her urgent need and said nothing to the man.

By now, most other doms would have her crawling along the floor with her openings red and raw and still dripping from their sexual exertions or encumbered by foreign objects designed to humiliate her, or they would have ordered her to kneel before them, mouth open, to be showered by the always surprising heat of their urine. They would have tested her limits, the depths of her abjection.

Somehow, Cornelia sensed something wrong about the situation.

But couldn't put a precise finger on it.

Looking back over the past hour or so, it now felt as if the man was being dominant to her by rote, as if he'd picked up his craft from a book, a novel even.

It made no sense. He was too relaxed, playful almost. There was a necessary harshness missing from his actions, a natural streak of sadism. Normally, this would have come as a relief to her, unfond that she was of the necessary ratio of pain that submission often encompassed.

What the fuck was he waiting for?

What did this man truly seek of her?

She had to remain alert, she realised; not allow her lust to blind her.

He moved closer to her. Towered above her as she sat, still sprawled, on the floor. He leaned over and picked up the leather belt he had earlier used on her.

'So,' he said.

'So?' she risked.

'I do believe you are truly submissive, my dear... You should wear a collar, I think,' he suggested.

'That is a belt, not a collar,' Cornelia pointed out in a respect-ful tone.

'Of course,' he answered. 'We can pretend, can't we?'

'It's not the same thing,' Cornelia said quietly. 'When a sub is collared, it's a mark of honour. It indicates that she is now fully owned, a slave to her Master's whims and commands...'

'Well, no matter, DeathAngel,' he interrupted her, 'maybe I just want to see something circling that sweet neck of yours while I fuck you. I've always liked women who wear chokers. Now, on your knees, facing the window...'

Cornelia raised herself and began assuming the position he required of her.

'Raise that arse higher, girl...' he indicated.

Cornelia was now on all fours, rump raised, eyes fixed on the sky outside through the cream coloured curtains. She could feel the man's eyes feasting on her indecency, her two sexual openings in full view, ripe for the taking. And the reddened criss-cross pat-terns of blood and bruised skin across her flaming cheeks.

AngelTamer positioned himself behind her and threaded the harsh leather of the belt around her neck without, at first, tighten-ing it. She heard the swish of his trousers sliding down to his ankles and the man swiftly unceremoniously stepping out of them.

Then, with one rough thrust, he had forced himself into her. Fully. Just like that. She'd been wet enough and well lubricated from the treatment earlier.

'Hmmm...' he grunted. 'What a nice and welcoming harbour. For now. Maybe later I can sample that pliant arse of yours.' He began his movements inside her, his heavy balls slapping against her bum as every push forward impaled her further against his bulk.

The improvised noose around her neck was still loose, as the man concentrated on fucking her, his breath floating down her back as he attacked her from behind with energy and rage. His cock drilled its way through her cunt with metronomic regularity like the natural ebb and flow of a wave, breaking against her bowels and raising her own inner tsunami from its unknown depths. Suddenly, with one hand he slapped her rump hard, drawing further fire and pain from the marks he had inflicted just a short while ago.

Cornelia bit her lips.

'Your cunt feels like sheer velvet, DeathAngel,' he whispered in her ear, bending slightly to reach her, his embedded cock forcing the walls of her sheath downwards, stretching her as he moved. Cornelia shuddered involuntarily, not because of the compliment, but because she was energised by the change of rhythm of the man's fucking.

She was about to dutifully thank him, but he continued his monologue.

'But a damn shame you allowed your curls to grow again down there. I so liked that small tattoo of a gun you're now con-cealing from public view, or should I say private view?'

As he said this, AngelTamer began slowly tightening the belt around her neck.

Cornelia knew there was an urban legend about the increased level of pleasure some form of asphyxiation could procure at the moment of orgasm, but somehow she guessed this was not his object right now. The tone of his voice had changed and it had nothing to do with the fact that his cock was now labouring deep inside her. There was an icy determination at work here.

Like the mood she dutifully wrapped around herself when the time came for a kill.

He pulled on the belt again and the leather began to dig into the skin of her neck.

'Stop,' she gasped, attempting to overcome the rivulets of sexual satisfaction already running through her blood and permeating every corner and nerve end of her body. He did not respond, but just continued ploughing her insides implacably.

How could he have known about the small tattoo of a gun she had gifted herself with following her last job? The manager of the club where she had been dancing that autumn hadn't liked it and she had, accordingly, allowed her pubic hair to grow back. Abundantly curly as ever. The image was so small it would have been impossible for him to glimpse it today through her bush.

It meant he knew her from before.

Their meeting here was no accident.

One of his hands was now circling her neck, checking how well the belt was now adhering to her skin.

Cornelia took a deep breath, in anticipation of the worst.

On one hand, her whole being ached for the pleasure the man was about to unleash inside her, she yearned to collapse downhill towards oblivion, but she was now distinctly aware the man had a different gaol in mind.

Still, the noose restraining her grew harder and harder.

Cornelia closed her eyes and, as if responding to the belt being tightened a further notch, let her whole body suddenly go limp.

The man was visibly not expecting this to happen so soon and stopped fucking her. Just as he leaned forward to check on her breathing, Cornelia savagely straightened herself out and leapt forward, scraping her knees against the floor in the process. His cock slipped out of her and without allowing him a second to respond, she kicked backwards with her left leg and brutally connected with his balls.

As AngelTamer, or whatever he was really called, caught his breath while the pain in his genitals began to spread rapidly through his body, Cornelia was already on her feet and quickly untied the belt from around her neck and now loomed over the man.

'Who the fuck are you?' Cornelia shouted at him.

His hands protectively cupped his now bruised and aching balls sack, as if he expected her next blow to reach for the same target. He didn't reply. Or rather, Cornelia didn't give him the time to do so, as her foot flew up again and before he could move his hands up to lessen the blow, connected with his chin. He fell backwards, dazed. Again Cornelia kicked him with all the energy that her anger now fuelled her with. This time, his nose caught the brunt of her violence and she heard the bone break and saw blood spouting across his face.

Cornelia had unthreaded the belt from his neck and quickly bound his legs at the ankles while he was still in shock. Despite the pain, the man tried to wriggle out of the uncomfortable position in which he was now immobilised. Cornelia was aware he would soon get much of his strength back again and rushed to the nearby bedroom where she found a bunch of neckties in the open wardrobe. She was back in a flash and used them to tie his hands as tightly as she could. Then she stuffed a damp cloth deep into his mouth. He was, for now, bound and silenced.

She dressed quickly.

She had to get out of here fast.

But first she checked the bedroom where she had spied his briefcase a moment ago. It was locked, but a sharp meat knife from the kitchen soon forced the flimsy lock.

Yes.

Concealed between some lifestyle magazines was a photo of her.

Long lens. Taken from a distance. New York.

Damn!

She impatiently pulled out the few clothes he had hanging in the wardrobe and emptied the two drawers full of shirts and underwear, seeking more information about him. A passport, further papers, anything. But it was fruitless.

There was even no sign of a laptop computer in the flat. And she knew the man had used one, if only to contact her online earlier today.

There was nothing further to learn about him or his identity here, she realised.

She could try and get information from him, apply pressure, even torture him, much as she disliked the idea, but she knew all too well he was unlikely to provide her with any of the information she wanted.

Had she not sensed something askew in the admittedly bizarre situation, she knew the man would have ended up killing her. He had just been waiting for the right circumstances. And strangling her during the course of a fuck would have been so appropriate, wouldn't it?

The perfect way to combine business and pleasure.

He was a professional.

Like her.

THE ALGEBRA OF DESIRE

Cornelia slammed the phone down.

No one in New York appeared to have a clue as to what was going on. This was to have been a simple assignment, almost domestic, and no trouble could have been expected, she was assured.

'But this guy tried to kill me,' she insisted.

Ivan, pensive on the other end of the transatlantic line had earnestly suggested there might even not be any connection between her investigation and the encounter with the American.

'I'm positive, Cornelia, that this has nothing to do with the Korzeniowski manuscript. The matter just can't be related. The job was passed on to me by a colleague in the organisation, so I didn't have the opportunity to meet the primary client. But I was given a strong impression she was kosher, previously unknown to our, shall we say, realm of activities...'

She.

A woman. Cornelia made a mental note of this negligently-leaked piece of information. It might prove useful at a later date.

But it didn't answer any of her current questions. She had pointed this out sharply.

What she naturally didn't reveal to her New York handler was the nature of her initial contact with the presumed assassin and what had intervened between them. She had just mentioned she'd met him in a bar. Which wasn't too far off the truth. Wasn't the Internet the new common ground for randomly meeting people these days?

'He knew who I was,' she said.

'And which Cornelia was that?' Ivan had asked. After all there were so many sides to her, not all of whom he even knew.

'He'd seen me dance…' she replied.

'I see,' Ivan nodded.

'And this would have been earlier this year,' she continued.

'Why?'

'He knew I had this particular tattoo. And I've barely danced a few days while sporting it.'

'Interesting.'

'So, what do you think?'

'I'm not sure. I just can't believe it has any connection with your current job… Maybe… just maybe…' he hesitated. 'Listen, let me think, make a few calls. Might be that this links to an earlier assignment…'

'You mean someone seeking revenge for one of my past hits?' she asked.

'Give me a few days. I'll ask around. In the meantime, be careful Cornelia. We'll talk again. Take care of yourself.'

As a precaution, she had moved out of the Groucho and found a just-about acceptable room in a cheap bed and breakfast in Bloomsbury, where she could blend anonymously into the tourist crowds milling the streets.

The Belsize Park episode annoyed her; it just shouldn't have happened. She had let her guard down. But, on the other hand, she felt a strong buzz of excitement racing through her veins. The adrenaline was flowing freely. Life was interesting again.

Maybe she was just a damn junkie for danger after all?

Yet another component in her curious jigsaw.

Would she ever understand all these conflicting compulsions that made her tick, she wondered?

There had been a message from Kerith, the literary agent. She called him back, but didn't inform him that she had now moved out of the Groucho. He still sounded somewhat confused about their evening together and had no clue or clear memory about what might actually have occurred between the two of them. Consequently, he was wallowing in a pit of embarrassment. How English, Cornelia reflected. He somehow couldn't come up with a direct question that might allow him to clear the air, had Cornelia been in a mood to provide a truthful answer. Fool that he was. It amused her to know that he was still uncertain as to whether he'd fucked her or not, and couldn't summon the courage to ask her directly, for fear of either offending her or giving her the impression she had not been sufficiently memorable!

He also had to confess that he had not primarily been fully handling the literary affairs of Conrad Korzeniowski during the course of the writer's final year. He'd allowed a junior agent in the firm to look after the client. Maybe she could help Miranda, he offered. The young woman had recently been away from the office because of a family bereavement, but was returning the following day. Her name was Sarah Sparks.

This at least provided Cornelia with a name and an introduction.

He made no reference to a break-in at the company offices. She was unlikely to be under suspicion.

Cornelia thanked him and cut the conversation short as Kerith was about to muddle his way through to a further invitation to meet. Libidinous old bastard.

She then rang her computer guy and agreed to meet him down

in Vauxhall in his local pub the following day after he'd finished at work. He'd salvaged most of the material on the stolen hard drives. Did she want it in print-out form? She did. She'd provided the hacker with a number of key words to identify material that might prove relevant. There was a fair bit of stuff, he said. 'Good,' she'd told him.

The house was a modest, though large, semi in Tufnell Park. The front lawn had gone yellow from lack of water and attention, and there was something unfinished about the building, as if it had undergone a whole series of revamps and extensions but none had been properly completed as the occupants swiftly moved on to another project or adjustment. The bell didn't work properly; its ring was intermittent and weak, and barely capable of raising whoever was inside.

The woman came to the door and opened it.

She was striking. Even though her hair was grey and cut short in an approximation of a pageboy style, she could not have been more than mid 50s. She wore a tiny pair of glasses and a long, flowing dress in an assortment of pastel colours.

'Hello,' Cornelia introduced herself. 'I'm Miranda Woolrich. We spoke yesterday. I do hope I'm not disturbing you.'

'Not at all,' the woman said. She had a very slight accent. Could have been Swedish. She would ask later, maybe.

'I realise this isn't an ideal time,' Cornelia added, genuinely uncomfortable about her pretence now that she was confronted with the older woman's dignity and serenity.

'It's OK,' Conrad's wife said. 'Do come in.'

'Thank you.'

'Maybe a talk about him will do me some good. Catharsis, you know? That's how newspaper columnists would put it, isn't it.'

'Maybe,' Cornelia agreed.

She followed Conrad's wife inside.

There was a long corridor, with rooms on either side, full of bookshelves crammed with volumes in all shapes and sizes, that led to a large kitchen a few steps down on a further level. Cornelia saw that the kitchen gave on to a large garden, where the grass was still verdantly green, unlike the small square at the front of the house.

'I thought we could sit and talk here,' the woman said.

Cornelia realised that this room belonged particularly to the woman, as if the others in the house were still too much possessed by her dead husband. The woman offered Cornelia a cup of tea. Cornelia accepted.

She had pretended she sometimes worked freelance for a small American literary magazine and was hoping she could convince the editors to let her write a long feature on Korzeniowski. This was just a preliminary sort of interview. As she happened to be briefly in London. His widow had kindly agreed to meet her.

Following the necessary small talk about the garden outside, London, the weather, New York, the house and a veritable panoply of lies that Cornelia weaved together to establish her persona and the questions she was hoping to ask, the two women grew comfortable with each other. There was something about Frederique Korzeniowski that, to Cornelia, didn't match the sort of woman who would live with Conrad for almost 30 years. Not if you had read his books.

His novels and stories were so full of women of all kinds, meticulously portrayed, etched in the ink of heart blood and emotions, but his wife visibly did not belong in that world. She was beautiful in a mournful, ethereal way, not a participant or victim in the war of the sexes which he had obsessively mapped time and time again.

'So, tell me how you first met,' Cornelia inquired.

Frederique Korzeniowski smiled gently, her eyes clouding just a little and said 'Ah, that's a long story…'

Cornelia nodded, indicating she had all the time and patience in the world and was truly interested in the story the woman was about to tell her.

The man she spoke about for the next couple of hours was not the man Cornelia had perceived in the books and her conversations so far with the few people who'd known him. This was the prosaic tale, warts and all, of a family man, a good father and husband, who just happened to write books on the side that were brimming with excess, passion and mortal sadness. His wife joked about the way people would always confuse the man with his characters. She genuinely believed, it appeared, that he didn't lead any secret life that could have given birth to his stories. How it amused him, she thought, to play on his reputation, perversely adding to the legend in each new book in a mischievous attempt to confuse friends and readers. Or, if Cornelia was right, to muddy his sexual tracks even further.

There seemed to be two Conrads. Each supremely different. For both private and public consumption.

In theory this could have made sense, she knew. Cornelia herself had divided her life into strictly isolated compartments. But when it came to Conrad, her gut instinct kept on telling her she was right. That there was a massive cloak of deception unfurling here. That his life had also been his masterpiece, and the books could not help reflecting its mirror image for those who knew how to assemble the clues, piece the puzzle together.

But it was difficult for Cornelia to be too direct in questioning his widow. After all, she was pretending to be a literary journalist, not a scandal mag hack. Some things she just couldn't ask.

'There are some who still believe there was usually a strong autobiographical element in Conrad's stories. Did that not bother you?' Cornelia asked.

'He had imagination,' the widow said. 'I've heard it said too. But I was married to him for nearly three decades,' she continued. 'Surely, I would have known if some of the stories were true, wouldn't I?'

As she threw the question back at Cornelia, the two women's gaze crossed. Frederique Korzeniowski blinked first. This was enough of an answer, an admission, for Cornelia.

Better not raise the subject of Conrad and other women again in the conversation. His wife was now protecting his memory and drawing a veil on his failings. Wasn't it always the case with womanisers everywhere that their dearest and closest preferred to ignore their actions, tolerated the infidelities and the pain they caused? Cornelia couldn't fathom it. But then, this was none of her business. She was here to find out about his last book.

'Was he working on anything at the time of his death?' she asked Frederique.

'Of course,' she answered.

'Do you know what?'

'He was always working on something, you know. That's what writers do. Even if they appear idle, there are thoughts, ideas swirling inside.'

'I know,' Cornelia assented.

'Some books, some stories, he'd mention one day and then they wouldn't be written until years later. There was a long gestation period. He was unpredictable that way, you see.'

Cornelia nodded sympathetically. The tea in her cup was now cold and she'd barely touched it.

'Did you ever talk about his work in progress?' she continued.

'Not really,' Frederique Korzeniowski answered. 'He very much kept things under his belt, so to speak. Felt that by discussing his unfinished work it might block him, change his course. He was a very private person. You know, even after all our years of marriage, there were times I had no clue what he might be thinking of. Of course he was very much a man of silences.'

'You didn't mind the fact he seldom took you into his confidence?'

'No. I just got used to it. You just do. Better silence than empty phrases, don't you think?'

'Maybe,' Cornelia said.

She was reaching a dead end, she could sense.

'There were some books I know he always wanted to write,' Frederique admitted. 'But they were just vague ideas he'd sometime bring up in conversation whenever he was unsure about what to write next. And those are the books he always put off to next time.'

'I see,' Cornelia said. 'Did he ever mention titles?'

'No. It was just THE science fantasy novel and the one about Paris. But I don't think he ever wrote a single word of either. He didn't do much research, you see. Every new novel was a sort of improvisation.'

'That's so fascinating,' Cornelia commented, allowing the widow to reflect further.

'Oh, yes…' Frederique's voice faded away.

'Yes?' Cornelia asked.

'Last year, he did mention an idea; it was at a party, I remember. Someone asked him if there was new book in the pipeline and Conrad mentioned a false memoir, a book that would once and for all clear up all the misunderstandings we were talking about earlier. You know as to whether he was always the main protagonist of the stories. '

'And did you ever see him at work on this particular project?' Cornelia asked her.

'No. He just worked in his study. I never knew what on. But in the months preceding his heart attack, I think he had something important in progress. You sort of felt it. He was even more distant and pensive than usual. That was the way he was when a new book was underway.'

'John Kerith, his principal literary agent, knew nothing about it,' Cornelia pointed out.

'He wouldn't,' Frederique Korzeniowski said. 'Conrad didn't hold him in very high regard. He mostly dealt with Sarah Sparks. Kerith mostly occupied himself with the foreign sales side of things. Seldom saw any new book until it actually had been published in Britain and the States and he could submit it overseas.'

'Interesting.'

'It was sad that Sarah could not attend the funeral,' the widow said. 'Her grandfather died, and she had to fly over to France where he had retired, to make the necessary arrangements. Too many deaths… We spoke at length over the telephone. She was very affected by Conrad's passing.'

'It was very sudden?'

'Yes,' Frederique confirmed. 'He was in perfect health. It just happened. Out of the blue.' She paused.

'And so early,' Cornelia said. 'Only fifty nine?'

'Yes. But he'd never looked after himself, you see. It's only yesterday that I spoke to the family doctor and found out Conrad had seen him some months back and had been diagnosed with hypertension. He'd never even told me. He'd been given some pills to adjust his blood pressure. But I'm not even sure whether he was taking them regularly. If he did, I never saw him do so.'

'I'm sorry,' Cornelia said. Continued: 'What about his computer. Did you or anyone look at it maybe, afterwards?'

'Oh yes. Our son did. He's the practical one in the family. It was strange, he said, Conrad must have somehow wiped it clean just before he died. There was nothing in the memory. It had all been wiped. New stuff, old stuff. All gone. But then Conrad was never good with computers. Came to them late. Always preferred his electric typewriter.'

'Curious,' Cornelia said. 'You're going to miss him, aren't you?'

'What's done is done,' Frederique sighed. 'Our children are grown-up, adults now. We're financially secure since that film deal of the other year. Almost as if he'd chosen the right moment to fade out of our lives.'

'But at least you still have all his books,' Cornelia said, in consolation. 'Not many people leave that kind of heritage…'

'I suppose so,' Frederique agreed reluctantly. 'But still, it's not the same as having him around, even saying nothing, is it?'

'I know,' Cornelia opined. She had gone as far as decency allowed, she felt. 'I'll leave you now,' she said, 'You've been so kind to talk to me so long. Especially now. '

'I'll be interested to see if you get your commission for the article,' Conrad's widow said. 'And reading it of course. It would be nice to get a new perspective on his writing. So much of it was so one sided.'

They both rose.

'You're driving?' Frederique asked, as she opened the front door for Cornelia.

'No.'

'I can call you a mini cab,' she proposed. 'We have a good local service here.'

'No need,' Cornelia said. 'The tube is just around the corner. Convenient. I can collect my thoughts better when I'm walking.'

Frederique extended her hand towards Cornelia.

Her grip was firm and warm.

'Miranda?'

'Yes,' Cornelia queried.

'I think Conrad would have liked you very much,' the woman said, with a curious twinkle in her eyes. 'I'd say you're very much his type...'

'Because I'm blonde?'

'Not only,' the widow said. 'And...'

She hesitated.

Cornelia slowly withdrew from the handshake.

'He did mention a title once, I recall. Might be what he was working on. It was going to be called *Confessions*.'

The front door closed.

Yes, Cornelia thought, walking briskly towards Tufnell Park Underground Station, with the occasional look over her shoulders to check she wasn't being followed. Just like a jigsaw: one piece fitting into place at a time. A veritable labour of patience. But where did AngelTamer figure?

Chapter 5

She used to come with me to foreign cities.

The ways of lust were impenetrable as it turned us into involuntary and incurious tourists. After all, we couldn't quite spend the whole duration of every trip barricaded in our hotel room fucking like rabid rabbits, could we?

So, between the hours of sex, we walked, explored, I dived into any bookshop I would pass and she would buy lingerie (on my credit card). We ate too much, saw lots of movies. The Grand Canal in Venice smelled; maybe it was because we were not in season. In the bay in Monterey the otters were silent. In Amsterdam, we had a rijstaffel which made our stomachs churn for hours after. In Barcelona, the Ramblas were overflowing with foreign soccer fans. In Brighton, mecca of dirty weekends, television cameras were everywhere for a forthcoming party political conference as opposed to a blue movie capturing our sordid exploits, but somehow every city felt the same as it harboured our frantic fucks. They had no shape, just a strange presence dictated by the intensity of sex.

Of course, eventually, she tired of travel, of me.

All I now have left of her is this photograph. Black and white. Of a woman naked against a dark background. A hotel room, no doubt. It's not even her, I am ashamed to say. Just an image in a book that somehow reminds me of her. I never had a talent for photography, couldn't even master the simple art of snapping your lover with a Polaroid. Sad, eh?

This is the way she looked as she stripped for me in a hotel room.

Maybe it was in Paris, a hotel on the rue de l'Odéon with wooden beams criss-crossing the rough texture of the walls and ceiling. Or then again it could have been the Gershwin Hotel, just off 5th Avenue in New York City, where the smile of a Picasso heroine illuminated the wall next to the bed and watched our lovemaking through the walls of darkness. Or whenever we also kept the light on. Maybe it was a small hotel in Amsterdam, windows overlooking a murky canal, with the noise of drunk revellers and cars parking keeping us awake at night. Oh yes, we frequented many hotels. Those sometimes elegant, often sordid final refuges of illicit sex. The one in Chicago which was being renovated and where she preferred to sleep in the second bed because I snored too much (in fact, the final hotel that harboured our pathetic affair; maybe the excuse was just an early sign of her fading interest in me), or the St Pierre on Burgundy Street in New Orleans, far enough from the hubbub of Bourbon Street, where I forgot to take her dancing (she only did in Chicago, but it was with other men).

Or the one whose memories I cherished best. Our marine and pastel coloured room at the Grand Hotel in Sète, where the balcony looked out on quite another kind of canal, where local jousts on long boats took place at the weekend. A coastal port where she took a shine to the limping waiter who served us one evening in a seafood restaurant, and seriously suggested we should invite him back to the room later. Nothing happened, but for months on end after that I would fantasise wildly of watching her being fucked by another man and even got to the point of lining someone up when we next visited Manhattan, only to have to cancel it because she had her period that same week.

In my terrible dreams I wasn't even jealous to see her in the throes of pleasure as another man's cock slowly entered her and I would listen to her moan and writhe, and watch in sheer fascination as her so pale blue eyes took on a glazed sheen. After our first time, as I walked her back to the train station, she had told me her partner would know immediately she had been with another because her eyes shined so much. No, I felt no jealousy at the idea of seeing her perform with a stranger. It would be for my pleasure and edification. I would position her on all fours on top of the bed, her rump facing the door and would let my fingers slide across the cleft of her buttocks and dip into her wetness as I would introduce the new man to the beauty, intricacies and secrets of her body. See how hot she is inside I would say, how that sweet cunt will grip your cock and milk it dry. I would be the director, set it all up, orchestrate their movements, stroke myself as her lips would tighten across his thick penis and take him all in, sucking away with the energy of despair (hadn't I told you how good her blow-jobs were? She sucked with frantic energy as if her whole life depended on it but still retained that amused air of innocence in her eyes as she did so, demonstrating her sheer enjoyment of the art of fellatio, much as I hoped I did when I went down on her and tasted her and shook while the vibrations of her coming coursed through her whole body and moved on to my tongue, and heart, and soul, and cock).

So, she stripped for me in a hotel room. Now down to just her stockings. Delicately undulating, thrusting her pelvis out, shaking her delicate breasts, allowing her hanging arms freedom, her hands caressing her rump in a parody of sexiness, just like a stripper in a movie. No music, just us in the otherwise empty room. A jolt, a jump, a shimmy, there just like Madonna in that video, just a tad vulgar but sufficiently provocative, there exuberant like Kylie Minogue, but never as frantic as Jennifer Lopez or Destiny's Child.

And I drank in every inch of her body. The pale flesh, the moles, and blemishes, the sea of those eyes which appeared bottomless, the gently swaying breasts, the ash blonde hair now growing down to her shoulders, the trimmed triangle of darker pubic curls through which I could easily see the gash of her nacreous entrance, the thicker folds of flesh where her labia, lower down, grew ever so meaty and protruded, the square regal expanse of her arse which looked so good in the thong briefs we had purchased together at Victoria's Secret on Broadway.

Then she would look down and see me, no doubt with tongue hanging out and my erection straining against the dark material of my slacks, and she would smile, and my heart would melt. And though I right then wanted to fuck her until we would both be raw and out of breath, I would also strangely feel so full of kindness, a sensation that made me feel like a better man altogether.

This body I have known so intimately that I could describe every minutiae of her sighs, the look in her eyes when she is being entered, the stain on the left side of her left breast, the dozen variations in colour of the skin surrounding the puckered entrance of her anus and the hundred shades of red and pink that scream at me when I separate her lower lips and open her up. And the memories come running back, like a hurricane, rapid, senseless, brutal. Of the good times, and the bad ones too. Of the time we went naked on a beach swept by a cold wind. The visit to the Metropolitan Museum when she felt so turned on by the Indian and Oceania erotic sculptures that we almost fucked in the nearby restroom (I was the one who felt it would be too risky and by the time we had reached the hotel again, the mood had evaporated…). The email informing me she had shaved her pussy and then a few days later another terse communication informing me that she had found a new lover and my anger knowing he was the one who could now see her bald mons in all its erotic splendour. The first time she allowed me to fuck her, doggy style, without a condom, watching myself buried inside her and moving to and fro, our juices commingling. The evening we ate oysters, she for the first time, and she recognised their flavour when she swallowed my come some hours later in the hotel room.

That hotel room where she stripped for my entertainment and amusement, eyes lowered, a sober gold necklace around her slender neck, where once down to her fishnet stockings she slowly moved towards me – I was sitting on the edge of the bed – and, the delicate smell of her cunt just inches away from my face stepped onto the bed cover, towered over me and opened her legs wide, the obscene and wonderful vision of her visibly moist gash just a couple of centimetres from my wide-open eyes, teasing me, offering herself, my naked lover, my private stripper, my nude love.

'You like it, Mister?' she asks, a giggle stuck in the back of her throat.

I nod approvingly.

She lowers her hand and, digging two opposing fingers into her wetness, she widens herself open.

'You want, sir?' she inquires of me.

I smile with detached and faint indifference. Somehow come up with some relevant joke which I can't for the life of me recall now. She bursts out laughing. Once upon a time, I could make her laugh like no other. I warn her to temper her hilarity and remind her of the time on the Boulevard St Germain when she had actually peed a little in the convulsions of laughter. She hiccups and lowers herself onto me. The hypnotic warmth of her naked body against me. I am still fully clothed.

All now intolerable memories, of hotels, of jokes that were once funny.

Now, too much has happened since the time we were together and happy in our simple, sexual way, and she wants us to be friends, and no longer lovers. There has been a Dutch man, married, now divorcing, a Korean with dark skin, and God knows who else. And finally I am jealous. Like hell. Surely, she insists, we can still have times together, just be friends, no sex, it's better that way. How, I ask her, but then I would, wouldn't I? How can we spend days in foreign cities, share a hotel room and ignore the fact her body and her eyes and her smell and her words and her cunt just shout out sex to me and I know I couldn't accept that ridiculous compact of friendship any more.

You can go with other men, I say, and I will not blame you, hold it against you, I understand that I am not always available and that you are young and have needs. But she knows I am lying inside. That I would say anything to have her back.

In hotel rooms.

Stripping for me.

Laughing with me. Laughing at me.

In darkness she moves; I am deaf, can't hear the music she is dancing so sensually to. Maybe a blues, a song by Christine McVie or Natalie Merchant. Or 'Sing' by Travis. Or maybe it's Sarah McLachlan's 'Tumbling Towards Ecstasy' (the Korean man who later abandoned her for a Russian woman, after breaking her fragile heart, had introduced her to it; a man of melodic tastes, it seemed…). Or again that Aimée Mann song from Magnolia (we saw the movie together; oh, how she enjoyed seeing movies with me). I hear nothing. Can only try and guess the tune from the languorous movements of her body as every piece of clothing is shed to reveal the treasures of her flesh, her intimacy. The crevice of her navel, the darkened tips of her nipples (so devoid of sensitivity, she would always remind me), her throat, the luminosity of her face, her youth, her life.

I open my mouth but I can't even hear myself saying 'please' or 'come back' or 'forgive me'.

She dances, my erotic angel, my lost lover.

The silent words in me increase in volume, but she is lost in the music and no longer even sees her audience. Behind her, the hotel walls are all black and she is frozen like a photograph, her pallor in sharp contrast to the surroundings. Stripper in hotel room. A study in light and darkness.

Like in a nightmare, my throat constricts and words fail me totally. I shed a single tear of humid tenderness, all too aware of the fact that I will never again be able to afford a private stripper. Let alone a hotel room.

Sarah Sparks was diminutive. Facing her, Cornelia, who measured almost six feet, felt like an ungainly giantess. She'd agreed to a breakfast meeting in the dining room of a large, Victorian hotel that towered in tentacular fashion over one of London's main railway stations. Having been away from her office for a few weeks, she had no other time to spare.

This was no problem for Cornelia who was in the habit of rising early most days.

The young literary agent was like a doll and Cornelia took an instant liking to her. Long, straight auburn hair, brown eyes and delicate skin defined her. Cornelia's first thought was how Sarah might be in bed. Which surprised her; she'd never truly been into other women, even though she had dabbled both out of curiosity or when her cover had required it on past assignments. Sarah Sparks could barely fill an A cup, a failing which made the vision of her nipples somehow irresistible to men and women alike, Cornelia knew. The business suit she wore was shapeless and her childlike form swam effortlessly inside the pinstriped material. She wore flat shoes.

'Kerith said you wanted to speak to me about Conrad?'

'That's correct,' Cornelia said. 'I'm a great fan of his and I was thinking of possibly writing an article on him, now that he's gone.'

'Who do you write for, Miss Smith?' Sarah inquired.

'Oh, just some academic magazines back in the States,' Cornelia answered. 'But with this one, I'd guess there's a chance of finding a more general market, maybe. Esquire or Atlantic Monthly. Who knows?'

'If I may say, Miss Smith…'

'Oh, call me Miranda.'

'As I was about to say, Miranda, you don't strike me as an academic.'

'Appearances can often be deceptive, Sarah,' Cornelia said.

They both ordered a full English breakfast. For her small frame, Sarah Sparks certainly had a strong early morning appetite.

Cornelia decided to take the initiative.

'He was a man who loved women, wasn't he?' she asked the young agent.

'Oh, that he was…' she answered.

'Did you sleep with him?' Cornelia continued.

'And what if I did?' Sarah reacted. 'Is that the sort of article you had in mind, Miranda? I just don't think there would be that much of a market. The sex life of minor authors doesn't attract much of an audience these days. The public are keener on singers, actors and soap stars.'

'Just personal curiosity. You are quite striking.'

'Thank you. But then so are you.'

'Had I ever met him, I do believe I would have allowed him to fuck me,' Cornelia announced. A passing waiter did a double take as he brushed by their table. 'But I came on the scene too late, unfortunately.'

'How very forward.'

'So, did you?'

Sarah Sparks hesitated a brief moment, caught her breath.

Then provided Cornelia with an answer.

'Not technically,' she smiled wryly.

'Pray explain.'

'I did not sleep with him but I did once suck his cock. Is that what you wanted to know.'

'A technicality indeed.'

'Well, Conrad was awfully seductive. He was so unlike most men you come across in book circles. Reserved but so full of tension, sexual tension, very funny most of the time, witty, never hid the fact that every new women had the potential to be an adventure, a new project.'

'So why didn't you proceed further?' Cornelia asked the young woman.

'He was married, and I'd once sworn I would never fuck another woman's man. I was also in a relationship at the time anyway.'

'I see.'

'I'd drunk a bit too much. We'd gone out to celebrate a sale. Had a curry at the Red Fort in Dean Street. Maybe it's true what they say about the aphrodisiac power of spices...'

'I think I envy you now,' Cornelia smiled.

'He was a great kisser, but I knew his reputation. Look, I was often the first to read his books when they came in. Often knew who was who, and had to counsel him to make changes. He never played safe, old Conrad. He wanted to make love to me. Badly. I said no twice, and I think if he had asked me one more time, I would have given in and damn my principles. But he did not. He just begged me to undress fully. Wanted to see all of my body, he said. A once and only time. A sweet memory, he said. At this stage, I was already in a total state of disarray, half undressed anyway, so I thought why not. And did. The look in his eyes was beautiful as he gazed at me. But he did not touch me. Anywhere. So...'

'So ?'

'So, I undid his trousers and sucked him off. He never asked me to. And we remained friends thereafter. The subject of sex was never raised by either of us again.'

'A touching story.'

'A silly one,' Sarah added. 'Some might call it sordid, but I treasure the memory. But, I gather, you went to the funeral?'

'Yes.'

'Kerith couldn't tell me much about it. Were there a lot of pretty women there?'

'There were.'

'Of course. I would have loved to be there. Put faces to fictional names. Conrad was so transparent, you know. Just loved all those women too much to even disguise them well enough. In a way, I think he loved them all. In his own way. I'm going to miss him, you know. Like a friend, a lover I've never had. But then I'm sure every one of those women would feel the same. He had that effect on people. Well, on us girls.'

'Sounds like the opening sequence of that Truffaut film...' Cornelia pointed out.

'Oh, Conrad enjoyed Truffaut's movies. Tout à fait.'

There was a lull in the conversation, as each young woman explored her own thoughts.

'I'm sure she was there too,' Sarah then said.

'Who?' Cornelia asked.

'There was one woman who meant more to him than any of the others. Actually, I think that every one of us was only considered as a substitute for her. And poor ones at that. It was some years back. She was married. It didn't work out. No doubt for a variety of reasons.'

'What was she called?'

'I can't tell you that, Miranda. That would be betraying Conrad.'

'So you know?'

'Yes. Happened almost fortuitously. A man rang up the publishing house to complain that Conrad had brazenly portrayed his wife in his new book. That the similarities were unmistakable. And this guy was quite furious. He threatened a libel suit. Kerith was visiting New York at the time so I was lumbered with the problem. I called Conrad in and he blithely admitted every bit of the accusation was true.'

'What happened?' Cornelia asked.

'Conrad was clever enough to make it all impossible to prove without this guy, the husband, ending up as a cuckold with egg all over his face. So we convinced his publishers to counter bluff and just tell the husband to follow through with his threats if he was so incensed.'

'Did he?'

'No. He probably took on a lawyer who explained to him what would happen, and so decided not to proceed with the case.'

'Wow.'

'But she never forgave him.'

'How do you know?'

'Conrad told me. She fucking broke his heart into a million pieces. Ironically, I think it made a better writer out of him and he never looked back from there onwards. He also embarked on his new career as a womaniser from there onwards. Prior to her, he'd mostly been a predictable family man. But the affair had opened his eyes and, as much as he knew it was both wrong and foolish, every women thereafter was weighed and judged as a possible replacement, a new her! Sad, actually.'

'Yes.'

'Once you know all that, Miranda, you can even read all his books and stories again, and they make so much more sense.'

'Not just a hall of mirrors.'

'Exactly.'

There was now a sense of sisterhood between the two young women. The one who had known him and the one who wanted to understand him.

'Tell me, Sarah… The *Confessions* he was working on before he died…'

'How did you know about that?' Sarah seemed alarmed.

'His wife only knew the title,' Cornelia answered. 'Did he complete the book? Have you read it?'

'The plain answer is I don't know. We spoke over the phone three weeks back and he told me he was a day or so from completing the book. He called it a novel, but it was actually a form of memoir in which he said he was going to tell the truth about his life in his world of women. I'd warned him against writing the book. Too many people could be hurt. But he insisted he just had to write it. Almost as an act of penance.'

Sarah fell silent and gazed at her now empty breakfast plate.

Cornelia had barely made a dent in her eggs, tomato, bacon, sausage and black pudding mountain.

'Did you read it?'

'No,' Sarah answered. 'Conrad died while I was in France burying my grandfather. 'He never delivered the book. I haven't a clue what's happened to it. I'm told it wasn't on his computer or in his office. He never printed things out anyway; just filed copy, usually by email.'

'Strange.'

'Yes, for the past few days I've been coming to the conclusion he might never have actually even begun writing the book. Writers are like that sometime. The stories I've heard. The art of procrastination at its most deceitful.'

'Would anybody know?'

'Not his wife. But then you know that too.'

'Yes, I spoke to her.'

'Trust dear Conrad to leave us with a mystery on our hands,' Sarah chuckled. 'The case of the missing manuscript.'

Cornelia thought hard of any avenues left to explore.

An idea occurred to her.

'Women? Do you know if there had been any in his life recently, before his passing?'

'Good question, but I have no answer to it,' the diminutive agent answered. 'He didn't take me into his confidence. We remained friends but he was also very discreet. Small hints but nothing very precise.'

'How did he meet them?' Cornelia persisted

'I don't think he had any strict rules,' Sarah Sparks said. 'or type. Apart from Kay, he seldom hunted in book circles…'

'Kay?'

'I shouldn't have let that slip,' Sarah complained, annoyed by her slip of the tongue.

'The 'important' one?'

'Yes.'

A waiter lounged by their table and brought the bill. Both young women attempted to pay it and after some brief protests agreed to go halves.

They were waiting for change. The vibrations of trains moving in and out of the busy station below punctuated the growing silence of the grill room.

Sarah Sparks was picking her handbag off the floor and getting ready to leave. She had a final query.

'Miranda?'

'Yes?'

'Are you really planning an article on Conrad?' she asked.

'Possibly.'

'You've asked so little about his actual writing, you see…'

'I'm interested in the man behind the words,' Cornelia answered.

'Are you?'

'Yes.'

'Have you read *Kiss Kiss*?'

It was Conrad's last novel. Cornelia hadn't moved on to it quite yet in her catch-up.

'Hmm…' she muttered.

'There's a lot about the Internet, isn't there? That might be the right place to pursue, I'd say. It's obvious he met women there. I have a feeling he would juggle cyber relationships online. Long before he actually bedded them. The Paris episode with the American banker in the book is too fucking close for comfort. Feels just like Conrad spilling his guts in a rare moment of truth. I'd follow up on that if I were you.'

Cornelia nodded.

'Thanks.'

They were in the cab line, ready to go their separate ways.

'Bye,' Cornelia extended her hand towards Sarah as the literary agent was about to open the door to her waiting taxi. Sarah Sparks ignored the hand and, extending upwards on her tip toes, kissed Cornelia tenderly on her cheeks.

'Good bye, Miranda. Good luck,' she said.

Cornelia shuddered. The parting greeting was pregnant with the ghost of so many possibilities. They both were physically aware of it. Sadly, Cornelia knew there was no time right now. Maybe if she returned to London in the foreseeable future. She returned the kiss, indiscreetly grazing her lips against the other woman's as she quickly moved from cheek to cheek. Sarah Sparks smelled nice. Cornelia smiled enigmatically. Sarah did likewise and stepped into the dark interior of the taxi, closing the door just as it drove away towards Bloomsbury.

A few minutes later, as her own cab sped away from the

railway station forecourt, Cornelia instinctively looked back through the car's tinted back widow and thought she noticed AngelTamer standing on the sidewalk amongst a throng of commuters. A moment later, he was no longer there. Certainly looked like him. Another problem she could do without.

Sitting in her Holborn bed and breakfast room with its grey atmosphere and strictly bare essentials, Cornelia closely studied the reams of print outs she had acquired from the computer guy. He had trawled through the literary agency's hard drives and highlighted a number of words and subjects Cornelia had provided him with.

Most of the material was far from enlightening and no more rewarding than her initial speed read under cover of darkness through the filing cabinets on the occasion of her break-in. Financial matters, royalty discussions, preliminary contract discussions, a few minor conflicts with over-enthusiastic copy editors, minor publishing gossip padding out routine correspondence between Conrad and his agents. It all appeared quite fruitless and Cornelia had almost given up any hope of extracting anything of real value when the heading of one of the communications caught her failing attention. It was an email, from some two summers back, from Conrad to Kerith. The content was irrelevant – just a go ahead to the agency to reluctantly agree to a magazine's terms for a small feature. But the initiating email address was not Conrad's normal one. The message had originated from a Hotmail account.

Cornelia excitedly began to wade through all the previous correspondence she had already examined to ascertain whether this was just a one off. It wasn't. She found five such communications spanning several years. And each had originated during the summer. It seemed that Conrad, she assumed on holidays, was possibly unable to connect to his customary server and then had used another account to communicate with his literary agency.

She had a new address for him: 'londonwriter@hotmail.com'.

Cornelia grabbed the telephone by the bedside and dialled her computer accomplice in Wandsworth. He was still at work.

'I might have another job for you,' she said.

'Oh, yes?'

'Might not be as easy as the last one,' she added.

'A lad needs a challenge,' he chuckled.

'Good,' she nodded.

'Although I charge according to the degree of difficulty, you understand?'

'You know I can prove generous.'

'So what is it?' he inquired. 'Or is it something so secretive we can't discuss it over the phone?'

'Not at all,' Cornelia said. 'I want to break into a Hotmail account.'

She heard him laugh heartily.

'Piece of cake, lady,' he answered. 'Microsoft territory. Ideal for the plundering.'

'Good. I've only the name of the account. No password.'

'No matter. Can do.'

'When?'

'It doesn't require any special equipment,' he said. 'Whenever you want me to do it, and from anywhere.'

He was a young, nerdish black guy who breathed and smelled computers through every pore of his body. Like most men, his eyes executed an instant double take when he had first met Cornelia, but it was obvious he knew she was way out of his league, sex-wise, and was consequently no threat to her. It would be wiser not to meet in public, though, what with the other American, AngelTamer on the loose.

They agreed on his fee.

He would come to her hotel room that evening and bring his laptop with him, they decided. He was confident he could break into the account fairly rapidly and visibly relished the opportunity.

MY DEGREE OF UNCERTAINTY

The plane banked over the ocean and started its sharp descent towards LAX. From her window seat, Cornelia could make out the outline of the Atlantic coast below; was that Santa Monica or already Venice Beach or again Marina del Rey? They were still too high for her to make out specific features, spaghetti like highways, piers, reservoirs.

She sighed.

The land of palm trees. And past madness.

California held mixed memories for her.

She remembered some of the strip clubs she had worked in, scattered like pebbles in the central orbit of the airport, each one trying to outboast the others in its resistible appeal to wayward punters and other sad men of the night. And all mining a similar seam of loneliness and abjection, whether courted by punters or performers.

Neither could she erase from her memory the sometimes extreme private parties she had attended in the area, whether under cover on a hit or because her senses had prevailed over her sanity.

Of raw flesh exposed and defiled by the sides of shimmering pools in the Hollywood Hills. Of inert bodies. Full of drugs or bullets. The outward appearance had been much the same if you didn't take too close a look.

The plane hiccuped through a pocket of air and Cornelia looked down and noticed the rising goose bumps on her pale forearm.

She tucked her feet under the seat in preparation for landing. She'd managed to doze through most of the journey, oblivious to the movies, the piss poor meal and the other travellers in economy class. Private investigations on a budget! She smiled silently. Welcome back Cornelia, the wavering ocean beneath seemed to whisper across the muted roar of the Boeing's engines.

'Ivan, I'm calling you from LA.'

She could almost hear his eyes widen with amazement on the other end of the line, back in Manhattan three hours ahead of her California time.

'What the fuck are you doing there, Cornelia?' he asked.

'My job.'

'Last I knew, girl, you were looking for that book in London.'

'I was.'

'So how come the change of scenery?' he inquired. 'You were never noted for tan lines…'

'Looks as if all traces of Korzeniowski's final book have disappeared off the map in London,' she said. 'But I've ascertained he was in regular contact with various women in the US. So, I'm following up.'

Ivan coughed.

'That's what I call initiative, Cornelia. I just hope the client approves the extra expenses.'

'She will,' Cornelia said. 'She must have a damn good reason for getting to the book before it's published, I reckon. Maybe because she's in it.'

'Yours is not to reason why, Cornelia…' Ivan interrupted her.

'I know,' she answered. 'Anyway, I came over on the cheap. Even used up some of my own Air Miles. I was never going to use them otherwise. Do you think I can charge them back?'

'Good girl.'

'So, just reporting in,' Cornelia said. 'I'll keep you posted of any developments. Any news for me on the other front, Ivan?'

'Not yet,' he replied.

'I think I saw the guy again a few days later, in a crowd. He was definitely following me.'

'Are you sure?'

'I'm no Little Miss Paranoia,' Cornelia said. 'You know me.'

'True.'

'So please see what you can dig up. Please.'

'I will,' Ivan said.

The swimming pool at the Hotel Figueroa was like a desert in the impersonal landscape of Downtown Los Angeles. Hidden at the back of the building and surrounded by protective walls laden with a million varieties of plants and trees, it shimmered quietly in the midday sun, bordered by giant terracotta pots, wrought iron chairs and even two skeletal beds that stood to one end, like 1,001 Nights rejects, worn mattresses covered by frayed tapestry material. It was a weird mixture of styles, part Spanish, part Indian, an oasis where every element was quite disparate but nonetheless fitted together in unbalanced harmony. A couple of blocks South stood the massive Staples Stadium and its adjacent Convention Centre, like sleek, space-age creations that belonged to another world altogether.

Cornelia sat under the parasol by the edge of the rectangular pool and sipped her lemonade, while the other woman examined her suspiciously.

Her name was Valerie. She lived in Pasadena but worked a few blocks away as a typist for a large legal outfit who were on a retainer with both state and local authorities. She was anything but at ease in Cornelia's presence. She hadn't known of Conrad's death before the telephone call earlier this morning.

'How did you find out about me?'

'The emails,' Cornelia replied.

'Are you his…' she hesitated, 'wife?'

'No, I'm not.'

'So, how?'

'How doesn't matter, Valerie,' Cornelia said.

'It's just a shock, you know,'

'I understand.'

'He hadn't sent me any new mail for a few weeks, but that was nothing unusual. He often went on trips. Kept out of contact when he was travelling. I wasn't one of his priorities, I know.'

'It was only a week ago,' Cornelia reminded her.

'He didn't suffer?'

'I don't think so. Just a massive heart attack, I was told.'

'Were you also…?'

'No.'

'It's just that I know I wasn't the only woman whom he corresponded with on the web,' Valerie said.

'That's what I discovered,' Cornelia pointed out.

'He was quite open about it. Very honest. We were hoping to meet, you know. One day soon. Maybe on his next trip to America.'

Sadness and inner pain radiated from her grey eyes.

She gulped down her lite beer.

'So, you're from his publishers, you said?' she asked.

'Yes,' Cornelia lied. Struggling at best with her English accent. Today her name was Miranda Irish. 'Tell me about him?' she suggested.

The California sun was beating down on the swimming pool area and the rectangular stretch of water appeared particularly inviting.

Valerie had met him on a chat line in some Internet forum she would occasionally visit when the loneliness past midnight was often too much to bear. She'd noticed his handle several times but hadn't dared to page him. She was basically shy, one of those who remained in the kitchen at parties. She loved reading books and the name he adopted online had had pleasantly bookish connotations. She'd recently emerged, scarred and hurting, from an affair with a married man who was based in the Cincinnati offices of the law firm where she worked. Conrad's first confession, after they'd established something of a cyber rapport over a few weeks of easy conversations, was that he was married. Valerie had sworn she would never again get involved with that kind of man, but he put no pressure upon her and she hated the idea of relinquishing her late night flirting so soon. So far it was harmless, although a small, nagging voice inside the sensible part of her brain whispered to her at odd moments that, should he ever come to California, she would find it hard to resist him. Through his words, she imagined his voice. Hugh Grant like, of course; very British and warm and proper. And she melted inside. Already.

She spoke to Cornelia in a monotonous tone of reminiscence, her voice sometimes vanishing into the air as she sank deeper into her bittersweet memories of the affair that never was. Cornelia leaned closer to catch every fleeting word of the woman's story.

They had flirted so effortlessly, she was informed. He would talk to her of the wondrous places he had travelled to, always hinting that maybe one day, if circumstances were different, he might take her there, with underlying promises of tender fucks in exotic hotel rooms, bodies surrounded by the heady spices and violent fragrances of alien cities and rivers. And we would tell her stories, about men and women and the eternal war raging between them, and the misunderstandings and the passion and the deep sadness that punctuated relationships. Just the sort of things Valerie wanted to hear, so she could spin her own interpretation and fool herself that there was a genuine possibility of something happening with this strange, contradictory and fallible man, whose every word seemed to be pregnant with romantic potential.

She had even given him her telephone number when he had asked her, and, maybe once a month, he would call her, and his deep voice would confirm all of her wildest expectations, waltzing through the intercontinental cables like a potent spell, soothing, seductive, at times hypnotic. Not much would be said, but the feelings they kept from each other hung in the air of her bedroom like cigarette smoke, and she would silently touch herself under the darkness of her sheets as he joked or murmured sweet nothings about the weather or his books in progress.

'What books in progress?' Cornelia boldly interrupted Valerie's dreamy reminiscences.

'Oh, just stories, you know, like he seemed to write all the time.' Where the story was of no real importance when compared to the naked emotions racing through the lines and creating an indelible mood of poignant melancholy.

Before their online encounter she had never read any of his books, but had since located and greedily acquired most of them on Amazon, and in between contacts would try and translate the text on the page into an approximation or thereabouts of a real story or stories that lay behind the thinly veiled tales, with the added help of the enigmatic hints he would sometimes furnish her with.

And more recently?

Valerie smiled broadly as she revealed what Cornelia already knew. The fact that, on occasion, to apologise for his repeated silence he would email her random documents with advance copies of new stories or chapters from a novel that hadn't yet appeared. As a treat. Which she cherished.

Cornelia wished to know if Valerie had kept copies of these. Clumsily explaining that the author's estate had to check whether they already had copies of the texts in question in their files, as some had been misplaced due to computer error in Britain.

Of course she had kept them.

How could she not have?

It took much silence and sympathy for Cornelia to convince Valerie to let her have copies of these stories or novel chapters. Her computer boffin in London had discovered that Conrad Korzeniowski had been in the regular habit of sending stories and work in progress as attachments to some of the women he was corresponding with. However, unlike the letters, the attachments with these precious documents could not be retrieved from Hotmail's depths by his dubious magic. Which is what brought Cornelia back to America, to establish what of the material Conrad had actually donated to his Internet paramours still remained unpublished, and unrecorded.

Valerie agreed to make photocopies of the Conrad papers in her possession the next day at her office over her lunch break and to meet Cornelia for the hand over again at the Hotel Figueroa after work hours. As eager as Cornelia was to discover the new Conrad material, she knew not to press Valerie further, and didn't suggest visiting her at her home in Pasadena or copying the pages at a local Kinko's. The woman was already on the edge, and couldn't be pushed too far.

It was just another day and a half to wait.

Cornelia would find something to fill the time.

Although revisiting her old haunts was not on the programme.

She walked up to her room.

There was no convention or major sports event on for another week further down South Figueroa Boulevard at the Stadium and the Hotel Figueroa, a harbour of rococo excess in the tall and impersonal desert of Downtown LA was almost empty, hosting a mere handful of coachloads of Japanese tourists who were never there during the day as they were being ferried between the local attractions from Disneyland to Universal Studios or Knott's Berry Farm, then at night to the soiled sidewalks of Hollywood.

Cornelia felt uncommonly dirty, poking as she was in to the affairs of the dead man and the surviving flotsam of other people's lives. At least, when she used to deliver a hit, she had no knowledge of the emotional emptiness of the people whose paths she had to momentarily cross. It was better that way. Her soul was slowly being contaminated by this damn case.

She was unclean.

In flesh and thought.

Maybe she would have a swim.

Chapter 13

Last fall, two CD tributes to Kris Kristofferson were released at almost the same time on different small labels. Both featured a motley assortment of country and Americana artists with their interpretations of, mostly, the identical classic songs. It reminded me that I first came across Kristofferson as an actor in a much underrated film called *Cisco Pike*, which also featured his music, if my memory serves me right. And all these years later, I'm no longer even sure of that. Suffice to say, I loved the man and his music and, notwithstanding the fact than I am junkie music consumer, naturally had to buy both the CDs.

The opening track on `*Don't Let The Bastards Get You Down*' is a version of a rather obscure KK song called the 'The Hawk' by Tom Verlaine. Tom Verlaine used to be the voice and main guitar player (Richard Lloyd was the other) in neo punk group Television, whose *Marquee Moon* has ruled many of my air guitar daydreams since its release. Sadly, one hears very little of Verlaine these days (and the same goes for Kris Kristofferson too).

I was recovering from a serious bout of gastric flu and had been laid low by the bug for almost a week, losing a stone or so along with my appetite and much of my energy. Not that I was using this as an excuse for not having submitted the 'erotic fruit' story I had promised my American editor too long ago. To cut a long story short, my mood had been so low that I had barely been able to listen to music during my illness, let alone write, work or concentrate much on anything, bar reading popular entertainment magazines or feeling nauseous at the sheer thought of food.

Tom Verlaine's mournful voice is an acquired taste, even for such a fan of melancholy notes in Leonard Cohen and other singers as me, but his guitar playing is something else. And listening to the song which opens this tribute CD awakened me to life again. Such is the power of music. The barely there, hesitant vocals underpinned by crystal like, ever-so slow guitar arpeggios with a beauty and an economy I just cannot describe but that went right through to my still cramping gut and somehow gave me hope again that one day, in a story or a future book, I could attain just such beauty, such epiphany. Verlaine's guitar, Carla Torgerson of the Walkabouts' voice, sometimes Springsteen at his saddest. Oh yes, there is redemption in this world. Bliss.

But no story about fruit, I fear.

I had a vague idea when I'd accepted the commission, but somehow it didn't gel. Had I not warned Sarah when she first approached me with the offer that I'm actually not that good writing on an assigned theme, even if I've edited quite a few books of the kind myself (but the eager literary detective will quickly establish the fact those are usually the ones in which I don't force feed a story of my own)? Oh, I know the reason well, mind you. On the one hand I'm not disciplined enough; on the other, I don't have much imagination, to be absolutely truthful. For years now, much of my fiction has been about myself, under various guises, costumes, incarnations, alter egos and assorted subterfuges which I'm deeply convinced so many people can see right through and when I completed my last novel (blandly lying to questions and interviews that it was in fact my least autobiographical when in fact it was anything but – ah, aren't post-modernism and metafiction wonderful alibis?) I firmly decided that it would represent the end of that era and that my next book would be a total work of the imagination. After all, what with my imperfect life and the risks I've been taking for too many years now, surely one day my wife and others would begin to read through the lines better and realise there was no smoke without fire.

And, having resolved to change my bad pseudo-confessional habits, I promptly conjured up a great title for the new book which I pitched to my publisher and now he has it scheduled and I still have no idea whatsoever what the novel is going to be about (but, yes, it is going to be different from my previous ones; has to be). And I sit here, paralysed and unable to settle on an opening line. I'd hoped writing this little story would prove a useful distraction and would unblock me. I really did. But, fruit? As unoriginal as I usually am, I just can't descend to the obvious level of bananas and cucumbers, surely? Although I'm sure many of the other potential contributors will (and no doubt admirably transcend the innate vulgarity of the fruit in question). You see, I've only used fruit in a sexual context once. And, for a damn change, I'm now reluctant to tell the story. In a way, I've already betrayed in my writing so many women I've been with, had sex with, fucked, used, whatever terminology you prefer to use, that you'd reckon one final indiscretion now would make no difference. But something in me wants to turn a new leaf. I really do.

K, when she read the stories in which she featured, sent me a sad note accusing me of describing her, her sublime white body, her face, her cunt, her slightly out of kilter teeth, her heartbreaking small smile, as if she were meat. I was shocked. All I'd been trying to do at the time was evoke her sheer beauty, conjure the absolute truth of my love for her, even if it was adulterous... (And maybe, by magically transmuting my feelings into words, engineer her return; little did I know that the randomness of the alphabet just has no power to awaken feelings anew).

I should have learned my lesson there and then.

But did I ever say I was wise? In fact, I sometimes feel that I grow more foolish as I grow older.

I'm drawn to risk, to other women, to sex. They're just there, you see. Sometimes just out of reach, of course but at other times I somehow do find the right repartee, wry smile, and I plunge head-long into yet another affair. Sometimes at night I rationalise that maybe what I'm really looking for is the blinding nova that was K in my life, but I'm kidding myself. They have all been so different from her. Dark haired, auburn, ash blonde, every colour under the sun that she was not. Every shape and taste other than hers. Maybe I don't even remember the name of every woman I've been with since then, but I do recall the varied hotel rooms and the mechanics, the ballet of sex, the moans, the fears, the sighs and breaths taken. And… oh, the eyes when she peers into your soul as she comes, your cock still embedded inside her or your tongue or teeth on her clitoral jewel…

New York: Algonquin, Iroquois, Gershwin, Washington Square hotels. Paris: St Thomas d' Aquin, Bersolys, de l'Odéon, des Ecoles. Séte: Grand Hotel. New Orleans: Burgundy, St Pierre, Sheraton. Seattle: Stouffer, Inn on Pike. San Diego: Handlery. Amsterdam: Krasnapolsky, Singel. Los Angeles: Hotel Figueroa, Pasadena Hilton. Chicago: Hilton Towers, Drake, Inn on Grant Park. The list goes on. Which I bequeath to future divorce lawyers.

I have been a serial lover. By habit and conviction. Guilty to the last degree. Sometimes I was even juggling several affairs. But somehow I never got the names mixed up in moments of passion, never got my itineraries confused. Even now, as my long-distance relationship with the graphic artist in Prague moves into its second on and off year and to unheard of levels of intimacy (we've pro-gressed beyond hotel rooms and I've actually spent nights in her actual bed, in the apartment which she shares with her teenage son who sleeps in the room down the corridor), I am still hopeful of reviv-ing the embers of the great sex I had with A (who, for a change, really got a thrill from featuring in a story and a book of mine; although her erstwhile boyfriend didn't appreciate it the same way... but then he was a fool for allowing her to stray). I'm even curiously flirting with JR, who works in marketing just around the corner from my office and has a nice smile and a spark in her eyes. Or maybe I'm misinterpreting the vibrations. Somehow I'm always open to suggestions, my eye roving liberally around the myriad possibilities and my mind weaving absurd but so enjoyable webs of seduction, even if my body is these days unlikely to follow suit (weakened by the bug, in bed the other morning, my penis had never looked so shrivelled...).

So why am now all so suddenly shy to reveal my raspberry story, or any rate couch it in fictional guise? Yes, that was the fruit involved. It was an affair that only lasted a few days in New York, before we parted ways by common agreement, she back to Australia, me back to London. Talk about the safety of distance. She was a writer based in the Sydney suburbs who had submitted a story to me which I'd liked, published and we'd begun to correspond. One thing had slowly led to another. But enough of the story of my rather brief involvement with CF. She later set up home with another woman, although I'm fairly confident I didn't drive her in that direction!

The thought occurred while writing this roundabout letter of apology for the non-appearance of my story that, even if I had a better imagination than the muse provided me with, I'm no longer sure that fruit is truly inspiring or even erotic (similarly I declined last year to contribute to Greg Wharton's 'Meat' anthology). Now, food would have been another kettle of fish altogether! I love food. No reservations whatsoever. There was a section in a newspaper colour supplement here recently about sex and food which just made my lips wet, text and illustrations both. Did you know there is a restaurant in Tokyo, which has now opened a branch in Manchester in which you can dine off a naked woman's body? The recumbent naked woman is clothed only in strategically placed scallop shells and whatever you've ordered for supper. Not a new idea I know; the surrealists used it. However, the sensual quality of the UK version is restricted somewhat by the use of Cling film (don't they call that Saran Wrap in America, I think?) as a hygienic barrier between skin and the diner. But you can replicate the Tokyo experience at home: take one naked woman (men aren't appropriate, since food items can be lost in chest hair). Adorn with sushi, sashimi or other cold food-stuff. Do not try this with, say, sausage, potato mash and a rich onion gravy. You'll make a hell of a mess, and the gravy could be a scalding liability. Offer to wash up that night though.

Of course, beyond the parameters of taste, we all know since Mickey Rourke and Kim Basinger in 9 1/2 Weeks (or do you recall Tom Jones's gastronomy plus highlights?) that food and sex form an exquisite galaxy of erotic possibilities. Spaghetti dangling precariously between plate and mouth, cherries slowly penetrating the barrier of lips in a symphony of red and scarlet (oh, a fruit; hadn't somehow occurred to me until right now...), asparagus, the stiletto of the legume world, ice cream, chocolate of all kinds. Now, if Alison did want to one day put together an anthology of sex and food, count me in and I would not fail to deliver properly again. Oysters and New Orleans; yes, that's what I'd write about, and let your fertile imagination improvise on that one you, wicked readers of mine... There are some who say libertines don't mix sex and food; they reason that before sex, libertines concentrate on one thing. At that moment, sex is their only obsession. Also they need to keep their bodies light. I beg to disagree. Tell that to the Romans who were partial to some vestal virgins or even common whores feeding grapes into open throats before the traditional orgy. Tut, tut – grapes! Another fruit I'd hitherto neglected!

With food involved, I'd be in fine form. From the wonderful excesses of Marco Ferreri's follies in his movie *La Grande Bouffe* to the pornographic delights of sashimi slices against pale flesh, yellow-tail tuna shades contrasting with the rainbow of variations a nipple can move through in the throes of passion, let alone arousal. I just wouldn't know where to stop. Actually, CF's nipples in New York were delightfully dark, as were her labia. The Gershwin Hotel, corner of 27th and 5th it was, a Picasso sketch drawn across the far wall overseeing our frolics. Or was it a Matisse? Sorry for my confusion, I also took a Cincinnati bank female executive to that particular hotel some years later, so the precise details are a touch unclear.

OK, so I'll finally tell you what actually happened. Satisfied?

It's not enough of a tale to make a story, you'll surely agree. No motivation, conflict or even resolution. One to defy the rule book, surely.

We'd agreed to meet up in New York. A suitably halfway place as any, I suppose. I think that from the moment we lay eyes on each other at Newark Airport, we both realised that the attraction that had undeniably existed over letters, telephone and a perfunctory exchange of photographs, hers nude, mine clothed, was not going to translate that well into the arena of the bed. But we had committed to the escapade and we couldn't afford to get an extra hotel room. The sex had been poor the first couple of days. Lack of conviction and fire from both of us, no doubt. It was mechanical. As if we'd been married for years already. She was one of my first extracurricular women since K and she was still in recovery from the break-up of her first affair since her husband had left her for another man. You could say we were still beginners in the subtle art of the zipless fuck. Somehow, she didn't mind me fucking her, touching her everywhere, my fingers entering all her holes, but she refused to take my cock in her mouth. I've never felt that fellatio was obligatory or necessarily pleasurable to receive but the simple fact she denied me this annoyed me intensely (reminded of Maryann, an American blonde I had known in my early twenties in Paris, who would allow me to do absolutely anything to her, including fucking her mouth, but would scream if I even touched her nipples by accident; you always yearn for what is denied you…).

Between fucks, we'd explore Manhattan and the Village together and our lively conversation would conjure up in daring scenarios which might spice up our times together. She wanted me to pick up another girl and invite her to join us (a fantasy that, unlike many other men, had never turned me on) but I failed abysmally in my feeble attempts to connect with another woman in the bars I trawled that afternoon while CF did some shopping. Possibly the inner knowledge that I was disappointing to CF, sexually, intellectually, detracted from my attraction to others, let alone identifying or convincing one who was also bisexual. It was winter and I was surprised to see a Korean 24 hour deli on University Place selling small raspberry punnets at that time of year and decided to treat myself and brought a couple. They were even reasonably priced.

Back at the hotel, I greedily downed the first batch on my own and set aside the other. At the time, I had no ulterior motive, I swear. When I travel I always keep some chocolate in the bedside drawer. The sugar rush always helps me wake in the morning when my mouth is pasty and dry. On this occasion I recall with utter precision it was a few bars of Lindt, praline filled squares, which I'd picked up at Heathrow while waiting in line in the food hall of the departure lounge to pay for my breakfast sandwich and Coca-Cola. I casually put the remaining raspberries in the same drawer.

When CF returned to the room later, she didn't even question me about my efforts to find a third party. She seemed to be in a better mood than she had been that morning. Maybe the time spent without me had been good for her. We dined at a nearby Japanese place and missed out on the final movie performances at the Union Square multiplex. Back in the room, we undressed and she initiated the first kiss before we had even slipped between the bed sheets. This was a first. I had until now had to make the first sexual step.

Fifteen minutes later, she separated from a particularly tender embrace and, unbidden, went down on me. Things were certainly on the up. She sucked very well, a consummate expert with lips, tongue, whole mouth, even a delicate occasional use of teeth, slow, methodical, rhythmic. I abandoned myself to her ministrations. Maybe this was going to work after all?

Later, having moved into a sixty nine position and studiously attempted to pleasure her in turn, I marvelled again at the subtle, dark hue of her outer labia and was reminded of the evening I had borrowed K's lipstick and used it on the outer perimeter of her cunt to highlight the entrance to my then gate of paradise (I'd also darkened her perilously pale nipples and licked her clean but that's another story which I've too often told before, and is never going to bring her back anyway).

'Stay like that,' I'd asked CF, detaching myself from her.

She lazily acquiesced. By now, we had somehow reached a situation of quiet trust and sexual complicity.

I stretched my arm over to the bedside drawer and pulled out a handful of raspberries.

CF followed my movement.

'What are you doing?' she asked.

'Shhh…'

I dimmed the light and squeezed a few raspberries between my fingers, mashing them together, the ensuing juice trickling steadily down my wrist and onto her stomach. I spread the red liquid down to her cunt and adorned her private lips, the dark red enhanced the brown hue of her folds and highlighted the wetness peering through her opening.

'Kinky,' she remarked.

'You think so?'

I began to lick her moistness, her strong taste now blending with the acid of the mashed fruit. Then a mad thought flashed through my mind and without missing a tongue twist I extended my left arm again to the bedside and pulled out a couple of the chocolate squares and quickly inserted them into her cunt. Within seconds, the heat of her insides had melted it and it slowly began to sip through her cunt lips. I took hold of the remaining raspberries and carefully crushed them into pulp then pushed the gooey remains of the fruit into her with almost all of my hand, past the feeble barrier of her lips and the sticky, pliant wall of liquid chocolate bubbling there like volcano lava.

'Hmmm…' CF gasped. 'So what now? Are you going to eat me or fuck me?' she asked wickedly.

I fucked her.

Never had a cunt felt so hot and dirty and welcoming to my cock. I came quickly. Then couldn't resist lowering myself down to her ploughed entrance again to taste myself within the leaking residue of raspberry and chocolate seeping out of her, drop by lingering drop.

'Look, you're making the bed all filthy…' CF remarked, pointing down to my detumescing cock, dangling disgusting brown trails on the white sheet beneath us, just as if I'd thoroughly sodomised her and dislodged a cavern of faeces in the process (she'd allow me to do that on our last evening in Manhattan, but her ass was spotlessly clean). So she sucked me off again. Sucked me clean, and I'm being literal, not vulgar.

There you are. Korzeniowski's raspberry story. This is a true story. Do not try this at home.

*

CF and I parted friends and we still email each other a few times a year. After me, she had a long affair back in Sydney with another woman but right now she appears to be happily into another heterosexual relationship, with a man who doesn't mind her having two grown-up children. She hasn't submitted me any stories since though.

I never considered stuffing raspberries up a lover's cunt again, or maybe it was that I did not see any on sale at nearby stores when visiting strange cities with other lovers. I once tried to insert chocolate into AK but she didn't like it one iota. Was fearful of infection. Stated that her inside walls were too sensitive. Anyway, wouldn't have been the same without the magic ingredient: fresh raspberries…

So, reader mine, this is a secret between you and me. A future bond, maybe? A secret I gift you to compensate for the fact I have not been able to provide a decent fictional short story on the theme of sex and fruit for an anthology. Hope it makes you smile at least, and I'm confident the book will do well without one of my feeble, self-centred efforts. Good luck.

By the way, what's your favourite fruit? What is/was your relationship to it? I promise I won't tell.

Cornelia had swum almost twenty lengths of the pool while the afternoon sun beat down relentlessly across her exposed back. She wasn't usually one for physical exertion, let alone exercise. The dancing seemed to keep her alert and fit. But once she had initially dipped her toes, she had felt the compulsion to force her limits, speed through the green blue and refreshing water, if only to fully clear her mind and get a wider perspective on what was happening.

Was she about to get her first genuine breakthrough in this both curious and sordid case? Would she ever understand this dead man and his life of lies?

And what about AngelTamer?

It was as if she had all the pieces in the jigsaw puzzle balanced between her fingers but did not know how to assemble them in the correct order. She lacked the overall picture that would enable her to fix the details.

She took a refreshing shower and walked back into the room.

Like the pool's decor downstairs, it was a curious blend of styles. Pastel and terracotta colours, muted lighting, wrought iron chairs and bed frame, Arabian drapes and rugs on both floor and walls. At times, when she looked around the controlled penumbra she felt as if she were walking onto the set of a slightly upmarket porno film set, or a 1930s bordello bedroom. Or at any rate that was what her imagination conjured up from distant recesses she had never previously called on.

She dropped the terry cloth towel and faced the mirror. Her body.

Lean, pale.

Strange, she reflected, how a woman's body so quickly sheds all evidence of excesses past. How the bruises and blood just fade away like a chameleon shedding its skin. Or was it a Dorian Gray scenario? Would the years soon catch up with her? Would she one day wake up and see traces rising to the surface, lines, a hardening of the skin, the colour of shame making a first appearance, the long-delayed effect of too many indulgences: the men and women she had loved, or at least liked, the men who had used her, brutally, conveniently, systematically. Would her alabaster looks one day turn to grey?

Her breasts were still high and firm, no signs of droop, thin pink nipples alert and sharp, but then hovering as she did between A and B cupsize, this was unlikely to become an area of concern. Her neck was long and unmarked, her skin, taut. Her legs still flowed endlessly down to her narrow ankles, just the faint trace of a childhood bicycling scar above her left knee. Modest birthmarks or freckles scattered here and there across her shoulders; no new blemishes. So this was the dawn of her fourth decade.

And what had she achieved?

She had her books, her bittersweet memories, her looks.

Didn't feel like that much all of a sudden.

She avoided looking into her own eyes.

As if fearful of finding things, answers there she would rather not hear.

Cornelia flicked her hair back, sweeping out the last drops of water crouching inside her curls, from the pool or shower head. The overhead old-fashioned circular fan whirred quietly.

She still had a whole day to kill before meeting up with Valerie again.

The last time she had found herself with too much time on her hand, she had met the man who called himself AngelTamer.

Cornelia bit her lip, drawing a thin trickle of pungent blood.

Fuck if she was going to make that mistake again.

But idle time was her worst enemy, she knew.

Alone in a rococo hotel room, or sometimes even her own apartment with the comfort of her first editions, clothes and sparse furniture, her mind just wandered of its own accord, into areas it was better not to consider or explore. But that she was drawn to, nevertheless.

It wasn't loneliness, Cornelia thought.

It was more, like emptiness. A hole inside her that required filling.

Not just a lack of personal friendships, or even sex.

If all she wanted was friends, she knew she could compromise her erratic lifestyle and find some. No problem, really. As for sex, nothing was easier. Too easy, to be sure.

She trailed a finger across her stomach.

Extended it into the northern reaches of her thatch. Then an inch or so lower, where the tattoo lay concealed behind the thin, wiry forest that had grown back so quickly. Reminding her once again of her last kill.

Strange how the face of that man in her reluctant memories was now metamorphosing into that of Conrad Korzeniowski. Greenwich Village and London. The way the past always anchored the present, the future.

She headed back to the bathroom and dug through her wash bag and found a tube of hair-removing cream. There was just enough left to squeeze out and lather over her pubic area. Maybe it was time to resurrect the tattoo. The man who had attempted to kill her in London appeared to have fond memories of the minuscule gun she'd had etched into her skin, just a half finger away from her sexual gash.

The cream had an unpleasant smell but five minutes later she'd already scraped away her curls and was again smooth as a new-born baby. It was easier than shaving, which often left you with irritable skin, pimples or rashes within a few days. Also the hair refrained from growing back for a slightly longer period. She looked down to examine her work. The dark ink of the tattoo now stood out against the paler than pale expanse of skin enclosing her cunt. It had lost none of its clarity.

There was something shockingly obscene about the spectacle of her childlike mons and the postage stamp sized image now forever lurking like a guard dog by her most private opening.

She washed away the last slithers of the pungent cream and then slowly massaged in some baby lotion, to condition the newly unveiled region of skin.

Paradoxically, the operation now helped her feel like the decisive Cornelia of old. All she lacked was a real gun in her hand or handbag, and she could walk tall and dangerously again.

She dressed.

Immaculate, logo-less white shortsleeved T-shirt and tight DKNY jeans. Nothing else. She rang the front desk and made arrangements for a rental car. This was LA: she had no wish to become reliant on public transport, let alone cabs who would never be available whenever she needed them.

The club was a couple of miles away from the airport on the road that led to the coast. Cornelia couldn't remember whether when she'd been here last, it had just been normal work or if she'd been undercover on a hit job. A period in her life she'd tried, quite deliberately, to erase.

It was the late afternoon shift and there were few customers. It would liven up from six onwards when offices emptied and the first batch of men came out, those who stopped over on their way home to wives or live-in lovers, a sexual version of happy hour.

After eight, the second wave would begin filtering in. Those in need of stronger stuff.

Just one of the two stages was occupied. A black girl in sequinned bikini was dancing to a Beyoncé Knowles tune without great conviction or grace. Most of the men at the bar even had their back turned to her, attending to the more serious business of alcohol. The stripper paid no attention to them and concentrated on the handful of punters actually facing the stage and casually sipping their drinks.

Neither the barman or the security guy at the front door looked familiar to Cornelia. It had, after all, been a few years, and these were not career jobs.

'Dead shift, eh?' Cornelia said to the barman, ordering a soft drink which came with more ice than liquid.

'Yep,' he confirmed, barely looking up at her. As if lithe six-foot blondes were his typical sort of customer at any time of day.

'Do you have your full complement of dancers for later?' she asked.

'Looking for work?' his eyes finally settled on her and his attention awoke.

'Maybe,' Cornelia said.

'Done this before?' he inquired.

'Dancing?' she answered.

'No, taking your clothes off for men; stripping; showing pussy. We operate an all nude policy.'

'That's no problem,' Cornelia replied.

The barman looked her up and down, assessing her, checking out her body.

'Where?' he asked.

Cornelia mentioned some well-known West Coast clubs.

'But I've mostly operated in New York,' she added.

'That explains it,' the barman said, drawing a beer for another customer. 'You don't look like our type.'

'What is your type?'

'Sluts 'n' Silicone R Us',' he answered, with a wry smile spreading across thin lips.

'Silicone free zone, I fear,' Cornelia apologised.

'So I see,' he remarked, his eyes on the gentle elevations of her breasts behind the flimsy material of the white T-shirt. 'Any references?'

She mentioned the agency back on the East Coast who used to handle most of her bookings.

'I've heard of them,' he said.

'We have a couple of gals off sick, so I could slot you in for a few shifts later today.'

'That would be great,' Cornelia said.

'But from tomorrow, when the regular girls are all on stream, I can't guarantee you any juicy shifts. The other dancers wouldn't approve. You just take your chance on the rota they set up. You do your time, prove yourself before you get evenings or weekends on a regular basis.'

'That's fine with me,' Cornelia said. 'I understand.'

She had no intention of returning tomorrow.

All she wanted was a few turns onstage today. To feel on familiar ground again. Be in control of her destiny.

'What's your name?'

'Angel,' she said.

'No can do,' the barman reacted. 'We already have an Angel.'

'No problem,' Cornelia answered. 'Make it Miranda.'

'That your real name?'

'Of course.'

'Normally, I'd ask you for a sample dance. But I'm short of

time and staff, and you seem to know what it's about. I just hope you strut your stuff well and that I don't get complaints from the customers. We get a lot of regulars here, and after nine, they're quite picky.'

'You don't like what I do, you don't pay me,' she offered. 'But I still keep the tips.'

'Sounds fair to me,' the barman said.

'What time do you want me here, then?' she asked.

'Eight will be fine. How's your pole work? It's always a good earner, here. A lot of our late night guys mostly come from the airport, the computer joints or the studios in Marina del Rey. They enjoy good pole work.'

Cornelia downed her drink. 'I'll be your queen of the pole, then,' she said.

'Bring your own tape,' the guy shouted out at her as she moved to the door.

'I already have it here,' Cornelia gestured at her handbag. 'Never leave home without it.'

She manoeuvred her way out of the car's parking area, where her rental Mazda was now squeezed between an SUV and a vintage Caddie.

All she needed now was some sort of outfit.

She headed for Venice Beach. Surely she'd find something there that would fit her and the occasion.

The club's air-conditioning was on the blink and Cornelia came off the stage after her final shift bathed in sweat.

Like riding a bicycle, you never forgot the moves. The shimmies, the provocation, the twists, the way to seize the pole with one hand and swing around it like a stringless puppet. The splits between chairs or, head facing downwards, briefly holding the pole with one hand. The slow descent down the slippery metal surface once the talcum powder had worn thin. The men seemed to enjoy it, although she realised she stuck out like a sore thumb along the gallery of hardened pros who worked here, the Latina girls who had no other social horizon, the Hollywood wannabes who had by now given up all hope and turned to this rather than porno, in a vain attempt to conjure up some form of respectability. Sensing her outsider status, few of the other women even bothered to communicate with her in the poorly lit changing room behind the stage, amongst the Sargasso Sea of stale make-up, crumpled underwear, pills and the smell of cheap perfume where every single note – green, sweet, musk, fruity and so many others – clashed abominably with the natural odours of bodies, perspiration and foul breath barely tempered by chewing gum or mint pastilles.

But somehow it felt like being home again.

Every sinew of her body reacting with innocent, though sexual abandon to the rhythm of the music, of these songs, these tunes she had already heard a million times or so. Her mind, both switched off and drowning in the familiarity; her skin burning and acutely aware of every swirl in the fetid air of the stage's orbit, her senses sharply awake to the nudity she was offering freely around, displaying with pride and honour, as if she were offering herself to a Master capable of the worst excesses.

Again, by the end of her set, Cornelia was wet, both inside and out.

But even though her sexual senses were as aroused as they would ever be, she also was aware of her own absence, her distance from reality. It was always like this. Be it on stage or with men, lovers. She was part of the moment and also outside it. Like a spectator watching herself, observing her every move, her every inner tremor as if under a microscope. Never quite capable of letting go totally, of giving herself fully.

The adrenaline draining fast from her tired body, Cornelia dropped her black g-string on the make-up table and wiped her forehead with her forearm. Hopefully the shower cubicle would be free.

She wiped the make-up from her face with a tissue. The eye shadow and the scarlet lipstick that was obligatory on stage. Made her feel like a gypsy wife. Outside the clubs she never wore any.

She was about to walk over to the communal washroom she shared with the other dancers and shower when the night manager's voice sounded through the small intercom connecting the club's main room and the dancer's dressing room. 'Miranda, dance for you.'

A customer had requested a lap dance.

Her first instinct was to turn the request down. Normally, she only performed on stage, and it had been ages since she had given a lap or a table dance. They had never appealed to her, in spite of the extra income they could often provide. It was too personal. She looked at her watch. It was just past eleven at night. The club stayed open until much later, but she had completed the three sets she had agreed to do. Enough. But her skin was still tingling, and her breath was short. Maybe it would help her to wind down? Why not?

Anything to keep her mind off things.

Ten minutes harmless entertainment at most, she reckoned.

He looked hopelessly young. Twenty-five at most, but he would surely have had to present ID to gain entrance. Young-looking, then. Khaki pants, blue work shirt and slip on brown Hush

Puppy shoes. Wore glasses and probably didn't even shave on a regular basis yet. His hair was pale brown, a growing-out buzz-cut.

'I'm Miranda,' she introduced herself. She had slipped on a pair of thong briefs and her white T-shirt. She could still feel the sweat drying across her whole skin underneath the material.

'Tim,' the young man said.

'Nice to meet you, Tim.'

He hesitated. 'Likewise.' As if other strippers he had possibly hired on previous occasions didn't even bother with the basics of conversation. 'You were very beautiful. On stage,' he added.

'Thank you, Tim,' Cornelia said.

'I've never seen you here before,' he said.

'No. I'm just passing through,' she replied.

'Oh,' he said, unable to hide his disappointment.

'Shall we?' Cornelia indicated the chair he should sit in.

'Yes,' Tim said and installed himself. The armchair's leather was fraying on the edges. The small room allocated to private dancing was bathed in dubious red lighting from a 50 watt bulb hanging from the bare ceiling; the paint on the surrounding walls was peeling and its worst patches were covered by old Fillmore East rock posters. Not particularly inspiring, thought Cornelia.

'First of all…' she began.

'Oh, I know the rules,' Tim interrupted her. 'No touching and all that.'

'You've done this before, then,' she said.

'Hmmm… Yes,' Tim replied and she could have sworn he was actually blushing, although the red light bulb meagrely illuminating the room confused matters.

Cornelia smiled.

'How much?' he asked her. She was taken aback. It hadn't

occurred to her to find out what the going private dance rate might be.

'The usual, you know,' she improvised.

Tim drew some bills from his back pocket and handed a couple of twenties to Cornelia.

'There we are.'

Cornelia just stood there, facing him, the money still in her hands, as the young man's eyes kept on watching her, transfixed, his gaze moving up and down her legs, lingering with yearning at her barely covered midriff.

'Just a dance?' she asked.

'Yes,' he confirmed.

'Wouldn't you rather want more than just a dance?'

He didn't reply, unsettled by her continuing conversation and questions.

'My shift here is over for today,' Cornelia revealed. 'Where do you live? I'd rather get away from this joint'

'Santa Monica,' he whispered.

'Do you want me?' she asked.

'How much?'

'You're repeating yourself, Tim,' Cornelia said.

'I thought you were not allowed to... propose... intimacy to customers,' he mumbled.

'I make my own rules, Tim,' she replied.

'I'm not sure I can afford you,' he said.

'Who asked for money? Here...,' she handed Tim back the forty dollars he had paid her for the private dance.

'What do you mean?' he asked.

'What I mean is I come free, Tim. Just for tonight. It's my choice, my indulgence. I want to be fucked. I want you to fuck me. Let's drive to your place. I'll follow.'

'You sure that…' he said.

'No tricks, Tim. Just consider this your lucky day.'

She enjoyed the look of utter confusion on his face, as if he couldn't believe his luck.

'Only one thing…'

'Yes?'

'Afterwards, I just leave. No conversation, no heartfelt confessions. Just like Cinderella at the ball. Agreed?'

'Agreed.'

'I have to change. Get my things. It'll only take me a few minutes. Let's meet up in the car park outside. What do you drive? I've got a red Mazda.'

'A grey Opel.'

'OK,' Cornelia said. 'And don't you worry, this is not a joke I'm pulling on you. I'll be there; mark my words.'

And five minutes later, Cornelia drove out of the strip club's parking lot, following the rear light of Tim's car as he took the road to Santa Monica.

By mid-morning the next day, Cornelia was back in her curious room at the Hotel Figueroa. He hadn't been much of a lover. Too hesitant, even tender. But she had slept well in his arms afterwards, the taste of his come still lingering at the back of her throat when she had awakened him in the early hours of morning and sucked him back to life from his earlier, somewhat premature exertions. He'd make someone a nice, caring boyfriend or husband one day but she knew he would never forget this night.

She soaked in the bathtub and almost dozed off again. The jet lag was still bothering her.

She connected her laptop and checked on her emails.

Two of the other women she had hunted down from Conrad

Korzeniowski's Hotmail files had responded to her tentative, if carefully worded request. One was in Seattle, and the other just outside Baton Rouge in Louisiana. Both, she knew, were married and had done more than correspond over the Net with Conrad. There was evidence he had actually travelled to them and, she assumed, slept with them.

There was also an email from an unknown address.

Cornelia,

I think it's time we met, don't you think? Your friends are asking a lot of questions. Surely you don't mind if I provide the answers in person? You suggest a time and place, as I expect you're not in California for much longer, are you?.

AngelTamer

How the hell had he located her?

And he also appeared to know where she might be every step of the way. She was positive she had not caught a trace of him around, or been followed since she had arrived at LAX.

Well, two could play at this game, she reckoned.

This time she would be prepared, and the meeting would be on her terms. But first she had a job to complete.

That evening, she met up with Valerie again and was handed a couple of hundred pages of email transcripts. It was a business-like transaction, and neither woman cared much for further dealings. They separated fifteen minutes later, the shadow of the dead writer floating above them, disapproving, scornful. Or maybe this was the way he'd always planned it, slightly melodramatic, like a pulp novel on the skids, where the main characters are being manipulated from above by a sinister stranger who walks the walk according to his own agenda.

Cornelia grabbed a quick burger and fries from the 24 hour diner around the corner from the hotel and rushed back to her room to begin reading.

She was now in possession of the first missing piece of the puzzle.

The following morning, she dropped the rental Mazda at the airport and bought a seat on the first available shuttle to Seattle.

The woman there was called Liisa. She was from Finland but had lived almost twenty years in America. She had married a gallery owner but the marriage had gone sour and she now worked as a technical translator. Her house was in Redmond, barely a mile from the Microsoft campus. She was a small, thin woman with dark auburn hair, and asiatic cheekbones. She must have Russian blood, Cornelia thought.

She had read about Conrad's passing, so Cornelia was at least not the bearer of bad news.

Liisa had met Conrad at a book fair in Anaheim, and their relationship had continued for nearly 13 years.

Yes, Conrad would sometimes send her transcripts of books in progress, she confirmed. It took all of Cornelia's powers of persuasion to convince Liisa to let her see the material and copy it.

It was different material from the pages she had gathered in Los Angeles but already Cornelia could perceive the connections, as well as the inherent contradictions of the new stuff isolated amongst copies of stories and books which had long been in print.

A clearer puzzle.

Then on to New Orleans, a city she loved but hadn't been to for a couple of years now. Another place full of terrible memories and joys and past physical excess. A city that evoked sex like no other. In the air, the food, the music. The sort of place Cornelia might actually have liked to live in had it not been for the oppressive climate.

She met Marietta at the Café du Monde. They then moved on to the back dining room of an oyster bar, which was almost empty this early in the morning. The older woman had driven down from the outskirts of Baton Rouge and could only spare a couple of hours. She was married to a pastor and her affair with Conrad had been a beacon of hope in a sexless world of duty and children. Cornelia was curious to know how the two had initially met, although she'd surmised it was, again, through the Internet. Marietta was rather large and wore her hair in an outrageous bouffant crown, a style that no one in New York or London would ever adopt. She had almost never left the South. She was both awfully reserved and ebullient when it came to discussing Conrad, although she had, from the outset, got Cornelia to swear on her nearest and dearest that whatever they talked about must remain forever secret.

'I thought he'd find me too fat,' you know, she said, pointing at her generous waistline. 'But he didn't seem to mind. Although he never said much once we were together for that week end, you see, so it was difficult to know what he was really thinking about. I've always assumed he was just being kind, but he preferred slimmer women. Just like you... You're so slender and tall. Quite beautiful. Even when I was a teenager, I was never your size.'

'Sometimes I wouldn't mind being more opulent,' Cornelia remarked apologetically, nodding down with her chin at her seemingly shapeless chest under the thin fabric of her cotton blouse.

Marietta fell silent for a moment, diving inwards through her cherished memories of her one and only adulterous affair with this odd man who had come all the way from London to spend time with her.

'The first time he undressed in front of me, I just gasped, you know. He was… blessed. So thick. My husband has never filled me like Conrad could,' she revealed, colours rising to her cheeks. 'It's OK; I don't want to pry…' Cornelia said.

Marietta only had a couple of chapters Cornelia had not previously seen. She didn't mind providing them to Cornelia. She kept them locked away in a special wooden trunk back home, where she had copies of all his emails and other forbidden items her husband would naturally disapprove of.

Cornelia in her room at the Place d'Armes had just about finished reading the new pages and begun speculating as to the order of the chapters in the apocryphal book, when the phone rang. She had left a message with Ivan shortly after her arrival. It could only be him.

'New Orleans, Cornelia! Bloody hell. What's with all this globetrotting?'

'There is definitely a book, Ivan. I've now managed to assemble much of it. I was right, it's all about the women he knew. Very indiscreet…'

'I've spoken to the client. She's seen the LA stuff you mailed me. I had to let her see it. Evidence we were not squandering her cash.'

'Sure.'

'She called this morning. She wants you to stop this wild goose chase.'

'Why? It's all coming together, Ivan…'

'Not for us to reason why, Cornelia. It's over and done with. From tomorrow, you stop chasing the rest of the book down.'

'But…'

'No buts, girl. Listen, you've done a good job. The client has just had a change of mind. It happens. More often than you'd think. It's just the way things are. Just make your way back to New York.'

Cornelia knew she had no choice. She'd already dipped into her own funds to finance the search and knew she couldn't claim all of it back. Just her fault that she preferred to stay in nice hotels when she travelled. Damn.

Just when it was all beginning to make sense, a book of shadows slowly coming to life.

She put the phone down.

DRESS SEXY AT MY FUNERAL

New York Fall again, a recurring season of changing weather with the temperature fluctuating wildly throughout the long day. Made your choice of clothing more difficult when you got up in the morning. You never knew whether you'd end up shivering or sweating if you'd taken the wrong decision .

Cornelia needed the money so began stripping again, revisiting old haunts, rooms and stages still reeking of tobacco smoke, even months after the city ban on smoking. This had now become the main subject of conversation and arguments amongst the dancers as they chatted in the dressing rooms while changing clothes or methodically applying their make-up.

There were more lucrative jobs around. Ivan would still phone and offer her an occasional assignment, but Cornelia was determined to quit the killing game. Not morality, just lassitude. Once the Conrad wild goose-chase had come to an end, Cornelia had been substantially out of pocket and somehow couldn't be bothered to claim her full expenses, feeling as she did that the job had not truly been completed.

Sure, it appeared as if he had actually been writing that final novel – if you could call it a novel – but there was no evidence that he had finished it, or that a full version existed anywhere but in cyberspace or in lonely women's document files in computers scattered around the world.

Which was no doubt the conclusion the client had finally come to, deciding the threat the book represented to her was in all likelihood meaningless. So, she had called Cornelia off.

Eminently sensible.

She was working in a new club that had opened up six months previously, just a block away from the Soho Grand. It was a month's contract and even the low-key daytime shifts attracted a good number of punters of the flush with cash variety. Good tippers mostly. To celebrate her elevation to a more upmarket stamping ground, Cornelia had assembled a new tape for her set. She would open with Kristin Hersh's version of Cat Stevens' 'Trouble', its jagged rhythms and changes of tone allowing her to dance slowly and present her assets as gracefully and quirkily as she could, catching the men's attention. Halfway through she would traditionally shed her bra and parade dreamily for the next minute or so topless under the hot spotlight while providing generous hints of more fleshly revelations to come as her long legs danced, scissored and flexed in lazy harmony. Her second track was of necessity faster, a Neil Young and Crazy Horse tune which saw her thrash around the chairs she used in often perilous equilibrium, threading the g-string in repetitive patterns between her crotch, dividing her ass cheeks and allowing glimpses of her smooth intimacy in fleeting moments of sheer indecency, until with the last power chord she would drop the minimal piece of clothing, unveiling herself totally at last, standing regally, legs apart. This is me: take me, the stance said to the men eagerly drinking in every square inch of pale body. Her final song was an agonisingly slow ballad by the Walkabouts, during which she would dance as if in a daze, stretch with lazy abandon, ever flashing pink at the staring men, gliding around the metal pole at the centre of the stage like a compass out of control before ending up with her sleepy floor moves which now left nothing to the imagination, as she caressed and opened herself fully to the lustful rape of their envious eyes. The music would fade endlessly and there she would end her set, eyes closed, like a broken doll, crucified on the dance floor, quite motionless, almost sleeping, not quite dead, a staked-out, captive prey, ripe and ready to be plundered. Then the lights would fade out. It was an act she had long perfected. Some of the other dancers and management often remarked that she showed too much, didn't tease or flaunt enough, but Cornelia knew she managed to avoid the awful vulgarity that so many of the other women displayed. Whenever she drew too many objections, she just moved on to another club. If she danced, stripped, it was always on her own terms. There was always enough demand for a striking, ice blonde willing to open her legs and show her wares.

It was Thursday, a quiet mid-afternoon shift and she was dreamily drifting across the stage, lost in her own thoughts, while her body swayed to the poignant sounds of Kristin Hersh's voice moving between determination and baby voiced pleading, when she spotted him towards the back of the room, at the bar, nursing a glass of what appeared to be red wine.

The man from London. The one who called himself AngelTamer. Whose message she had ignored.

He saw her recognise him and smiled gently, as if they were sharing a private joke over the distance that separated them.

Cornelia could have rushed off the stage and run to the dressing room. There was a back door into SoHo there and she knew it would be easy to lose him in the warren of small streets of the neighbourhood.

But she also knew he could not harm her here. Yet.

She kept on dancing, barely registering the change of tune. She had to take her eyes off the room when she began twirling around the pole as part of her set. When she had the chance to look down beyond the lights again, he was sitting a row away from the small stage, observing her with ironic attention.

She rebelliously returned his stare, then deliberately looked away and concentrated on a man, stocky, balding, looked like a German tourist, sitting a couple of chairs away from AngelTamer. It almost became a private show, emphasising every bump and grind and squat as she drew his undivided attention, as if by arousing him to unheard of heights of desire she was also putting herself under his protection, away from the dangerous hands of the nearby AngelTamer.

She was lifeless on the wooden floor on the stage as the spot-lights finally faded on her act. It had seemed to go on forever today. She rose in the semi-darkness and forgot to even bow at the sparse audience she had attracted, usually the signal for men to throw a few bills onto the stage at her feet in way of tips.

But AngelTamer did contribute.

It would have looked odd had she not picked up his offering. It was a hundred dollar bill, wrapped around a smaller piece of paper.

In the privacy of the dressing room a few moments later, she read the note.

```
                          Angel,
        You can't keep on running. Mail me. Time to meet.
   It hadn't even been signed. There was no need for him to
                  identify himself this time.
```

Chapter 10

She was just another woman I'd met somewhere, as I searched for the million faces of Kay in every set of soft hazelnut eyes and the fleeting silhouettes of every female body I crossed in the street, on trains, in bars. Sometimes, I would recognise something of her, the way a curl of hair fell over a pale forehead, the turn of a lip, the curve of a slight breast beneath thin material, in the pink colours invading a cheek as I sustained eye contact just that one moment too long for innocence. But in all of them, it was evanescent and unseizable, and merely an ersatz dream of Kay. Never quite the real thing. But sometimes, a connection was made, and I took full advantage of it. You never knew where things might lead, and I was all too aware that what happened had been so damn special that I would be even more of a fool than I was already to even hope for anyone like her before. But a cunt is a cunt, and a bad man is still a man, and the allure of new flesh was something I couldn't resist.

Luba had a child of five, a small boy who lived with his father, a boyfriend she had fallen out of both love and lust with. So we stole time from our other lives whenever we could both afford it, concocting credible alibis for our lateness and absences. I have the nagging feeling that our respective partners guessed what was going on and sort of tolerated it, already knowing that it was the sort of affair that would only lead nowhere and that it was best to allow us to indulge in our wanderlust, rather than unnecessarily upset the apple cart and uncover a veritable nest of vipers that would complicate every one's lives too much and force us to cross that line in the sand after which nothing would ever be the same again.

We'd enjoyed frequent wet, sweaty nights, and even the occasional afternoon, in plain hotel rooms made for sex. But our desires screamed for more, and we had decided we needed to spend more time together. A whole few days somehow. Somewhere else. Even though we'd agreed on this course of action, I was distinctly nervous, but eagerly looking forward to the time we would have together, the ecstatic vision of her outstretched limbs on a bed, the prurient opening of her greedy mouth as she would feast on me, the dark folds of her openings dilating in the after-throes of pleasure. Because, between the fucking, we really didn't have much to say to each other. We came from different places, both geographically and socially and, past the obligatory life stories and tales of previous loves, there was little in the way of communication. I hated her taste in music and she, no doubt, found all my repetitive talk of books, travel and films rather boring. I'd initially warned her I was often a creature of silence, and this seemed to suit her just fine. We fucked like rabbits or any number of animal species locked in the eternal and empty dance of the beast with two backs. I loved the look in her eyes as she gazed at me while I ploughed her hard and she succumbed to the unstoppable waves of her pleasure. She enjoyed the fact that I had some imagination, perverse though it was at times, that I regularly took her in more than just the missionary position or doggie style, and enjoyed going down on her, making her come long before I even tried to penetrate her. She was an easy comer, her clit as sensitive to the gentle or rough touch of my tongue, lips or fingers as her dark, soft nipples were dead to most normal forms of sexual stimulation. Well, you can't have it all. But this was the extent of our communication. The affection we shared for each other was simple friendship and complicity, but we both knew it didn't come from the heart.

And we wanted more of that innocence alongside the sex.

On the pretext on a publicity tour sprung on me suddenly by my French publishers, I managed to liberate four days from my schedule. Luba pretended to her man she was visiting a girlfriend of hers who now lived in Paris. It would be our holiday. I didn't wish to spend the time in a large, busy city; we'd done that already one weekend past, a year or so before, sharing our time between feverish fornication, shopping, long walks and restaurants to banish the threat of any real conversation. The coast it would be; not quite the right time of year, late September, but hopefully it would still be warm enough to at least walk on a beach and watch the landscape of the sea as it ebbed and flowed, waves breaking on the sand time after time like Sisyphus climbing that damn hill, never quite making it fully onto the shore. A vision I had always found hypnotic and profoundly peaceful. We connected at Orly airport, south of Paris and, changing terminals through unending corridors and conveyor belts, caught a smaller plane to Montpellier. The sun was shining when we arrived in mid-afternoon. I'd made car rental arrangement and we were quickly on the road, racing down twisting lanes, between vineyards and hills towards Sète where I had booked us into the Grand Hotel, where I'd stayed for a brief night some years back following a literary festival nearby.

'It's so pretty,' Luba commented as we drove through the Languedoc valleys to our destination.

'It is, ' I agreed. 'Wait until you see the hotel. I'm sure you'll like it. It's unusual. An amazing glass covered atrium and sweet rooms.'

'Nice,' she said.

'And most of them overlook a canal. Almost like Venice, but without the smell,' I added.

'I've never been to Venice,' Luba commented. 'Will you take me to Venice one day, Conrad?' she asked.

'I will,' I said. Lying. I'd already promised her New York, Seattle and New Orleans. One more promise didn't cost me. Luba knew as well as I did we'd never do those things and that we'd eventually drift apart when we encountered new lovers who would satisfy more than just our genitals.

'Great,' she said.

The room we were given was just perfect: ultramarine-themed, with seashell motives scattered across the pastel coloured walls. The windows opened on to a small balcony big enough for just two on a thin day. The view unveiled the T-shape of the town's inner canal, cluttered with small pleasure boats on either side, a semi-mediaeval clock tower and a pattern of ever-receding bridges as far the eye could see. Dropping her case to the floor, Luba had rushed to the window to let some air into the stuffy room and, there and then, just fell in love with the whole place.

'It's so… beautiful,' she said, bending over the balcony's metal ledge to look down to the street and waters below, her already short skirt hitching up in the process, revealing the lower curve of her great arse and the thin fabric of her barely-there thong.

'Isn't it?' I agreed. 'And we're just a twenty minute drive from some great beaches.'

'Where you can go naked?' she asked, recalling a conversation we'd had a week or so back.

'Yes,' I said. 'Lots of space and privacy. Anyway, at this time of year, there can't be too many tourists or holidaymakers.' I'd been researching the area on Google. Illicit sex requires meticulous planning.

'Wow,' Luba shrieked, already looking forward to these few days of impromptu vacation. 'We can be like a real couple…' And leaned forward an inch or two further, as she shifted her weight from one foot to another, her hands gripping the balcony's metal edge. The diminutive strip of her thong panties was eating into the tight crevice of her arse crack, stirring up lust in me with every minute movement of her excited body. I moved onto the balcony in turn and touched her shoulders. She shivered as I breathed down her neck. The blue-green canal was a vision of peace, its surface uninterrupted by movement. I lowered my hand down to her partly-uncovered buttocks.

'A nice view behind you, too,' I remarked.

'Oh!' As if she hadn't realised the delightful spectacle she had been providing me with.

'Stand still,' I ordered, gently smacking her right arse cheek.

'Hmmm…' Luba sighed.

'Not a word,' I continued, pushing her black skirt up to her waist, fully uncovering her thinly-protected arse. I pulled suddenly on the thong's elasticised waist and tore the negligible material away from her body.

'You…'

'Quiet,' I insisted. 'I'll get you others.'

I stuck my hand between her thighs, forcing her to open her legs some inches further to my advance. As I expected she was already quite wet. Her curls were clotted with glueish secretions. I moved forward, pressing her whole body against the metal barrier. I was quite hard myself and unzipped my black jeans with my free hand.

'Bend,' I asked her.

'Here?' she feebly protested.

'Here. Now,' I confirmed.

I shimmied on the spot, allowing my jeans to slip to the balcony's floor and readied her with two fingers. Luba moaned gently. On the other side of the canal, I caught sight of a middle-aged man sitting fishing, a lunch box and a bottle of mineral water perched on either side of him on the stone edge of the canal. He had noticed our activity and peered at us, trying to see more clearly.

'Look,' I told Luba, 'that man, there, he's watching us.'

A mad thought occurred to me.

'Pull your T-shirt up,' I told her. She obeyed. I knew her well enough to realise this would excite her. I unzipped the side of her short black skirt and let it fall to the ground. The man over the stretch of the canal could now see all of her. And then I roughly pushed myself inside her. As I fucked Luba on the balcony, I did wonder what the man must be thinking. How much he could actually see. From where I stood, his features were unclear; even with glasses, my eyesight is far from perfect. Was Luba looking across at him while I mounted her or were her eyes closed? Was he enjoying an erection? Luba shuddered under my assault.

Possibly because of the circumstances we both came quickly. The man hadn't taken his eyes off us throughout. Deflating I slipped out her dripping cunt. I was about to walk back into the room, but Luba stopped me.

'Wait,' she said, and moved sideways and onto her knees and took my increasingly limp and damp cock into her mouth. 'I'll clean you,' she remarked. I knew this was totally for the benefit of our voyeur. I almost got hard again under the slow, meticulous ministrations of her tongue as she proceeded to lick our combined secretions from my cock.

'We taste nice,' she said.

'Time for real food,' I said, as we moved back into the room to wash and change. Fish and seafood restaurants were thirteen to a dozen half a mile further down the canal, in the approaches to the port, and I had determined to have a feast of oysters on my first evening in Sète. Luba had never tried oysters before and, after some hesitation, tried one from my platter, and found the texture and taste both revolting, much to my amusement. She stuck to salad and fish. Later that night, she remarked that even my come now tasted of oyster, which I found a tad far-fetched.

The following day, we took the car and drove down the coast and found a remote beach beyond an area of ponds where flamingos lurked in immobile silence. So long after the season, the sands were quite empty and we indulged in some skinny-dipping despite the lack of sun. The sea was turning to its duller autumn colours and melancholy filled the air as we surveyed the flat horizon of sea and beach, and fucked desultorily in the shade of a small dune. What with a quiet breeze fluttering around us, the sand got everywhere and what had seemed like a good idea on paper turned out to be both uncomfortable and even painful. So much for all the outdoor fucking my characters often practiced in numerous past stories, albeit generally in the Caribbean or the Maldives, and under a fiercer sun!

On our third day, we shopped in the small town and I bought Luba some fancy underwear which she, of course, promised to model for me later. I even found a dark brown button-down shirt in the local Monoprix. We walked all the way up the hill to the Cimetière Marin where local poets and singers were buried and looked out to the impassive sea that separated us from the coast of Northern Africa. By afternoon, we were both slightly sad as well as tired, and took a chaste nap, cuddled against each other in the narrow double bed. We woke as the sun was setting on the canal and Luba asked me what she should wear. I had her try on the new underwear and jokingly remarked that her pubes needed a trim.

'So do it,' she suggested. I fetched my kit and positioned her on the bed with thighs wide apart, and with a roving eye for the ever so dilated opening of her exposed cunt, began to trim the growth on either side of her lower lips with my sharp nail scissors. The sheer intimacy of the game visibly aroused her and micro filaments began to stretch stickily across her now-gaping cunt like a spider's chastity net. I'd once suggested actually shaving her, but she had refused as the aftermath often resulted in pimples and a bad irritation of the skin. By the time I had finished, she was almost bald, a sight I much enjoyed, her curls all shorn, with just a semblance of five o'clock shadow as evidence she was no longer a child.

'Voilà,' I said, admiring my work.

'Très bien,' Luba looked down and approved. 'Wow, you haven't left much at all,' she remarked. Her face was slightly flushed and the vision of her sitting on the edge of the bed with legs so wide open, her inner folds revealed, wondrously naked from the waist downwards (she still wore a book promotional T-shirt for an anthology of pulp fiction I had loaned her to sleep in) jump-started my imagination.

'You should go out like that tonight,' I suggested.

'Like this?' her eyes widened.

'Well, you can wear your long skirt, the one with the flowered motif,' I added.

'It's almost transparent,' Luba said.

'Exactly.'

'Are you sure?'

'Absolutely. I demand it, actually.'

'OK,' she agreed. 'So which top should I wear, then?,' Luba

asked, foraging through her small case. I retreated a few steps behind Luba as we moved among the narrow walkway between the walls and the canal as we ventured towards the port and its flock of welcoming restaurants and bars, and caught the final rays of daytime sun shining through the skirt, illuminating the sharp silhouette of her long legs. I wondered if others could also see she wasn't wearing anything under.

'It feels so sexy,' she whispered to me as we sat at a café sipping citron pressé and an exotic liqueur she had been speculating about earlier.

Her bare arse pressed against the metal of the seat, as her skirt spread across her legs, concealing her unusual nudity from the many passers-by.

'Makes me feel so horny, you know, Conrad.' She had wanted to fuck after I'd trimmed her pussy hair earlier, but I'd turned her down. Later, I'd promised. There was no rush. First I wanted to go out and eat. 'Fatten me,' she'd joked. 'Absolutely, and more,' I'd answered enigmatically, a crazy plan taking root in my feverish mind.

The restaurant we finally chose was beyond the port area. It specialised in Spanish cuisine, and served enormous portions. It was crowded. The service was slow. Time enough for her mind to wander as the itch below took hold of her senses. I'd never seen Luba in such a state of febrile agitation before. I would never have guessed that the feeling of being impudently exposed below would have such an effect. I was turned on too. Cause and effect. The meal took ages, even though the food was delicious, just spicy enough but lacking aggression.

Luba wiped a faint trail of tomato sauce from the corner of her lips as the waitress took the plates away. 'Any dessert?' the young woman, who walked with a limp, asked us. I looked to Luba. 'No,' she declined. 'I'm just too full.' The waitress moved away. 'Isn't she pretty?' Luba queried me. I had in fact found her plain and unappealing. 'Not really,' I answered. 'Anyway, didn't you once tell me that you weren't into other women?' Luba grinned back at me mischievously. 'Tonight,' she said, lowering her voice, although we were speaking English, 'I'd do anything. Just the way I feel.' Her hand moved under the table to her lap. She was touching herself.

All I could do was smile. 'Anything?' Luba lowered her eyes. 'Yes. Anything.'

I recalled earlier idle post-coital discussions of mutual fantasies.

'Are you absolutely sure?'

She nodded approvingly. The waitress brought the bill. I looked her up and down. No. Not what I had in mind.

There was a small bar facing the Grand Hotel on the other side of the canal. Not a tourist haunt, more of a faded joint for local regulars. There were half a dozen men at the bar and others in a back room noisily playing pool. The place had a familiar smell of stale cigarette smoke and alcohol fumes. We ordered a couple of espressos. I looked Luba in the eyes, determining that she was still willing to go through with any sort of madness I felt fit to inflict upon her.

'Look around and choose one,' I told Luba.

'Any man?'

'Any one.'

She turned and perused the small crowd at the bar. One of the men drank on his own, not part of a group or any conversation, nursing a half-empty glass of red wine. He looked slightly familiar and I thought I recognised him as the watching fisherman from the other day. Middle aged, stocky, florid. I couldn't be sure, but it could well be him. He noticed our gaze, held our eye contact and smiled enigmatically. Him being here would make sense; it was just a few yards from the spot where he had been fishing and it would be natural for this to be his café of choice.

Luba couldn't decide.

'Him?' I discreetly pointed him out to her.

'OK,' she accepted.

'This is what I want you to do, then,' I commanded her, providing her with specific instructions to follow. I handed her the key to our hotel room and she walked off towards the stone bridge that led across the canal, leaving me to settle the bill. All the while, the man at the bar had been watching us with quiet intent. I moved over to him, negligently dropping a ten Euro note on the counter.

'You recognise her, don't you?' I asked him.

'Yes,' he said. 'Impossible not to. That was quite a show you two put on the other day.'

'Do you find her attractive?'

'Of course,' he answered.

'You can have her, if you wish.'

'You're joking,' he responded.

'I'm not, ' I replied. 'For free. We enjoy variety, you understand. You can be her holiday present from me. Are you interested?'

'When?'

'Right now. But I stay to watch. That's not negotiable.'

He put his glass down.

'Let's do it,' he said.

The door to the room had been left unlocked and the only lights left on were by the side of the bed. Luba was on all fours on the bed, just wearing a T-shirt, her rear facing the door. Obscene and innocent. Her legs were held apart and both her cunt and anus invited the steady gaze of lust, exposed, raw, available. The

Frenchman stood on the threshold, as if hypnotised by the porno-graphic spectacle of the offering. I asked him to wait for an instant and walked over to the bed. Quickly delving into my own suit-case, I pulled out a tie and a black leather belt which I used to bind Luba's hands to the top corner of the bed. She had to adjust her position on the bed, her back arching to maintain her equilibrium and comfort and I spread her legs further. Her cunt now gaped. I found a silk scarf in her handbag and tied it around her head, denying her any kind of vision.

'Now,' I turned back to the stranger. He was already slipping his trousers down and pulling his cock out. It was a majestic specimen. Uncut, thick and veined like a delicately carved sculpture. He was already rock hard. He shot me a final glance, as if seeking my approval. I nodded. He positioned himself at her lips and with one quick thrust entered her. Despite his girth I was fascinated to see how easily he penetrated her and filled her, stretching her engorged lips to wondrous effect. Luba caught her breath, either surprised by his sheer size or momentarily seized by a brief moment of pain as he forced his way deep into unknown recesses within her innards.

He attacked her with unceasing force, burying himself inside her flesh with every in and out piston movement, metronomically regular and untiring, his large, heavy balls slapping against her pale arse cheeks. For a second or so, I had an abominable thought of that monster of a cock breaching her other, delicate opening and dilating it to unthought of dimensions like the aftermath of sodomies in some particularly revolting hardcore movies I'd sometimes watched.

The Frenchman put me to shame in the energy stakes I had to admit. He stayed hard, never losing his repetitive rhythm, system-atically drilling into Luba's cunt with ferocious ardour long beyond the time I knew I could myself sustain. I moved to the side of the bed and wiped sweat from Luba's glistening forehead. She was feverish, burning, but I knew it was from sheer pleasure, and the secret knowledge that what we were doing was off the map and wicked. This was the epitome of anonymous indulgence. We were using each other, just as she was being thoroughly used by the stranger.

He was now swearing under his breath as his attack on Luba increased yet in intensity, calling her a slut, a foreign whore. But she couldn't understand French and I was in no mood or position to contradict him. Then, with a roar, the man came. Luba shrieked. I held my breath, closed my eyes, imagining his mighty flow flooding her womb. Finally, total silence again. He was still deep inside her, his head bent forward, almost resting on her frail shoulders. I could see the overflow of his come pearling down her thighs. I wiped her face again and freed her eyes.

She looked up to me, still impaled on his cock.

'You OK?' I asked her.

'Yes,' she sighed softly, attempting a feeble smile. The front of her T-shirt was soaking wet and her nipples scraped downwards against the material, denting the grey fabric.

I experienced pangs of guilt now. We had crossed the border from fantasy into reality and it felt so damn awkward.

'We did agree anything…' I said, almost as an excuse.

The Frenchman stood silently behind us. Luba inched her way forward and his thick cock slipped out of her. He was still half hard and sizeable.

Her eyes shone as they always did after she had come. She looked at me as she straightened herself out. Asked:

'Absolutely anything?'

'Yes,' I agreed, somehow guessing already what she would

now require of me. Too many late night conversation over soft pillows during the course of previous encounters.

'Want to be sucked clean?' she asked the French guy.

He looked non-plussed. Failed to answer.

'By him?' she pointed in my direction.

He shrugged his shoulders. I moved to the back of the bed, dropped to my knees and took his still dripping cock into my mouth and proceeded to suck and lick him clean. It tasted of her, of course. How could it not? His seed just didn't count. It was the least I could do for her now. Eventually, the man retreated, just as he was about to get fully hard again, no doubt nervous of the fact that another man was now sucking his cock and initiating the same feelings a woman's mouth would produce. He muttered his apologies, pulled his trousers up and made for the door.

Luba and I slept fitfully after that night's encounter, and our conversation was at a lower ebb than usual. The next morning, shortly after breakfast, we drove to Montpellier airport to catch our flight to Paris where we parted and moved on to our respective countries and homes. We kept in touch for some months, half-heartedly assuring each other we'd try and meet up again, but somehow our calendars and hearts never quite got it together. She met the guy from Korea. I fucked someone in New York. And, monogamous adulterers that we were by habit and tradition, mutually decided our affair had come to its logical conclusion.

Luba and I still talk on the phone every few months, and when we are in the right mood for jokes, we both agree we'd had a most interesting holiday together.

But still now, I remain unsure whether this particular episode is one I cherish or am ashamed of.

Thanks for the memories, though.

Cornelia contacted AngelTamer the following day and agreed to meet him. A public place, she insisted. They settled on a Dominican bar on the corners of Stanton and Ludlow, a few blocks away from the Landmark Theatre. Mid afternoon on Sunday. Cornelia never danced on Sundays. It was her day of rest.

'So what is your real name?' she asked him, the moment they had both sat down. 'You know who I am. I don't like to be at a disadvantage.' He had greeted her as Cornelia from the outset, after they had stiffly and formally shaken hands, not Angel or Miranda or any of the other handles she had adopted on occasion, for reasons of work or pleasure. 'It would be nice, at least to know the name of a man who's both fucked me, and tried to kill me.'

He smiled. He was wearing a thin black leather jacket, a white shortsleeved shirt and jeans. There was distant whiff of aftershave drifting over from his direction. Old Spice. Not unpleasant.

'Fair's fair,' he said. 'I'm Christopher. But you can call me Chris.'

'Chris, then... '

Their drinks were brought to the corner table they had selected by a lanky waiter with slicked back hair. A Lemon Snapple for her and a Sprite for him.

'So who goes first?' Cornelia asked.

'Are you wired?' Chris inquired.

'No,' Cornelia replied.

He shrugged.

She pulled up her black T-shirt. She wore no bra.

Chris grinned. 'Ah, yes, I remember them well. Quite exquisite, if I may so.'

She lowered the T-shirt.

'Satisfied? Enough bullshit. Why me?'

'It's just a job, Cornelia.'

'What do you mean?'

'We share a profession, you see. We're both freelance agents. Most likely our respective employers have similar backgrounds.'

'There's a hit on me?'

'As I said, it's a job,' he looked genuinely pained to have to admit this to her. 'Not that I enjoy taking out women, particularly one as attractive and fascinating as you. But unlike you, Cornelia, I don't have the luxury of cherry-picking my assignments.'

'I see,' her eyes clouded, her brain frantically searching high and low for whatever reasons had landed her in this quandary. 'You're based in Manhattan?' she asked.

'Yes. Not far from you in fact. West Village.'

'Wrong side of 6th,' she pointed out. 'You know a lot about me?' she queried.

'I was provided with a very detailed dossier. You're a quirky woman, Cornelia. All this first edition book business. But I think there's something badly fucked up about your sexuality.'

'You can keep your opinions to yourself,' she reacted angrily, but immediately simmered down. She must keep her cool at all cost, she knew. Not allow him any further insight into her weaknesses.

'Had to do a hell of a lot of homework to get a grip on you. To bulldoze my way into meeting up with you back in London. Must say I prefer my sex more vanilla style.'

'If it's any consolation, you had me fooled all the way, until you committed a minor slip. But maybe I'd allowed my true nature to cloud my judgement,' Cornelia said. 'No one had ever exploited that weakness in my make-up before. I'd been so careful to keep it hidden.'

'I would never have guessed if I hadn't been provided with the information,' Chris remarked.

'Is it connected with the Conrad book?' Cornelia ventured.

'No.'

'You would say that, wouldn't you?' she reacted.

'Did you really think it was?' the man asked.

'Not really,' Cornelia gratefully admitted. 'It's a case that somehow hasn't quite resolved itself. I was just speculating, wishful thinking and all that, although I realise it just wouldn't make sense.'

'Methinks Cornelia thinks too much,' he commented.

'Feel free,' she said. Then, sharply: 'Who?'

'I can't tell you that, Cornelia. Put yourself in my shoes. People like you and me, we have standards, no? Client confidentiality and all that, no?'

'I just fail to understand,' she said.

'I don't even know who,' Chris relented. 'I guess, someone wants revenge for a past hit. The past does have a way of catching up with us.'

'I'd come to a similar conclusion.'

'There you go.'

'So why did you want to meet?'

'Call it professional courtesy. Once you became aware of me and my intentions, it was all out in the open. And I like you. A lot...'

'I'm charmed...' she replied. 'So what do we do now? A gun-fight at the OK Corral?'

Chris chuckled.

'No. I must say that the initial prospect of fucking you to death had a wonderful sense of irony. This thing of yours with unknown men, it's bound to get you into trouble one day. So sooner rather than later. And at risk of sounding like a two-bit psychiatrist, Cornelia, I even got the feeling that you were seeking a sort of oblivion. La petite mort and all that…'

'You read me like a book,' she ironised. 'So are you offering me a truce? Feeling unusually generous?' she asked him.

'No. Just playing fair. Makes me feel better that you're in the know. Otherwise, it would be too much like stabbing you in the back. In the dark.'

'How magnanimous,' Cornelia remarked. 'So are you issuing me with a challenge? Winner takes all?'

'Not quite.'

'Well, the way I see it,' she said. 'One of us is going to end up dead on the final page at the end of the book.'

'That's a blunt way of putting it, but… Yes,' the prospect genuinely appeared to sadden him.

'In which case, Chris, I think our conversation has come to its inevitable conclusion,' Cornelia said. 'I'll let you pay for the drinks, least you can do…'

She rose to her full height and walked out of the bar without even turning back and strolled briskly towards Houston where she hailed a cab running East.

Back at her apartment after a roundabout series of taxi rides to Gramercy Park and then back to Broadway and Astor Place, she loosened the floorboard under which she hid a weapon she should, by rights, have disposed of following her last job. She unwrapped the chamois leather pouch in which the gun had been kept protected, and systematically pulled the shiny weapon apart. A Sig Sauer. Her favourite kind of heat. Never required a second shot. Fitted her hand like a glove, her grip marrying the handle with easy grace. She slowly oiled every single component of the gun and then quietly assembled it again and loaded it with a handful of bullets she had kept in her refrigerator, buried deep into a tub of margarine.

By the time she had completed the necessary overhaul, her fingers tingled. Old habits just won't go away. She was about to move to the sink to clean her greasy hands when the telephone rang.

She took a pen and a clean sheet of legal paper in readiness.

Chris AKA AngelTamer lived on Greenwich Avenue. She now had his address.

Cornelia smiled.

His curiosity, let alone his sense of fair play, had got the better of him. He'd wanted to see her again. How unprofessional. It was going to cost him.

Once the other hit man had initially agreed to meet her on Stanton and Ludlow, Cornelia had arranged for old acquaintances, two doormen she had become familiar with while working the clubs and titty bars of the Lower East Side, to be lurking outside in wait. Both to look out for her but, more importantly, to tail him home after she had left and report back to her. Which they now were doing. She'd paid them in advance with the same hundred dollar bill he had gifted her with just a few days before.

Fool. Now they were on equal footing.

And she had no intention of letting the matter drag on any further.

That same night, she duped her way into his apartment building and stood outside his door. She knocked gently, and waited for him to answer. He suspected nothing.

The first bullet caught him right between the eyes, as he peered in astonishment at her pale face and her tousled Medusa hair before briefly looking down at the Sig Sauer held firmly in her right hand, pointed right at his face. He knew immediately he was about to die. The second bullet pierced through his heart a fraction of a second later, before he could even crumple to the ground. Cornelia pocketed the gun and briskly pulled the now lifeless body into the apartment and closed the door behind her. It had barely taken a half minute from the moment she had knocked on the door.

He had been alone. The other bullets would not prove necessary, which was a relief.

She dropped Chris's body in the entrance hall and, slipping a pair of gloves on, did a quick recce of the apartment.

She quickly found a buff envelope which contained her file and photographs and stuffed it down her jacket. She would read it later.

She then systematically thrashed the main room and his bedroom, upending the wardrobe and the mattress. Pocketed whatever cash was lying around or hidden in obvious places.

Hopefully, it would look like a break-in gone bad.

Had she had time to plan more thoroughly, she would have also planted some drugs in the apartment to confuse the issue further for the plodding investigators soon to inherit the scene of the crime. As it was, she doubted she'd even make page five of the New York Post.

She walked back East at a leisurely pace and even did a detour by the Strand Bookshop's rare book room and treated herself to a first British edition of F Scott Fitzgerald's *The Beautiful And The Damned*, thanks to the money she had stolen from her would-be killer. Waste not, want not. She deserved it.

Chapter Twenty

I'd killed her. Or so I believed. Then her ghost began to haunt me.

Or, then again, maybe it was just me going mad. Slowly, surely, finally. Ah, the ravages of love!

It began at night. It always begins at night. I woke in the heart of darkness, my mind racing like an old vinyl record somehow accelerating abnormally from 33 to 78 rpm. One part of me sought with terrible desperation to erase all memories of her. My once and past, beautiful, touching, vulnerable Kay. But, alongside in abominable coexistence, another rebel section of my mind did its best to cultivate that fruitful field which could summon back the smell of her body, the sound of her voice, the heart wrenching sway of her hips, the gait of her walk down a busy London road or wherever, all the hundred things that were her, the essence of her being, of her death. My heart would tighten, my cock would grow hard, my breath no doubt began to smell and the bitter fragrance of my sweat would metamorphose into a bilious stench in all likelihood designer-devised to attract all the minor demons and torturers of the lowest level of hell. My tormentors.

Was it guilt? I couldn't even be sure. After all these years – nearly ten – I could no longer be sure I actually had committed the dreadful act of erasing her from my life in such a definitive way. Time is such a convenient cleanser.

'If I can't have you, then no one will.'

A childish, petulant attitude, with murderous consequences.

So, I took a vacation. The Caribbean. A harbour of heat and

indolence. Where my eyes could feast on the shapes of a thousand other women in meagre attire, compare curves, opulence, posture, the million variations in the shape of breasts both in repose and in motion. We'd never been anywhere hot when we had still been together, so the only colour I'd seen her skin host was the pale hue of porcelain, an alabaster white that had no equal for me, just a wondrous shade that captivated my attention even more than the varying shades of green and blue of the becalmed sea before the wind took flight over the coast, usually around eleven each morning, and I had to wear a baseball cap to prevent my hair flying awkwardly in all directions, defying gravity and elegance. At least I still had a full head of hair, however recalcitrant it was. I assumed that by now Kay's erstwhile husband was approaching the terminal stages of baldness.

I sat daytime on the beach reading my one book per day, roasting in the sun, allowing the constant breeze to soothe the sweat pearling down my front. The palm trees swayed. The German girls ran topless across the sand of the cove we had adopted for the duration. The heavy hips of the Dominican women swayed lazily as they walked slowly across the sand, shoals of adorable kids with ribbons in their hair drawn in their wakes. The British teenagers ambled down the beach and the hotel's stone and wood promenade overlooking the ocean, with their navel piercings on display and their nascent cellulite squeezing out in folds from their bikini bottoms. I was not alone, of course. My wife was there with me. As ever. But by the fifth day I also came to the sad realisation that we had barely spoken to each other so far, beyond the excruciating banalities of food appreciation and respective greetings for the time of day. I had somehow given up communicating altogether. Maybe she had even noticed? It made no difference. I had never been that much of a conversationalist. Economical, you could call me. Or worse. I just had run out of things to say.

We ate early in the dining room that overlooked the ocean and traditionally watched the sun set around 7 pm between the mountains to the west (or were they volcanoes? I'd never bothered to find out). We took drinks from the bar and walked back to our air-conditioned ersatz-wilderness hut. We were asleep within an hour at most. Sometimes a desultory fuck, more often not even that, just a friendly peck on the cheek and an affectionate 'goodnight', as the sounds of disco music filtered feebly towards our room from the hotel's main entertainment plaza where the festivities for the evening were only just beginning. Not our style though.

Sometimes on the beach when my eyes strayed from the written page or the eternal movements of the waves and the sea ahead of me, I would follow an arse and approximate its shape to that of Kay's. But more and more, the memory of her, her texture so to speak, was fading with every passing week. Soon, I knew, all I would recall of her would be her face from that photograph they had featured in the newspaper, and I would no longer be capable of evoking at will the sadness of her eyes, the texture of her pale skin, the hundred variations of her cunt. It was enough to make me cry inside.

Invariably I'd wake in the heart of the night. I'd discreetly move to the terrace and close the door to the bedroom. The sky was always pitch black and there would be no stars. I could hear the chirrup of ever-present insects, the sound of the palm trees waltzing gently in the night wind and, just a hundred yards away, the monotonous ebb and flow of the sea on the sandy beach. And I felt alone like never before. So, so lonely. Like in the song.

I sat in the reclining deck chair I'd dragged over from the beach on our first day here and waited for day to break, expecting the slow metamorphosis of the sky from pitch black to navy blue and then ever-paler shades, until the moon disappeared altogether and, over the impossible horizon of the ocean, the sun would make an early appearance behind a curtain of thin clouds.

Which is when she whispered to me.

In the darkness.

In the silence.

'You always promised to take me to a tropical beach, didn't you, Conrad?'

I had. I was in love with her then. A love she ultimately rejected.

'It's not you,' I replied quietly. 'You're not here. You're dead.' Refusing point blank to turn my head even an inch and face her voice, her improbable face.

'Go figure,' she said.

'It's me, ' I remarked, subdued, resigned to the impossible, 'I've just read too many books, seen too many films, or maybe it's just a case of bad digestion. Those tortillas at the grill tonight did have a strange taste, didn't they?'

'I wouldn't know,' Kay said. 'One good thing about being dead is that food is no longer much of a concern.'

'I'd hate to be dead,' I answered, the faint trace of a smile no doubt colouring my thin lips. 'Food is good, food is nice. Probably why, since you, I've put on so much weight.'

'You don't look any different,' she replied.

It was then I turned to face her at last.

It was her, unchanged, eternal, the same she always was in my dreams before her image had begun to slowly fade as the years had taken their toll on my ageing grey cells.

'Neither have you changed.'

She advanced a finger towards my face and touched my cheek.

he breath of her contact was ice cold.

'You're warm,' Kay said. Or was it actually the ghost of Kay?

'That was always the case,' I said. ' Remember?' I'd been more han just a lover. I'd also been able to warm her in bed.

Her hand retreated and fell to her side. She sighed. Her eyes vere still as deep and sad. And alive.

'You killed me,' she stated. Again.

'I know.'

'You killed me I think a dozen times. At least.'

I made no comment.

She continued, 'and if killing me was not enough, you insisted ɔn killing me over and over again in your stories, your books. I vas just a slab of meat, a body, a thing you played with at your ɹeisure, that you twisted the knife into. How could you be so cruel, Conrad?'

'Try to understand me,' I pleaded. 'It was a way of keeping you ʌlive. And fuck the paradox. Surely you of all people would ɹnderstand that.'

'No. You were bitter and mean and cruel and insensitive…'

'So be it,' I interrupted her. 'Is now really the time to argue ʌgain as we did so often over the telephone after you broke free ʌnd returned to your husband?'

'No,' she agreed. I was surprised.

The sounds of the nearby sea died on the deserted beach and ʌad now faded into the backdrop of our futile conversation.

'So, why have you returned?' I asked her. 'To haunt me?'

She just stood there in the heart of the night's silence. I could ɹust about guess the vertical shapes of the trees behind her, ʌnchoring the beach like thin, dozy giants. Her gawky shape ɔbscuring the ivory darkness of the sky.

'There is no need to haunt me, Kay,' I continued. 'No need to manifest yourself for that. You've haunted me ever since you rejected me. Every bloody night, every bloody day and there hasn't been a minute when at least a corner of my mind hasn't been preoccupied by your absence, by the depth of your missingness.'

Again she failed to answer. A sphinx.

I was still sitting where I'd been all along, in the blue recliner on the room's terrace, just wearing a pair of washed-out green shorts.

'Talk to me, Kay.'

'Yes?'

'So why have you come? Today, tonight of all times?'

She appeared to be lost now.

'I don't know,' was all she could say.

'You've had almost ten years, you know. Actually it will soon be our anniversary. August, remember.'

She lowered her eyes. The night breeze ruffled her hair.

'That hotel,' I continued, 'that Tuesday in August. How I picked you up in Camden Town, opposite that cinema that's no longer there. How you told me you were both hoping I'd not come so you could be supremely angry at me but also that I would so we could officially become lovers in the illicit sacraments of the flesh. I still remember that first time. How could I ever, ever forget…'

My turn to sigh and feel the weight of the passing years on my shoulders, descending in overdrive towards my heart. It was all flooding back. All of it, every embrace, every word, every shard of inconceivable pain. I held back my tears.

'So why the hell are you here?' I asked her, raising my voice, oblivious to the possibility it might wake my wife up, beyond the closed terrace windows or the whole damn resort.

'I just had to,' she finally said.

'A sad case of haunting,' I remarked.

'Yes,' she agreed. 'I'm not very good at it, am I?'

'No,' I replied. Then: 'Maybe it requires training?'

'But you were responsible for my death, time and time again, Conrad and how can I forgive you that? How can I?' she protested. I'm here because of you.'

'I know,' I agreed with a heavy heart.

And I knew that, however prosaic her ghostly appearance was right now, that the haunting was only just beginning this very minute in time and her apparition this particular night would inevitably open the floodgates of my life again, allowing the pain to live and prosper in strength and intensity and keep me awake every single night for the years to come. If I lived that long.

'So,' I said, ' what now?'

She furrowed her brow. Her cold hand touched my shoulder. I shivered uncontrollably.

'A last fuck?' she said.

'A mercy fuck,' I answered.

'You could call it that,' she agreed.

'The one you were going to allow me that night,' I said. 'But I went and betrayed you first, so I wasn't even granted that.'

'Maybe,' Kay's ghost said.

I was overwhelmed by sadness. And exquisite tenderness.

Her hand took mine.

'Come,' she said and led me towards the beach.

There I am. It's four or so in the morning, on a beach in the Caribbean, following a woman who doesn't exist any longer. I know I'm not dreaming. No way. But then, don't the insane always argue that they are the sane ones as a clinical proof of their insanity? It's not Kay and it is Kay. My mind balances between denial and a crazy kind of acceptance.

'Lie down,' she asks me once we are just a few yards from the ebb and flow of the night waves sliding feebly against the shore. Just like *From Here to Eternity*, only everything is dark. But the moon is full and illuminates her face, like a spotlight on an eerie stage that only has me as an audience. She, of course, is the star. The ghost of honour.

I kneel down. The sand is powdery, still warm from the day's unending sunlight. Her hands swiftly pull down my shorts and Kay, in turn, gets down on her knees and takes me into her mouth. My cock is surrounded by ice. But still manages to react. Weakly, but soon I accustom myself to the chilly embrace of her tongue, recognise the frozen softness of her lips as she teases my cock so well. She hasn't lost her touch, I see. Her hair brushes like silk against my stomach and I slide my errant fingers through her myriad curls, counting, caressing every twist and turn of her blondness. It's like she was before, I note. Her soft perm, unlike the photograph in the newspaper (a feature about young women who had to balance career and children, where she expressed her regrets about reaching her mid 30s and being childless and having lost all those years to a job she had now given up) where her hair was now straight. Do ghosts still go to the hairdresser?

I close my eyes and will my erection to fullness. To do so, despite the coldness that now seeps through my cock, I cheat on her mentally. I think of the other Kay, of who she was when she was still alive, and the way her tongue used to coat my cock with her saliva as she sucked me in all those hotel rooms. Trust House Forte at Heathrow, Cumberland near Marble Arch, the Old Ship in Brighton, a room on the top floor of the Groucho Club in Dean Street.

My cock grows and now almost reaches her throat. Her teeth nibble my glans with danger and tenderness as she enjoys my

exture, feels my girth invading her mouth with every lick, every
movement. Her hands, glacial, kneed my balls, a finger trailing
outh to tease my perineum as she allows me one long, agonising
hrust that almost has her gagging.

She knows what I am thinking of. The hotel rooms of our
hared past.

She speaks. Impossibly as my cock is still buried deep inside
er mouth, impaling her throat.

'You had this thing about hotel rooms, didn't you?'

I nod silently in response.

'You promised me rooms in the South of France, in
msterdam, in New Orleans, in New York, in Seattle, in
'ancouver, even in the Caribbean...' the last with no measure of
'ony.

I did.

But all our fucks were within a hundred mile radius of London
t most. We were both married. We were both cheating. Promises
ome cheap.

I'm quite hard now as her chilled lips continue their mechani-
al ministrations. I open my eyes and pull my fingers from her
ingled hair, move one hand to her shoulder. Her skin is wet,
lammy, polar.

She draws back and allows my cock to dangle out of her previ-
usly welcoming mouth.

'Fuck me,' she orders.

She lies down on the sand, arms outstretched, legs wide open.
n the penumbra I can barely see her cunt, that opening I once
new so well, like a map of my infamy and her inner beauty.

I position myself above her. I'm already losing my erection. I
old myself in one fist and force myself inside her. The unbearable
oldness of her innards hits me like a refrigerated hammer and I

hopelessly deflate. I hold myself inside her and will my cock t
live again. Again, eyes wide shut, I conjure my better memories c
the other Kay, the way her pubic hair curled like a hundre
whirlpools as I played with her, the shattering colour of her inside
as I explored her systematically with eyes and tongue and finger
time and time again in all those rooms that were my memories.

'Fuck me,' she shouts.

And I fuck the living Kay with all the tenderness in the world
can summon from the depths of my soul. The dead Kay does nc
respond to my vain thrusts. No expression of pleasure or pain illu
minates her face. Her body is like a block of ice against which
am obscenely throwing myself.

'Fuck me harder,' she insists, frantic.

I do. Again and again and again. My cock is so cold I ca
barely feel it any longer, as if it were no longer part of me. A
distant part of my mind recalls articles about Polar explorers wh
lost fingers, toes, ears. Can a penis freeze off, I wonder?

I remember the sweet, lovemaking sounds of Kay, the sighs, th
endearing 'Oh, God!'s, the depth of longing in her eyes as w
rutted like animals on office floors or in bathtubs. Dead Ka
accepts my assault with indifference.

'Like a slab of meat, huh?' she reads my mind.

My anger rises and fuels my desperate erection and fightin
against the pain in my extremities I at last manage to call up som
distant and forgotten synapse and a pitiful wavelet of lust an
release courses through my weary bones and muscles and make
it snail-like to the general area of my near-impotent genitals.

'Fuck me one last time,' she screams, a sound that could rais
the dead, and then at lower pitch : 'It's what you wanted, Conrac
a final fuck, a closure fuck, no?'

I come.

I'm surprised my ejaculate doesn't freeze at the moment of release. I feel it spread across my stomach. Viscous. Gooey. Guilty. Soon my balls are actually dipping into it as Kay fades away, little by little, feature by feature into the navy blue fabric of the tropical night.

'You should never have killed me in your books, Conrad,' she whispers, almost gone, evaporating like the ghost she is. And, bathing in my own emissions, I realise with horror I never even had the opportunity to see her cunt close-up again, or the poignant small dunes of her breasts. But ghosts are creatures of the night, manifestations of darkness, and their purpose is surely to raise yearning from the dead and make us sinners suffer. On and on.

Kay is no longer there. I try to pretend I can still smell her, a familiar fragrance I once would buy for her at duty-free franchises in foreign airports, but I'd be lying to myself. There's only the lonely smell of the night about and that of the nearby sea.

Soon, morning comes. Cemetery blue makes place for lighter shades of blue. Soon, the moon disappears in one quarter of the sky and a shy sun makes a fleeting apparition behind a bank of clouds in the East.

It's just me, naked, with my shorts pulled down to my ankles, my cold cock all shrivelled and glistening with my come, and in the sand, proof again that this was no dream, the very shape of Kay's crucified, fucked body where the ice is slowly melting into the sand.

I accept the evidence blithely: I am now haunted.

And the only release from the nightmare will be my own death. That was her message. Pure and simple, no translation required. Could it ever have been otherwise?

How Can Moments
Go So Slowly

Cornelia had expressly demanded a face to face meeting with Ivan.

She knew she had to tell him about AngelTamer and how she had, for now, dealt with the problem. Otherwise, he would be replaced by others and it would become an unceasing nightmare.

There was a code of honour.

He was surprised, not so much at the way she had acted so decisively, but by the fact that somewhere in the complex layers of the organisation, the left hand had not been communicating with the right.

He appeared more concerned by the fact Cornelia had used a weapon supplied for a past hit and which she should have long disposed of. She had to assure him that this time she would get rid of it. Let him believe what he wishes.

He then assured Cornelia immediate steps would be taken and to no longer worry about the threat.

He certainly had no wish to lose her talents.

Cornelia realised she would have to pay for her peace of mind, and would no longer, for the foreseeable future, enjoy the privilege of turning down assignments. That was the way it worked.

She even wondered briefly if the whole set-up had been devised o that effect: once 'in', never 'out'. And perhaps the appearance of AngelTamer on the scene had been closely connected to her partial retirement. This was the way the organisation was warning her that it wished to keep her in the fold.

She wouldn't put it past them, after all.

Who else could have compiled such a detailed dossier on her and her proclivities?

Next time, she would be warned.

But for now it was better to leave certain things unsaid.

He assured her, following a few telephone calls while she waited in another office, that the matter had now been laid to rest and she wouldn't be bothered again. The other parties understood the situation and an agreement had been reached to rescind the contract. As Ivan put it, you don't piss in your own soup. His interpretation lacked a modicum of elegance but Cornelia tried to appear grateful. No mention was made of future assignments. For now.

She was off the hook.

Not the way she would have hoped, but she didn't think there was an alternative.

She could live with it.

She would have to.

As she ambled down Madison, the chill in the air carried a forewarning of a harsh winter to come. Maybe there would be snow shoulder high on the canyons of Manhattan this time around? Cornelia remembered the last time this had happened, and how much she had enjoyed it. A winter wonderland like an added archeological layer covering all the grime and noise of the city, momentarily concealing its sins and anguish. She was sure there was an appropriate metaphor at play here, but what the hell, it had been fun, roaming the white, newly-created boulevards, the parked cars buried under heavy mountains of snow and the city cleansed of its inhabitants as so few ventured out. She buttoned up her jacket as she began to shiver.

Spring came. Cornelia had extended her gig at the joint by the Soho Grand and stripped and danced there throughout the Winter. It was still new enough to have reasonable standards of cleanliness and the heating system never went on the blink, as so often happened in the older, more downmarket clubs. Ivan hadn't come up with any new assignments. Was the recession also affecting the killing business, she wondered? No matter. She had no need for extra cash right now and was still reading her way through her over-burdened shelves, catching up on all the books she had somehow accumulated, hoarded over the previous years.

She came across a short story she hadn't previously known by Conrad Korzeniowski in a back issue of Tin House.

Memories of her unfinished job the previous year came flooding back.

The piece felt like another random chapter from his final book, although it stood up well enough on its own. She could recognise his idiosyncratic touches, his sometimes-overbearing melancholy, but there were also new names, events dispersed throughout the flimsy plot that, as ever, seemed more concerned with emotions rather than the limited obligations of an original story line.

She had kept copies of the excerpts she had picked up on her curious travels in Conrad's online footsteps.

She read them again, in the context of the newly-discovered story and it felt like another configuration of the jigsaw emerging before her eyes.

Yes, there were things she had missed. Coincidences. Clues

scattered mischievously between lines. Flip references which now were beginning to make sense.

Cornelia smiled.

It wasn't a job any longer, but a challenge.

A pleasing one.

A way to exercise her imagination and powers of deduction, talents somewhat badly underused in the course of her daytime occupation.

'I'll Watson you yet, Conrad. Oh yes I will,' Cornelia whispered to him. 'Oh yes…'

She spread the pages out over her kitchen table, switched on her laptop, connected to a search engine and grabbed paper and pencil.

It took her two hours. Of guesswork, approximation and instinct.

But she had a name.

Two names, in fact. Also the husband.

All the right clues had been present in Conrad's writing all along. It was just the piecemeal way she had read and interpreted his material that had prevented her from narrowing down the evidence she was seeking. Or maybe she hadn't been curious enough back then.

She had neither the time nor the inclination to go back to London, and hoped that a carefully worded email would smoke one of them out.

Odds on that it was the woman acting on her own initiative and her husband was not involved.

The client who had wanted Conrad's last book located.

She was staying at the Washington Square Hotel. Had she known that was the same hotel Conrad often booked himself into on some of his visits to New York?

She looked much like Cornelia had expected her to look. After all, she had read so many descriptions of the woman, many of them passionately intimate, intensely private, in Conrad's pages. She felt as if she already knew her well, from the way the colour of her eyes shifted in the light, the words, the gentle obscenities she let slip in the throes of lovemaking, the hues of orgasmic flush coursing across her skin as she came in response to his touch. But in truth, she didn't know her either. She still came as a mystery package, visibly ill at ease with this forced visit to New York to discuss an old, painful affair with a total stranger. But, beautiful she was, Cornelia had to admit. Poised, if fragile; elegant, and at the same time tentative; dressed plainly in an opaque silk blouse and fawn cotton skirt and a patchwork waistcoat of many colours.

She could be me, if another road had been followed somewhere along the way, Cornelia thought.

The inner recognition of another damaged soul under the polished veneer of every day reality and appearance. A prey to inner demons that would never go away.

She felt an immense wave of sympathy flood her senses as the young English woman sat herself down in the dark leather armchair of the hotel bar, facing Cornelia.

'Am I here to be blackmailed?' she asked.

'No. Nothing like that at all,' Cornelia replied.

'Good. Because I have nothing to hide… I didn't think I was to meet another woman, mind you.'

'What did you expect?'

'I guessed it was something to do with Conrad. That's why I came. Beyond that, I was trying to keep an open mind.'

'I know about you and Conrad.'

'I realised that from your mail summoning me to New York.'

'For a time, I had somehow come to the conclusion you were dead…'

'Really?'

'The way he wrote about you, in the past tense.'

'Well, it was almost ten years ago.'

'But he couldn't erase the memory of it.'

'Do you think I could?'

'Why were you so interested in his book, the *Confessions*?'

'You knew about that?'

'Yes. That's how I assembled the pieces of the puzzle. The two of you, the real story. I was the one who was given the job of research-ing it, whether it in fact existed or was even to be published.'

'You don't look like a private investigator, I must say. Maybe I've read too many thrillers and had the wrong mental image in mind. So I suppose I owe you a word of thanks?'

'You know as well as I do that I was not allowed to complete the job. You called it a day.'

'I know. The stuff you found. I just felt it was enough. Couldn't bear reading more; and by then it was obvious the book was never going to be published, wasn't it?'

'I don't think he even wrote it for publication.'

'I came to the same conclusion.'

'It was more like a letter to you, which he never sent…'

'He wrote me hundreds of letters in the years that followed our break-up. I never answered any of them. But I did read them, though. What else could I do?'

'You tell me.'

'I was married. That's the reason I couldn't continue the affair with him. It was just going too far, too fast. And he was so intense and unpredictable. There were nights when we weren't together that I couldn't sleep for fear that the whole pack of cards that was

229

my life was about to collapse because Conrad would lose
patience and do something drastic and I would be thrown out of
my own home.'

'But your husband found out, didn't he?'

'Yes. I still suspect it was Conrad who wrote to him breaking
the news.'

'Did he admit to it?'

'Of course not, he always denied it. That's what so many of his
initial letters were about. But he lied well.'

'What if it wasn't him?'

'It would have made no difference, I suppose. It painfully
brought my husband to his senses and he changed his lifestyle. He
was desperate not to lose me. He changed. We even tried for a
child...'

'And...'

'We didn't succeed. Lots of reasons.'

'I'm sorry.'

'He gave up his job as a financial journalist and became an
investment analyst for a major bank. For the first time, we had
money to spare.'

'So where did you hear about Conrad's new book?'

'A coincidence. He was on the radio, a late night chat show on
a regional channel. He mentioned a project which, he said,
would, once and for all, reveal the truth about the autobiographical nature of his books. He was almost jovial discussing this, as if
it was a big joke, the way people always confused him with his
characters.'

'But why did this worry you so much? He'd already written
and published so much about you elsewhere. What would yet
another book change?'

'I panicked. My husband and I had just decided to adopt.'

'Why the panic?'

'I don't know. I just did. For a moment, I thought the final story would contain all the real names, the sordid facts. Having saved my marriage once, I was determined not to let it fracture again a decade later as the wounds were reopened and allowed to fester.'

'So you initiated an investigation and search for the book?'

'Yes. Only to hear of his death barely one week later. But none of the few obits mentioned whether the book even existed.'

'You read the material I managed to recover?'

'Yes.'

'And?'

'It was sad.'

'Is that all?'

'What do you want me to say? That I enjoy being responsible for the way I affected his life? Turned him into God knows what? I'm sorry, it just happened.'

'Is that all?'

'We met, we fucked, we parted. End of story. Satisfied?'

'Not really.'

'Why are you so interested now? You've been well paid, I have no doubt.'

'Call it personal curiosity. It's not my customary sort of case. It just caught my imagination.'

'Why do you think the whole book had just disappeared? Apart from those random chapters which he threw out like messages in a bottle?'

'Haven't you a theory?'

'I suppose I do.'

'And?'

'Conrad knew he was dying somehow, and this was a final plea for forgiveness.'

'So why didn't he submit the book for publication? Did something happen?'

Kay smiled, her thin lips creasing, her brown eyes clouding.

'It's just a theory.'

'Tell me,' Cornelia asked.

'Of course, since we parted so suddenly that night, I'd monitored his activities. Kept up with most of his publications, seeking signs, messages that were just meant for me. I observed him silently. I witnessed how the anger – he once reviewed a set of books I'd edited in his column and tore each of them viciously apart, quite unjustifiably – and then the pain coloured his stories. It was excruciating for me to follow, but I also think that he came into his own as a writer. Our pitiful affair had given him an excuse, a foundation stone upon which to build his incredible house of cards. Soon, I think, he came to realise that he couldn't even distinguish himself between the fiction and his embroidered and tricky version of reality. So, the last book, these *Confessions* as he wanted to title the book began as a genuine attempt to level the field, finally admit to the naked truth. But somehow, as he began writing the book, it became evident to Conrad that he was no longer capable of revealing the truth. Fiction just interfered, dominated. The liar inside him had taken over from the writer, the man. So his final demonstration of honesty was to destroy the book. Maybe he considered it a failure, by his own standards or intentions?'

'Quite a theory!'

'And I'll stick to it.'

'You're still married?'

'Yes.'

'Happy?'

'Serene. We had a few difficult years after the affair with Conrad, but we patched things up. What's happiness, anyway?

Conrad always said reproachfully I had a cold heart. He was right.'

'Did you ever see him again?'

'Yes. Twice. Across the Charing Cross Road, we were browsing at different bookshop windows. He never saw me. The other time was at a gallery opening, I was with my husband and noticed him in the crowd just as we arrived; I pretexted a headache and we rushed back home.'

'Were you afraid he would make a scene?'

'Not Conrad, not his style, but I know my husband would have been well capable of it.'

A family of Italian tourists entered the bar, noisy, exuberant.

Cornelia realised the conversation was coming to an end. Did she have answers, finally? Regardless, she felt a surge of relief having reached the end of this particular road. She had one final question for Kay.

'You know he loved you madly, don't you?'

'I know,' the young woman replied, with a heartfelt sigh. 'But he betrayed me.'

'I think you both betrayed each other,' Cornelia said. 'Feels like a total waste.'

'You can't change the past,' Kay said.

On which note, Kay and Cornelia parted, never to meet again.

Chapter 1

When I was a child, well actually when I reached my tenth birthday, my mother allowed me full use of her library membership card which provided me entrance to the adult section. I had long exhausted the library's junior shelves and both she and I agreed that I required more intellectual stimulation. I was given carte blanche to roam between the stacks and read whatever caught my fancy. I will always be grateful to her for this wonderful act of both generosity and trust. Never did she query the books I was borrowing or reading in situ. Censorship was not part of her arsenal. It made me who I am.

During the course of the first couple of years, I explored those library shelves like a child possessed, intent on reading every single page I had until now been denied. I devoured trash and classics with equal enthusiasm, I plunged headlong into arcane philosophy, history and every primer the library stocked on sexuality. I was allowed to bring home three books a week, only two of which could be fiction, and by midweek, school homework duly expedited, I had usually run out of reading material. No matter, I would then spend a few hours before the library closed for the day speed-reading further volumes. There was a universe of books, a world of stories, and I was totally in its thrall.

At thirteen, two years earlier than normal, a letter from my school certifying my seriousness and moral probity no doubt, convinced the library to grant me my own membership to the adult section. I'd been exploring it from shelf to shelf already, but this extraordinary derogation now entitled me to borrow double the amount of books per week, and I now walked home every Monday afternoon with six books in all. It was intellectual bliss.

My father wasn't too happy seeing his son and heir always deep into a book – as it is I already had to wear glasses, which for him was not an evident sign of masculinity; he would have preferred me to be more of a sports enthusiast or keen on girls, but my mother silenced most objections and pointed out that in this day and age he was lucky I read books at all (though I also collected comics and sports magazines with a minor vengeance) and did not spend my time in the street with local hooligans and good for nothings who were bound to turn out badly one day soon. As for girls, she pointed out wisely (and presciently) I still had all the time in the world to turn that particular page.

Having provisionally run out of science fiction novels and whodunnits, and awaiting the library's imminent autumn delivery of fresh titles, I distractedly found myself one afternoon in the lit-crit section, not until then one of my familiar haunts. Here I came across a fascinating set of five volumes by some rightfully forgotten academic from the 1950s which analysed in the most minute detail the opening paragraphs of almost two hundred and fifty novels, both famous and obscure. I never actually borrowed the set but would spend literally hours standing between the shelves leafing through the books at random.

Already then, the thought had crossed my mind that I actually wanted one day to become a writer myself, and this pedantic treatise felt to me like an indispensable 'how to'. From Sartre to Spillane, first lines and paragraphs were dissected mercilessly, and even though now, many years later, I cannot recall either the name of the critic or the actual titles of any of the books thus reviewed, I still remember the indelible lesson that the beginning of a book should be something special.

It should grab the reader and not allow him to put the book down.

You must catch his attention.

Through shock effect.

Through wit.

Through surprise.

No novel should start out in a dull fashion.

In the beginning is the end and from the very first line, the author must hook the impressionable (and receptive) reader once and for all.

This made a lasting impression and maybe explains why so many of my books have somewhat unusual openings. The Conrad Korzeniowski touch, I prefer to call it.

Yes, I've set novels on their way with obscenities, with images designed to make you think twice, with descriptions that are unusual, with dialogue that intrigues from the outset. I have no shame. It's my stock in trade and, by now, is usually expected of me.

But this is not a novel.

And I'm not sure how I should begin.

Let's see.

Atenolol.

Does that grab you, maybe? Intrigue you?

No?

Well, it's not a four or five letter word, I know.

Not much I can do about that.

Sorry to disappoint.

Atenolol 50 mg tablets.

Take *one* tablet in the morning. Do not stop taking this medicine unless specifically directed by your doctor.

That's what it says on the pharmacist's label.

And maybe the reason I have decided to write this book.

Until now, I've rarely suffered from illness. Even common colds seldom affected me. Just an occasional headache from time to time. I don't smoke or drink and have always enjoyed near perfect digestion. So my eye sight is poor, but even that appears to have stabilised some decades ago and I always felt that glasses made me look more intelligent, interesting, intellectual – tick the appropriate box.

I would joke in public that I followed the precept of living now and paying later (just like the principal character in an old Jack Trevor Story book, a sadly neglected writer and himself something of a character; we never met but had friends in common), and now have the nagging feeling that this is the later. A time of reckoning has finally come.

My term life-insurance policy had expired and I'd fished around for a replacement. Having settled on one, my wife had suggested we expand the terms to include a major illness and incapacity clause. I thought then that she was just displaying her customary hypochondria and gave in to her without too much of a struggle. Hell, we could afford the added premium. We both knew that what with her medicine cabinet already bursting at the seams with a solution to every woe she would inevitably outlast me by many years. Women usually do, don't they?

Before signing the documents, the woman from the insurance company, a fast-talking, unpleasant salesperson with an ill-fitting dress, asked to take our respective blood pressure, as prescribed by the policy. I hadn't even visited a doctor for nearly twelve years, and couldn't remember if I'd ever had my blood pressure taken. I was in perfect health, wasn't I?

Turns out I had a severe case of hypertension.

The policy would have to exclude heart attacks or stroke and it was advisable for me to visit my GP as soon as possible.

I'd always assumed before that being a particularly calm and pragmatic sort of person, who took so much in his stride and seldom panicked, let alone suffered from stress, spared me absolutely from the possibility of high blood pressure. I was mistaken.

I duly researched the subject. Calmly, in my own time. The very next day.

The risk of heart attack, stroke or thrombosis rises in hypertensive patients to six times the average for your normal punter. When one's daytime diastolic pressure remains abnormally high, it increases quite considerably the cumulative stress on the vascular system. As a result, in the majority of cases, vascular damage does occur and there is a thickening of the heart wall. This indicates the heart is having to work harder than it should. And the heart is like an engine, which if overworked can just break down.

Am I blinding you with science?

Hypertension is also a part of the natural process of ageing, meaning it won't get any better.

Beta blockers are a solution. They work by slowing your heart, and thereby reducing the force with which the heart pumps the blood around your body.

Usually, people begin with a relatively low dose, of five milligrams.

I'm on fifty.

Atenolol.

I was in between novels, working on a series of short stories American anthology editors had asked me for. I've always enjoyed working to a set theme or subject; it's good discipline, a challenge to conjure up a gripping yarn from the blank screen with just a word, a single idea to hold onto. I felt I did a lot of my best work that way. I was also churning out newspaper columns, reviews and articles, all the while quietly ruminating on what my next book would be.

I could always do another of my gently-pornographic love stories full of sound, fury, hotel rooms and noir grinding in the night. People would expect it of me, I knew, and I was good enough that I could vary the ingredients many ways and offer new angles, shed fresh if lurid light on the torturous private lives of men and women. Then there was also this idea of a book about English and American expatriates in Paris in the 1950s, in the years of existentialism, St Germain des Prés in its heyday, bohemianism, jazz cellars and all. This was one I'd had in mind for nearly a decade now but never got down to writing. Maybe the research required discouraged me or the fact I wasn't quite ready to write in what was now an historical period. Or again, the great science fiction epic I'd always promised myself I would write, an impossible tale of love lost, found and lost again set against a time travel background, my Orpheus in outer space. Just another heartfelt project I kept on putting off year after year and which no doubt my editors had long given up on.

But there was no rush.

The right idea would come along and even though every new book was more painful to write than the one before, I'd manage it again, conquering the doubts and the inner fear. Just don't believe anyone who tells you that it gets easier. It just doesn't. For me at least it's fucking agony, I tell you. Maybe that thickening heart was the result of a dozen novels too many I'd sweated and suffered over. I knew the reams of non-fiction I'd hacked out certainly weren't responsible for my present state of health.

Whatever.

Actually, I cheat.

I now take my daily pill before going to bed. So the possible drowsiness the beta blocker sometimes induces does not inconvenience me in the daytime. Am I tempting fate?

Nothing like a daily Atenolol pill (so small: sometimes orange, at other times shocking pink or even white) to make you feel melodramatic about all the books you'll never find time to write. Roads not taken. Mistakes made. Women past.

As a writer, I've always tried to be too clever, providing clues aplenty, but also deliberately introducing contradictions so as to scramble the facts, the tenuous intersection where fiction and reality meet. Where I am no longer the character, if ever I was. A 'hall of mirrors' a critic once wrote. But I also liked to tease and confuse and complicate and allow the reader the benefit of the doubt.

I suppose now is the time to unravel it all.

Tell the truth.

Once and for all.

In the guise of fiction, naturally.

Time to say sorry and thank you too. But mostly sorry to those I've hurt because of my selfishness, my overflow of love, my controlled madness. So there will be no index, no dramatis personae revealing who was who, and who did what in my past books. They exist and that's enough. Anyway, most of it was rather transparent, don't you think?

And even if you knew that A was in fact B, that X was Y, K was K and that, naturally, I was me, would it change the way you read my past books? The stories remain. The emotions. The heartfelt feelings. I seek no forgiveness for those, and will offer no apologies.

Atenolol.

There are 28 pills per strip, which should last a month. Often each one before you pop it out is marked on the shiny surface of the strip with the day of the week it should be ingested orally. I never respected that order in the early weeks and took the pills at random. Now it matters even less.

Dead man walking, with a hidden stockpile of multi-coloured pills slyly hidden in a drawer full of past, redundant print-outs of long-published books…

As I was writing some of the chapters in the book (which you will of course read later) in haphazard order, I began to realise a lot of things. Too many for comfort.

Too much pain in all those memories I have tried in vain to suppress. A realisation of a life that others might well envy but that today brings me little satisfaction. Too many what ifs.

Where are they now? I wonder.

Will any of them read these lines, this book?

So here you are, the truth and anything but the truth: the lying confessions of a rom

Kiss Me Sadly by Maxim Jakubowski

1

She said pussy.

I said cunt.

Just a minor misunderstanding in our confused exploration of the world of lust.

Sexual semantics the way Brits and Americans differ on their pronunciation of the word 'tomato' maybe?

For her, pussy was playful, gently sexy, fond as well as provocative, almost an endearment.

To me, it just sounded downright vulgar. A word used too often in bad X-rated movies with inane and damn inappropriate canned muzak on the soundtrack to accompany the vaginal hydraulics on open display, or whatever other orifice the action chose to feature in intimate close-up. A very American word.

Maybe she'd had too many American correspondents or cybersex partners on the Internet.

Pussy just reminded me of cats. I hated cats.

In her opinion, cunt was too direct, too offensive, too raw.

For me, it was something natural, honest, and a matter-of-fact word to describe the female sex, a body part which never failed to fascinate and obsess me. I was naturally aware that there were a further hundred or more names for it, descriptions and euphemisms and such. I even had a book on my shelves which gloriously listed them all, with origin, language and etymology analysed in cod scholarly fashion. Don't ever fault my research.

I did not believe in fancy words that skirted the subject: a cunt was a cunt was a cunt.

And each successive one I encountered was so blissfully differ-ent, a brand new experience, a source of wonder and delight, shapes, colours, shades, odour, variations, taste, texture, all worthy of a thousand narratives. There was little need for words to map a woman's sex as far as I was concerned. Just too many words to describe it that confused the issue.

Don't get me wrong: some men are born tit men, leg fetishists or arse lovers; and, for me, the eyes and the face were always the first features to catch my attention in a woman. Cunt, of course, came later. Or in many cases never, as my relationship didn't always necessarily carry me so far.

It was a body part you graduated to with honours in your rite of seduction. A supreme reward and thus unique. Private. Shockingly incomparable.

So, imagine my surprise when, towards the end of a routine e-mail one day in late spring, Milduta wrote me that she had just shaved her pussy.

Three weeks earlier we had been in New York, staying together at a small hotel on the borders of Greenwich Village. We had spent almost a week there, her first ever visit to Manhattan, and between feverish bouts of fucking, had walked miles, browsing shops, me gleefully buying her clothes and silk thongs from Victoria's Secret, eating too much Japanese food, seeing movies, visiting museums, hunting down bars where they served fresh carrot juice which she could down by the gallon, discovering to our mutual surprise how well we fitted together sexually and emotionally. During our sex games I had often trimmed her, taking voyeuristic pleasure in thinning her pubes so that her meaty gash was openly revealed in its full glory behind the protective curtain of her curls. I had, almost jokingly, suggested not for the first time she shave her genital area. She had declined with a knowing smile, yet again pretexting the discomfort of the hair growing back afterwards and how her skin often reacted with undue irritation and unseemly pimples. She'd had experience of this when she had briefly lived with a Swiss banker in Zurich. A dominant personality, he had required her to be shaven below. She had, initially, obligingly played along with his desires, still at a stage when she was testing the nascent relationship, unsure whether it held the prospect of becoming a permanent one.

With a laugh, she had also revealed that the banker shaved around his cock and balls, so that their smoothness had matched. An image that often fanned my erotic imagination.

My first reaction when I read her mail was to guess she had met another man.

Surely, when a woman reveals her intimacy so openly, it is for a man. Why him and not me? But she assured me she had only done it on a whim. Waxing her bikini line in the bathroom one morning, she had miscalculated and depilated unevenly. Getting rid of the rest was just a way of putting things right, she said.

And it felt so sexy, she added. Not like in Switzerland where it was part of sexual compact. Now it was just for herself and no one else. She felt so naked below when riding her bike to the nearby town where she did her food shopping, and arousal came so easy in the knowledge of the secret she harboured down there. She sounded both amused and amazed that it should be so. I could have told her that long before, my fascination for smooth pudenda having steadily progressed from airbrushed models on pornographic playing cards to hardcore movies and evocative nude photography.

I wondered when I saw Milduta again what the effect on my libido would be to witness her naked cunt without its curtain of soft, darker curls. The only women I had ever known with smooth vaginas had been so from the outset of our affairs. Would knowing the 'before' and the 'after' of a woman's genitals have the same erotic effect on me? A thought that nagged me for weeks to come.

I wrote back, asking her to stay shaven until we could find the opportunity to meet up again.

'I'm not sure,' she answered.

It was that hesitancy that triggered my suspicions and the fear soon gripped me of losing Milduta, that I would never rest my eyes on the wonderful vision of her cunt in all its splendid and utter nudity.

I'd always known our relationship was far from exclusive. There was no way it could ever be, due to our personal circumstances.

<… oh, u know, I just shave my pussy… lol… is feel so sexy…>

Well, she certainly chose her moment, didn't she?

2

Life is not a movie.

The choices are always far from clear cut. The villains walk in various shades of grey and the solutions to problems are complicated as hell.

Actually, films make it all look too easy and their subtle art of deception warps the mind, soon beginning to affect your actions in most insidious ways. You are not a character in someone else's plot, and there is no certainty of three acts and a happy-ever-after ending. You have no control of the situations, whether good or bad.

Life is a mess and makes no sense and often feels like an accumulation of clichés; at any rate, that's the way it looks if you consider the whole thing with some degree of cynicism (some might actually say realism). So it is no sin to accept the ambiguous romanticism and peacefulness of the images flickering on the screen, because you aspire to goodness, to happiness, and the conscious retreat into daydream or fantasy is such an easy road to follow.

Life made easy.

So...

It begins like a movie. With a wide screen and a sumptuous wash of music, massed strings – or more likely synthesiser chords in this day and age of budget consciousness – eventually rising to a majestic crescendo. Random images coalesce and a melancholy sort of melody emerges from the unformed wall of sound... 'Porcelain' by Moby maybe, or the sad tones of Nico as orchestrated by John Cale, like the soundtrack for an imaginary western, the climax of which might prove particularly bittersweet: a gunfight, lovers parted by fate, hearts asunder, a desert, a ravine, a tear.

It's a tune that aims straight for the heart but hints at further sadness to come, further down the highway. Sadness, yes; because tragedy is much too strong a word and the world we live in is so full of incomplete people, with small hopes and minuscule epiphanies that pale against the true suffering that always seems to occur elsewhere in the lives and countries of others. Some might even state that there are no tragedies for people like you and me, just minor inconveniences.

The credits of the movie roll at last, rising from the heart of the music, and indistinct shapes emerge out of the blurry chaos that occupies the screen and its rectangular geometry. Panavision format, just like in the good old days.

A woman's voice is heard, plaintive, across the gradually fading sounds of the poignant music.

Is she singing? Crying? Sighing?

Has she a quaint, breathless and somewhat exotic foreign accent to your practised ears?

A voice that evokes longing.

To which you invariably respond with open heart. Lowering your defences. Revealing your fundamental vulnerability.

Fool that you are.

To read further you will need a copy of the book.

KISS ME SADLY by Maxim Jakubowski
is available in paperback and hardback from most good and
a few bad booksellers. In case of difficulty please check out
our website:
www.thedonotpress.com
where you'll find a range of excellent books by a wealth of
wonderful authors.